Dead Horses

A Peter Romero Mystery

Table of Contents

Chapter 1

Al-Fadi, The Redeemer, lay dead over blood-clotted sand.

I had seen this Polish stud last year at the Scottsdale Arabian Horse Show. The Missing Livestock Report described this horse with mirror precision; champagne and white tobiano patterns like big commas over the neck and chest.

I usually paid little attention to the online livestock-theft notices, but my pueblo, the Cochiti Pueblo— halfway between Albuquerque and Santa Fe—exercised concurrent jurisdiction with the New Mexico Bureau of Land Management over this park. The *Kasha-Katuwe,* also known as Tent Rocks, is a set of unique pumice formations southwest of the pueblo. Bands of gray volcanic tuff and beige-pink rock layered the cliff face. Arroyos, wind-scooped slot canyons, cut into cliffs. The beauty of this place always left me in awe.

Except for now. The carcass decayed at the base of a cliff. When some picnickers had complained of the smell, I drove down to the site with my own horse and trailer in tow.

And, I needed the diversion. I still felt the sting of the divorce papers slapped in my hand two Mondays ago.

Al-Fadi had been dead for at least three days evidenced by the flies buzzing by the thousands and the mass of wriggling maggots. I gagged as I circled the carcass to get upwind. White ribs protruded from his torn hide like an open picket gate. Coyote. The Arabian's bloated legs stuck out straight and stiff. Hollow cavities stared from the eye sockets. The stud's mane and tail fluttered in the wind, then straightened as a dust devil twisted by, throwing grit in my eyes and topping the carcass with sand.

A bullet between the eyes had finished off the stud point-blank. Burnt hair surrounded the wound. Maggots continued their feast among the wounds.

Holding my breath, I pulled out my pocketknife, an eight-in-one do-everything-but-feed-the-horses model and dug around the back of the horse's throat. I sliced through hesitant soft-tissue and scraped along bone until I got lucky. The bullet, wet and slightly distorted, had distinct land-and-groove marks.

It looked like a .357, but I wouldn't know for sure until the lab examined it.

I stepped back for air, took a deep breath towards the sky. I couldn't imagine anyone still being here, but I checked the pale tuff cliffs to make sure I was alone. Phallic rock formations, ninety feet high, offered unlimited hiding places. Tricky breezes sent a shiver cold down my spine. Even Crowd Killer danced and snorted where I'd tied him. I pocketed my knife and rubbed his nose. He settled down as I talked to him, and after a while he started munching the brush he'd stashed inside his cheek.

A pebble scraped from above and Crowd Killer alerted. I scanned the cliffs. My horse was skittish as hell, and maybe I acted jumpy, but that didn't explain the hair raised on my forearms.

Watching and listening exposed nothing, so I went back to surveying the ground. Wind and a light rain last night had muted the critical characteristics of boot prints but tracks in the sand still showed that two assholes had driven a trailer to this spot. They probably then unloaded the Arabian, led him to the base of the cliff, then shot him in the head.

Tent Rocks was only one of many good places to hide a carcass in the Southwest. *Al-Fadi* came from a ranch north of Santa Fe. So, why here? They had to trailer the Arabian forty miles to this place and that didn't make sense.

A flash of light jacked my heart. I scanned the cliffs. Twenty years on this job had netted me plenty of enemies and a healthy dose of paranoia. But I didn't see a damn thing except Hawk, perched high and regal on the cliff.

The FBI, BLM, and Sheriff needed notification, but my cell phone showed no bars. I strung yellow tape quickly and got ready to leave. The cliffs flashed again, but this time I caught the source at the top. I played dumb and mounted up. Crowd Killer made his usual protest by twisting away as I legged up but settled down soon. We trotted toward my truck and trailer like I was going home. Once Crowd Killer was loaded, I would track down that son-of-a-bitch watching from the edge of the cliff.

4

I hopped into my Jeep, a red and white '53 custom, and drove down Route 92 towards Cochiti Pueblo, Crowd Killer in tow, for two miles until out of sight of the cliffs. I pulled into a ravine and hoofed back toward the place where I'd noticed the flash. I doubted the watcher was still there, but I needed a sign. Marks on the ground often speak with a clear tongue.

I slogged uphill slowly. I needed to work out more. Hugging ravines and vegetation, visions of *Al-Fadi* in life passed before me. Fifteen hands high and over twelve hundred pounds. Muscular beauty. Flowing mane. A showy prancer in the Scottsdale Horse Show arena who had owned the crowd and knew it.

On high ground, I stayed off the skyline until I reached where I thought the watcher had to have been. An overlook above the carcass showed footprints and scuffing where someone had crouched. I figured the snoop had to be some weirdo or maybe a cop-wannabe who'd picked the missing horse off the online missing livestock reports and got his kicks by watching the scene. But these tracks created a path that showed the man had enough savvy to stay completely out sight. He was gone, leaving only traces of footprints behind.

Shadows lengthened and I didn't want to chance a broken leg in this rough country after sunset. Seeking out an unknown at night didn't appeal, either. I trotted down the ridgeline to my Jeep.

The carcass would still be there in the morning. And if the snoop was there, I would nail him.

Chapter 2

Next morning, I called the FBI's Albuquerque field office. My usual contact was on assignment, so I talked to an agent who was new and not enthusiastic about investigating a livestock killing. "I'll get right on it," he said, after consulting his boss.

I took that to mean later. Much later.

Then I called the Sandoval County Sheriff's Office in Bernalillo. Deputy Robert Bowditch was an old friend. More often than not, the sheriff would jump on livestock cases.

"Got a dead horse at Tent Rocks. FBI's not enthusiastic, how about you?" I asked him.

"You mean that missing Arab stud from north of Santa Fe, what, Rancho Camino de Rincon?"

"The same." I filled him in on the details.

He said, "Weird dump site. Why drive a horse all that way just to shoot it? Plenty of places for that up north. Why here?" he asked.

"Nothing comes to mind. Doesn't even make sense to steal a horse like that. Can't show it. Can't breed it. Can't even sell the sperm without papers. An Arab without registration is worth zip."

"That all you got?" he asked.

"Questions is all I got."

"I'll let you know if I hear anything, but FBI and BLM is up each other's ass more often than not. Sorry, I'm not jumping into that hornets' nest. Enjoy." Bowditch hung up, off to protect and serve.

The Bureau of Land Management's Rio Puerco field office in Albuquerque had jurisdiction over wild mustangs, so I called. Special Agent Raphael Torres seemed interested until I gave details.

"This horse is wild or stray?" he asked.

"No."

"Not my problem."

"Okay, I'll bury it."

"Not at Tent Rocks, you won't," he said.

"You said it wasn't your problem."

"It is if you bury it in my national monument," he huffed and hung up.

Great. I reported a crime, and nobody came.

Last, I punched in Rancho Camino de Rincon's number. The ranch foreman, Tyler Richman, answered.

"Found your horse." I told him when and where.

Richman exhaled. "You're gonna tell me *Al-Fadi* is dead."

"You knew?"

"Second one this month. A filly, *Mahbouba*. Found her up in Colorado a week ago. Shot in the head. Horrible thing. *Fadi?*"

"Same. What you want me to do with the carcass?"

"Damn. You got a trailer?" he asked.

The image of the stinking remains flashed in my mind. "Carcass is in bad shape."

"Mr. Romero, the owner has great affection for that horse and wants him buried at the ranch. Believe me, he doesn't take no for an answer. You will be well compensated for your time and any damages."

"I'll get back to you." I hung up.

On the far wall of my office, my eyes caught sight of a framed photo I'd hung of me in my dress blues thirty years and that many pounds ago. For whatever reason, it grabbed my attention. Next to it used to hang our wedding picture. A rectangle of unfaded paint emphasized its absence. Costancia must've taken the photo with her; a gesture that meant maybe she didn't think the whole marriage a disaster. There were good days, for sure, and we'd raised a fine son.

A picture of Costancia hung to the left of the bare spot. She was nineteen then, with long, thick hair; black and radiant. Her smile delighted everyone she'd ever met. Her voice calmed. Her eyes captivated. She had tried to make it work for twenty-five years. I did, too, but I fucked it up by putting more effort into my work than into our relationship.

I glanced at the divorce decree and pushed it to a far corner of my desk and hoped it'd disappear. Regret closed my throat and tightened my chest, so I directed my attention to a situation I might be able to fix. Dead horses.

7

I sat wondering why someone would kill a beauty like
Al-Fadi. Not rustlers because those outlaws have connections
and the Arabian would be in Mexico by now. People who knew
horseflesh wouldn't kill a pedigree stud that might bring in
over a few hundred grand. Kidnap for ransom? The owner
would've received demands and threats. And there'd be no
missing livestock reports.

The murder of this beautiful animal bothered me more
than I thought. Animals have souls and killing them without
need pisses me off. An old man from my pueblo, had to be a
hundred, told me something that stuck once.

"When our ancestors traded hunting for farming, they
lost respect for animals once equal. To justify themselves,
when Man enslaved the animals, they had to deny the animals'
intelligence, deny them their souls."

The next day, I motored to Tent Rocks, this time with
my Winchester lever-action, because he that is forewarned best
be armed. I usually carried my Ruger Blackhawk .30 carbine
revolver. A good piece in a frontal assault but it would be
ineffective against a threat from the top of the cliffs, if it came
to that. I felt for the shells on the seat for comfort.

The dead stallion lay as I'd left him. Coyote had visited
during the night again and Buzzard sat on the cliff watching
me. Nothing else had changed. Neck hairs under my braid
tingled as I scoped the bluffs. My head felt naked to the
likelihood of a riflescope, its crosshairs making pin pricks on
my skin. Maybe this time it was just paranoia screwing with
my head, but I still kept my rifle close.

I had work to do and couldn't spend all day scanning
the scenery. My thoughts turned to the carcass ahead of me. I
love horses, always have, and wasn't happy at the thought of
desecrating such a beautiful animal, but I admit I was a little
excited to use the new winch I'd installed last month. I flipped
my braid over my shoulder and ran the cable through the hook
then around the horse's chest. God, it stunk.

When I'd almost winched the whole mess into the
trailer, a hind leg snagged on the gate and tore off, landing in
the dirt. I threw the leg inside, thinking I should've kicked

8

myself in the ass with it. The image of this magnificent
Arabian, trailing banners of long radiant hair, now minus a leg
and jammed inside a small trailer, burned my gut. To destroy
an animal like this, a man had to be twisted.

I headed north on Interstate 25. Ten miles south of
Santa Fe, a hot sun shimmered the highway and the
surrounding grasslands of La Bajada Mesa, the juniper-studded
flat top where wagon tracks of 17th century travelers are etched
into volcanic rock. Interstate 25, a modern overlay of the *El
Camino Real de Tierra Adento*, the Royal Road of the Interior,
obscured the original road, the principal trade route between
Santa Fe and Mexico City. The route bustled with traders,
thieves, and mercenaries for nearly three hundred years, but
history enjoys little respect in the modern world.

I breathed in the story of this mesa as I motored up its
slopes. La Bajada nurtured my people long before the Spanish
came. Pre-contact footpaths, stone piles, and agricultural grids
bore witness to settlers, farmers, and conquerors.

Anthropologists say my people arrived as early as
twelve thousand years ago. The anthropologists are wrong,
though. My people are not new arrivals. We have been here
forever. I am not merely *from* this place; I am *of* it.

My awe of this land's past was deflated by the thought
of the regal animal, descendant from a line of horses five
thousand years old, loaded in my trailer.

I glanced in my rearview and noticed a truck five
hundred yards behind me. I watched him for twenty minutes in
the rearview. It must have been amateur hour because when I
slowed, he slowed. When I sped up, so did he. I shook him
loose at the Cerillos exit with a quick off-and-on.

North of Santa Fe, up US-84 past Pojoaque and south
of Nambe, I turned onto a road shaded by gnarled cottonwoods
and marked by a timber arch that framed the Sangre de Cristo
Range. At the end of the pasture-lined road, I spotted a two-
hundred-year-old stucco hacienda built in traditional pueblo-
style. I knew the inside without even seeing it: lots of fancy
tile, fountains, twelve-inches-in-diameter vigas supporting the

latillas crisscrossing the ceiling, and skull-cracking door frames
built for shorter people who lived two centuries ago.

Ranch Foreman Tyler Richman greeted me under the
shade of a hundred-year-old cottonwood canopy. A breeze
rustled the leaves. I appreciated the opportunity to cool down.
The day was a scorcher.

Richmond looked forty; a skinny horseman in his
Wranglers and white, long-sleeve, snap-button. A sweat-ring
soaked through his Stetson. Beat-up boots and a lame gait
confirmed my opinion; anyone who's ever broken horses ends
up broken, too. Richmond had the used-up expression of the
over-stressed on his thin, tanned face.

I told Richmond what I'd observed at the crime scene
including the suspicious gawker.

Richmond said, "The weirdo gets his kicks watching
crime scenes?"

"Who knows? Drives a '72 Chevy C-10. Blue, patched
and primed bomb. Beat to shit. Not smart enough to tail
undetected. Couldn't read the plate numbers, but it looked
Colorado. Ya know, red and white. Veteran's plate, maybe."

Richmond nodded.

"How does something like this happen?" I asked.

Richmond dropped his eyebrows. "What do you mean
by that?"

I'd stepped in it a little deeper than I wanted to. I had to
sympathize with the guy because his job was threatened. "I
mean, how do two expensive horses get stolen within a week?"

He glared at me. "Where you get off, Romero? You
find one horse and you're in my face with it? What the fuck?"

"Just asking questions."

"How 'bout minding your own fucking business."
Richmond spit the words, upped the volume.

I was surprised by his reaction, but I matched him for
volume. "I just drove a rotting carcass forty miles and made it
my business." My face in his. His breath quickened, and I
braced for a fist.

A man in a dark suit ran out of the home's front door,
yelling, "Hey, hey! Knock it off!" The man pushed his way

between us. Richmond backed away. So did I when I spotted the piece under his jacket.

"Who's this?" The man in the suit asked.

Richmond said, "Some wannabe cop from Rez Nowhere."

"I brought up his horse at his request. Who are you?" I asked.

"Name's Palafox. I've been hired to investigate the thefts. You two hotheads cool off." He swiveled his head between the two of us, acting like he wanted to take us both on at once. A set of biceps pulling at his coat sleeves hinted he had the muscle to do it. His chin said, Try me. "You Romero from Cochiti?" Palafox said calmly.

"Right," I said.

"I'm sorry for the misunderstanding, Mister Romero, but Tyler's been under a lot of pressure as of late. Tyler, you got work to do?"

Richmond turned to go but not before throwing a nasty eye-lock that told me we would knock heads again.

"Tell me what you know about this incident, Mr. Romero," Palafox asked.

Again, I described what little I'd found at the scene, the stalker, and the vehicle he drove.

"We have a perplexing situation here." Palafox paused. "*Al-Fadi* was out of *Bask*, the sire of 196 national champions. Stud fees for him range around ten grand plus. Studs like that would sell for three-fifty grand or more, easy. Theft of an expensive Arab I get, but kill one? Got any ideas?" He asked the question deadpan, but I suspected Palafox was fishing. I get it. Too often the finder is the killer.

"Well, you got two valuable horses killed in a week and your friend Richmond is more than a little touchy about the subject. But this is *your* case."

Palafox nodded, gave me a knowing smile. "Send us an invoice for the hauling," he said as a ranch hand drove up a front-end loader, scooped him up, and took *Al-Fadi* behind a barn. Sounds of the front-loader faded into silence.

11

The dead horse's stench of rotting cheese and feces flooded my nose. But, it smelled more like insurance fraud. I focused on the door that Richmond had disappeared into.

The dead animal haunted me as I drove south on Interstate 25. Part of me hoped to spot the Chevy pickup that had tailed me earlier. I kept an eye out for it, if for no other reason than to relieve the tedium of driving. No such luck. Monotony stuck with me until I sighted home.

Adrenaline replaced boredom when I spotted the beat-to-shit Chevy parked in my driveway. The man leaning against it hung an AK-47 from his shoulder.

Chapter 3

I parked short of the man, the grim reaper himself for all I knew. An Indian but not from here. Black hair, forties, but younger than me, five-ten like me. He carried a few extra pounds, needed a shave and a bath. He didn't gesture or speak, but I caught from his nasty scowl he meant unpleasant business.

The Jeep's V-8 grumbled like Bear in the quiet afternoon. I shut the engine down. Nothing but a dull hiss filled the void. The man waited while growing a grin that revealed some missing teeth.

My wife always insisted I was trouble-prone and I could never deny that claim. I'd already been jacked up enough today with the dead horse and that asshole Richmond. Now, trouble smiled a big fuck-you with a Kalashnikov.

Six years of active duty in the Corps as a military policeman and fourteen in the reserves had earned me duty during the ass-end of Vietnam and a call-back for Desert Storm, so facing armed hostiles was nothing new. Twenty years as a cop had introduced me to all kinds of unpleasant characters in its own right. Seeing the armed man sent me into full alert. My heart red-lined, nerves tingled, muscles swelled, eyes became clear and quick like Hawk, ears sensitive like Deer.

Being within shooting distance of a military firearm did not encourage my sense of well-being, however. I swallowed my heart, stepped out of the Jeep, and walked toward the man as sweat rolled down my back. "I'm sorry, sir, but there's no open-carry on this reservation unless you're a resident and we prohibit automatic weapons."

The man glared from under his eyebrows. "What?"

"Place that weapon in a carrying case or lock it in the rear of your vehicle." If logic won't work, bullshit might.

"You shittin' me?"

"Do it now." As I stepped closer, he seemed puzzled for a moment, then amused.

"Where I come from, the fella who's armed gives the damn orders," he said.

13

"I'm Pueblo Officer Romero and you are in my jurisdiction. Pack the weapon away and leave this reservation."

"Or what?"

I stepped forward but stopped when the stranger jerked away from the truck and planted both feet. "Identify yourself and state your business, sir. Place your weapon on the ground," I said.

The man slipped a hand into his hip pocket, said, "Do believe it's fine where it is. You got a badge?"

I ran, more like flew, the ten feet it took to get to him and jammed an elbow to his Adam's Apple. He dropped fast, grabbing for his throat. He gagged, flopped like a hooked fish.

Kicking the weapon away, I leaned over the gasping body.

"I said state your business!" I stepped away and waited for the man to find air. Maybe I'd been too heavy-handed and hurt a guy that didn't need it, but I'm a cop first, nice guy second.

"You understand me now?" I glared down at him.

The man nodded, not able to speak. He tried to rise but collapsed into a wracking cough.

"Tell me your name."

The man tried to talk between gags, then pointed to his hip, so I fished out his wallet from his pocket. An ID card displayed the name of Clement Ouray Pokoh. A gold badge dangled from the inner flap.

"Shit, man. Why didn't you say something?" I had just cold-cocked a detective of the Southern Ute Indian Tribe Department of Justice and Regulatory, CID, headquartered at Ignacio, Colorado. I helped the man to his feet and led him toward the house. I fumbled with my keys and helped Pokoh inside to the living room couch. I went to the kitchen and filled a glass with water. "Drink. Jesus, man."

Pokoh sat without speaking until he could find air. "Damn, you're fast." He sipped water, took a breath.

"Why the hell didn't you ID yourself? Going for your pocket like that put a shot of cold piss through my heart. I'm sorry as hell, but goddamnit, man, I told you who I was."

14

"Saying it don't make it true. My mistake. I was going for my wallet. I should a
said something." He palmed his throat and swallowed. "Don't think anything's broke. I'll live."

"Now that I damn near killed you, how can I help?" I tried to grin.

Pokoh showed what could pass for a smile, but his eyes stared cold. "Horses. Dead horses."

"What I saw over in Tent Rocks?"

Pokoh nodded.

"Why the interest?"

"Someone dumped a filly on the reservation last week. Could tell she was Blue List just by looking at her." Every Blue List Arabian traced directly to ancient Egyptian Bedouin bloodlines and were bred according to strict rules. Pokoh shook his head. "No doubt in my mind."

"That filly from the Rancho Camino de Rincon up near Santa Fe?" I asked. He nodded. The man knew his horses.

"Tracked leads to this area. Figured you might be one of the perps. Bad call." Pokoh massaged his throat, swallowed.

"Any idea who the horse-killers are?" I asked.

"Talk says wackos got a beef with Muslims, Arabs in particular. Horses included. Some sort of crackpot theory, if you ask me. Survivalists, and the like, who hang around the Colorado-New Mexico border. Cortez and Durango, mostly. Make money selling drugs. Legal marijuana put a kink in their style, so I think they're looking to branch out, but I don't know what. Gotta be big."

"Why?" I asked.

"Any dumbshit knows an Arabian horse is walking money. Ransom, extortion, whatever. What moron fucks up that kinda opportunity?"

"Well, I wish you luck on finding these perps but not much I can do except tell what I know, which is less than you." His investigation might prove useful to me later, but my gut said to play dumb for now.

Pokoh started to rise, took my outstretched hand. "Well thank you, sir. For the water…not the throat punch."

I opened the front door, trailed him to his pickup. "Good luck. I hear more, I'll let you know."

"I think you're gonna hear a lot more," Pokoh said, driving off.

The rest of the afternoon, I was too busy to wonder what he meant. Routine tasks demanded all my time: chasing kids throwing rocks at cars on Highway 22, mediating a recurring argument between neighbors over a rooster, discussing a surveillance plan of suspected TV signal theft with a local media provider, and an hour trailing a suspicious auto with dusty Colorado plates and redneck decals—guns, NRA, second amendment—on the rear window. The driver finally understood he was not welcome when I blue-lighted him and crowded his black Hummer H3. The guy, hair high-and-tight with bushy beard, did not belong here and was most likely up to no good. The man departed the pueblo at high speed after rendering a middle finger salute. Off the rez, the asshole was someone else's problem.

At home, I hung my Stetson on a peg and dropped my car keys on my desk. I shuffled through paperwork and read emails. About the time the routine had me bored to death; the phone rang. The readout showed *unknown caller*, but I picked up anyway.

"Yes sir, Officer Romero, this is Tommy Palafox, Santa Fe County Security Consulting, we talked earlier today at Rancho Camino de Rincon."

"Right."

"I'm afraid we have another horse theft," he said.

"Sorry to hear that."

"This time it's a mare, *Rababa*. Pregnant, too. Hell of a loss. Sheriff found her up near Ignacio, Colorado. Shot in the head."

"Terrible thing. What can I do for you, Mr. Palafox?"

"Well, we've sort of run out of ideas. I need someone on the outside. You know, outside looking in."

"I can recommend someone."

"How about you?"

"Can't help you there, these thefts are outside my jurisdiction. This sounds like multi-state crimes. I think you need to call the FB —"

"We're willing to offer you a substantial stipend, Mr. Romero. Rancho Camino de Rincon's owner is a man of means and is determined to put a stop to this."

"Plenty of private security and investigative contractors in New Mexico," I reminded him.

"I've done my research, Mr. Romero. You've been awarded the Public Safety Officer Medal of Valor recently, you have an excellent reputation, and come highly recommended."

"Thank you, Mr. Palafox, but my job keeps me busy." I'm the pueblo's only policeman. "Recommended, you say?"

"Yes, Special Agent Jean Reel said you were the man for the job."

Hearing that name caused my heart to jump. I had worked with Reel on several cases and we'd grown close. Almost. Meaning she wanted to hop into bed, and I didn't. I had a wife then. I pictured Reel's body, imagined her naked, wished I'd accepted when I had the chance.

"She speaks highly of you."

Reel had been detailed out of state, but it seemed, was still looking out for me. "Give her my regards, but no, I'm happy here." I lied.

My job resulted in divorce. Daily police work bored me shitless. The pueblo governor drove me nuts. All for pay that was less than previous offers from the Sandoval County Sheriff and Albuquerque PD.

Flat-out quitting wasn't an option. I'd used my car as collateral for my horse and the loan payments hurt. The idea of taking some of my banked vacation and moonlighting, like every other cop I knew, appealed to me.

And this case was strange. Who would shoot expensive horses for no obvious reason? Criminal activity can be boiled down to either passion or profit and no such motives were apparent here. This case was trouble, something I never had to look for. Trouble usually walked in the door or called on the phone. Like now.

17

"We'll talk again, Officer Romero." Palafox said goodbye after an off-hand mention of a retainer that caused me to fumble the handset like a third-string JV running back. I hung up, stared at the phone. What had I just refused?

Chapter 4

My police line rang at 3:00 a.m. I padded across the hall from my bedroom to the office.

"Peter! Peter, come quick. There's been a—my God." It was Marta Pecos, the wife of a lifelong friend.

"Marta, what?"

"Oh my God! Oh my God!" She screamed, then dropped the phone.

"What is it, Marta?" She sounded terrified. My chest tightened as I listened to her wracking cries. "Marta? Talk to me!" More crying. "I'll be right there!" I hung up, threw on clothes, and ran for the Jeep.

I drove ten minutes to the oldest part of the pueblo which dated back to 1250. The Pecos' home, located on Cedar Road, was a detached single-story adobe with a few windows on each side and a single door, front and rear. Vigas supported a flat roof.

The front door was open when I arrived, and neighbors milled out front. Marta wailed as I shouldered through. She was huddled on the couch wrapped in a blanket over pajamas. She pointed to a bedroom.

Marta's husband, Juan, lay in bed. Blood covered his chest and upper arms. The wound, clean and quick, sliced deep across his throat. Arterial blood had sprayed up the wall behind the headboard. The bedroom showed no signs of struggle; Juan had died while asleep.

Juan Pecos and I had attended school together from kindergarten through high school. I'd joined the Marines and Juan, the Army paratroops. That was worth a lot of ribbing when I still drank, when we hung out. Lately we hadn't seen each other much, except for the less-than-occasional trouble with his son, Jason.

The feds had jurisdiction for major crimes on the reservation and my only responsibility on such cases was crime scene protection until the FBI arrived. That pissed me off because I have more badge time than many of the kids, they called Special Agents. I hit speed dial. I swore and wanted to fight someone, but I needed to talk like a professional over the phone. I took a calming breath.

The agent-on-duty promised a team from Albuquerque, fifty-five miles from here, in less than fifty minutes. "Forty minutes," I demanded.

I sat next to Marta on the couch. My face heated, my vision blurred. My eyes stung.

Marta's skin had drained of color except under her eyes. Her tear-streaked and puffy face aged her twenty years. Her fingers pinched at the sofa's fabric and she stared at the opposite wall. Framed pictures of men in uniform, her husband, his father, her father stared back.

I hid my rage as best I could. Acting professionally in the face of tragedy is agony. Especially a personal one. No matter how long you wear a badge, no matter how many times you observe inhumanity visited upon victims, it's never easy to keep your heart at bay. Juan was my friend since we were pups. We played, schooled, hung out, drank, and even duked it out a few times. A real friend.

"I need to ask you some questions, Marta," I said.

Marta shook her head, wiped her face, and started to cry again. She pointed to the other bedroom.

There, the copper smell of blood and the odor of shit permeated the air. The lights were off, so I used my flashlight. Marta's son, Jason, twenty-one, lay on his bed. He stared at the ceiling; a glistening gash opened his neck. His skin stretched tightly over a scabby face. Peeling lips bared decayed, stained teeth. Husky as a kid, Jason's now skeletal, almost fully sleeve-tattooed arms crossed his chest in a defensive move that had failed to protect him. His spiked rings never finding purchase in his assailant's face. And, he'd seen it coming. Back in the living room, I asked, "Can you tell me what happened?"

She tried to talk, broke into tears. "I don't know," she said between deep sobs. She shuddered when I put my arm around her.

"Please, Marta, talk to me," My voice cracked.

Marta inhaled, held her breath, then exhaled. "I fell asleep on the couch, I got up to get a glass of water and go to bed. When I returned from the kitchen, something was wrong. I turned on the lights and saw—" She started shaking. Her vacant eyes stared off somewhere.

"It's okay, keep going." She shook her head and fell deeper into grief. She lay on the couch, clutched her stomach and quaked with silent cries, then rolled into a fetal position. She covered her head with her arms.

A crowd had gathered in front of the house. Through the doorway, I spotted Marta's sister, Rose, and motioned her over. "Rose, Marta needs you."

Fear distorted her face, but she only had eyes for her sister. She sat on the couch and cradled Marta's head. She murmured softly in our language, Keres, and rubbed her sister's hair. Marta seemed to calm. Her breath slowed and the shaking subsided.

I took time to examine the two corpses more closely. In the master bedroom, there were no signs of forced entry in the windows, no disruption of furniture. Juan's glasses lay undisturbed at the edge of a bedside table. There was less blood on the bed than I expected. Juan had died quietly.

In Jason's bedroom, the victim had been killed with a violence that roiled my stomach. Blood spattered the walls. I'd seen the terrible things humans do to each other often enough, too often, but the callousness of this act surprised me. Given the efficiency and orderliness of the crime, it seemed the perp knew what he was doing. The FBI would glean details from the blood spatter, but I doubted they would find fingerprint evidence. This was professional.

The disorder of Jason's surroundings, however, echoed his life. Trash, old pizza boxes, and crushed coke cans littered the room. His thin jaw slacked open, the brown, ragged edges of his teeth hinted at a lifetime of bad choices and one in particular: Meth.

Jason had been busted by County for possession, spent time in lock-up. I'd arrested him more than once and turned him over to his dad. Jason was my son's age. While Junior had gone to UNM and the NFL, Jason had gone downhill. I knew, but never wanted to know, how far it had come.

Rose came up. "Marta wants to talk," then shook her head when she entered the room. "Stayin' up all night, sleepin'

21

all day. Knew he'd come to no good," she said. Rose showed no sign of grief over her dead nephew. People show grief in different ways, but I tucked her reaction away for future reference. I returned to the living room and sat next to Marta.

Marta teared up, leaned toward another break down, but sniffed, then composed herself. "Juan knew Jason was doin' terrible things besides drugs. To get them, you know. He wanted to turn Jason in. I told him to give the boy a break. He'd pull out of it." She started crying again, this time she couldn't stop. "Now both are gone."

Rose sat and hugged her close. It didn't seem to help.

I asked Rose to take her into the kitchen and as far away from the bodies as she could, give her some water, make some coffee. "The FBI will be here, soon," I said.

As I walked toward the master bedroom, Rose came out of the kitchen and I asked her how Marta was doing. "She'll make it," Marta said, weakly.

Outside, dash-mounted flashers lit the crowd. Someone yelled, "Step back folks, step back!"

Two men entered the home, both dressed in black coveralls with FBI embroidered on their breasts in yellow. I knew them both, Special Agents Michael Crutchman and John Zagorsky.

"Okay, Romero we got it," Crutchman said with a dismissive wave-off and belligerent tone. Whenever I saw Crutchman's wide cheekbones, broad forehead, and pronounced jawline, I had an urge to rearrange them with my fist.

"I got two adult males, dead," I started to brief him, but the agent had little time for me and was inspecting the master bedroom before I stopped speaking.

"I got it," Crutchman said over his shoulder.

Crutchman needed a knee in the balls every now and then. Like now. A slow burn rose from my stomach. Zagorsky motioned me outside. "Tell me what you know."

I told him what I'd seen in the bedrooms, then said, "Jason had a substance abuse history."

"Know the family?"

"My whole life."

22

"Tough like that," Zagorsky said. "People you know. Any family we need to talk to?"

"Younger brother Matt lives in Albuquerque. Marta, the mother, and her sister, Rose. Talk to Rose, for sure."

"Tell me what you think." Zagorsky tilted his head.

"I run off an H3 earlier today. 2007, black, with Colorado plates, white mountains with red background, a veteran's plate. Decals on the bumper; NRA, love guns, cold dead hands, that sort."

"Numbers?"

"Too dirty to read," I said.

"Description of the driver?"

"Hispanic, high-and-tight haircut but full beard, like I've seen on hipster snowboarders."

"Zagorsky!" Crutchman yelled from the doorway.

"Stay near the phone, Romero," Zagorsky said as he walked away.

Crutchman yelled from the house. "Hey, I said you're out of it."

"Right." A lifelong friend and his son. Throats slit. Stay out of the investigation, my ass. It doesn't work that way.

Before I left, Rose came out of the house and I asked her how Marta was doing.

"She's a tough woman, but Peter, please check on Matt. She told me he hasn't been home in two months. She's worried. He's all she has left."

I hadn't seen Matt for years and didn't know what he could contribute to the investigation, but I would find out. "Yes, of course. I'll talk to him this morning."

Chapter 5

The early sun bled scarlet and rust along the back wall of my home office.

I listened to the messages on my personal line. A computer voice instructed me to press one if I was Peter Romero. I deleted it.

I dialed Junior's number. My son's voice boomed on the other end. "S'up, Dad?"

"Good to hear your voice, son. Stayin' healthy? Is the coach beatin' you up?"

Junior played tight end for Dallas and was not easy to get on the phone, especially when training camp started, this year in Oxnard, California. I got lucky and connected before he walked out the door for morning training.

"Hey, what can you tell me about Jason Pecos?" I asked without segue.

"Didn't really talk to him much after he got into drugs. Haven't seen him in years. Sad case, that guy. Even Matt would have nothing to do with him. What'd he do now?"

"I hate to tell you this, but someone killed him this morning. His dad, too."

"Oh, man. That sucks. Wha—"

"It was awful, son. Seein' Juan cut like that upset me. I can't..." I choked up without warning.

"Don't worry, Dad. I get it, but I don't envy your job."

"Your mother always said the same thing."

"How you and Mom doing?" he asked.

"Haven't heard from her after the papers were served." In fact, it appeared Costancia was not going to talk to me again. I had left messages on her phone. "You?"

"I talk to her about once a week. Says Grandma's as ornery as ever."

"Things are going well, then." Costancia lived with and cared for her aged mother on the southern edge of the Navajo reservation, a place without running water, electricity, or phone reception. But that was not the reason she never called. I was the reason.

"I gotta go to practice, Dad." He paused. "Listen, you and Mom. You really gotta try and work it out."

"I know, son."

Junior clicked off. His absence on the line brought home how empty my life had become.

I was so proud of my boy. Good kid, great student, extraordinary athlete. Costancia always said he looked like me, called him Mini or *waasht'i* when he was a toddler. As a man, he stood taller and broader. Built in a muscle factory, friends said. Smarter too, but I never let on.

I pushed away from my desk. Even though I'd been up most of the night, I wanted to interview the surviving Pecos boy, Matt, before the FBI got to him. Whatever the FBI learned from him; they would not tell me. And there was always the chance they would tell him not to speak to anyone, especially me.

Matt lived in Albuquerque and a police database search gave me Mateo Pecos's address, but his cell number was not listed. The report of a death is not best done by phone anyway, so a visit was in order. I hopped into my Jeep and motored south on I-25, thankful it was too early for Albuquerque rush hour traffic.

Matt's home, a single-family ranch, was located across from a Target. A black Dodge Ram with tinted windows parked out front. I studied the ride. A lot of truck: tricked-out grill, fog lamps, auto-bumpers, side steps. All black-on-black. Had something epic under the hood, too, I bet.

Breathing deeply, I walked to the front door. On active duty in the Corps, I had accompanied the chaplain on death notices, and I'd given death notices as a cop. There is no easy way to do it, so I always tell the family quickly and directly, in no uncertain terms, that their loved one is dead. They are going to be wrecked no matter what, so there's no sense in sugar-coating it.

The most difficult thing is not knowing how the family is going to react. In some cases, family members have fainted, slammed the door in my face, or pulled out a gun. Or asked for the money. Some will want to hug you while they cry, some will lose their mind and tear their place apart, and some just sit in stunned silence.

Matt answered my knock. He was four years older than his brother but looked younger. Matt had avoided drugs, held a steady job and, from the looks of the house, led a productive existence.

"This can't be good, Mister Romero," Matt said. "It's Jason, isn't it?"

"You and I need to sit down."

Matt let me in, motioned to the living room couch, and sat on a chair across from a coffee table. Looking around, I admired the neatness of the place, or maybe I was just putting off the inevitable.

I always struggle to find the right thing to say during notifications, what I tell them they'll remember for the rest of their lives. "Matt, Jason and your father were killed last night at 2:45 a.m. The cause of death appears to be stabbing with a sharp instrument. They both died instantly. The FBI is at the scene investigating and your mother is safe with your aunt."

"No. No." He said straight-faced. "There's some mistake. No, not both."

I watched him then shook my head. "Matt, I am so sorry, but there's no mistake."

Matt blanched. "Aw, shit." He shook his head, exhaled, said, "No surprise. Jason hung with bad dudes." He'd focused on his brother and had not, I assumed, processed the death of his father. I said nothing. Matt would need no reminder.

He put his head in his hands. The color drained from his skin. My heart went out to him. I have known this young man since he was a baby. Mateo Pecos rocked back and forth on the couch and rubbed the nape of his neck. He clutched himself. "Who did it?" he asked through clenched teeth.

No soothing words came, but I managed a weak, reassuring smile. "FBI's working it now. I'll tell you more when I know." I looked away when I spoke, relieved I got through it without fumbling the words.

"I'll kill those bastards!" he said, neck muscles like cables. His breath came in bursts like a sprinter.

26

"Kill who, Matt?" A probing question at the wrong time can hurt. Matt was a victim of this crime, too, but his comments made me curious.

"He was a good kid. Funny. Laughing all the time. Good in school, too. Had a wicked pitching arm. We practiced 'til my catching hand hurt. But now, shit, nothing but trouble since he was twelve." Pecos sniffed back tears and snot. He wiped his face with a handkerchief. "My parents tried everything. It just got worse."

"Know anyone who would harm Jason?"

"Damn near everyone he met." Pecos held a handkerchief over his eyes.

"Who, exactly?"

"Wanna start with pushers?" He sniffed, wiped his face. "Locals?"

Matt took time trying not to lose it. "Mostly, but talk is he owed so many dealers he had to buy out of town."

"Anyone specifically who might have it in for him?"

Matt sniffed again, paused. "Heard a loudmouth talking in a bar. Seen him around. He's a meth cooker. Said a tweeker stole his car, a lowrider. Cooker found out later it was Jason stole it. Dumbshit ripped off a fucking cooker to pay a dealer." He dropped his head into his hands. "Jason couldn't do anything right."

"This cooker gotta name?"

Matt said, "No, never heard a name."

Matt twitched while talking, poor kid was wound up. He grabbed a table lamp, jerked out the cord, and threw it against a wall.

"Stay with me, Matt, I know your hurtin,' but stay with me. I wanna help. Any ideas where I can find this cooker?"

His shoulders slumped. Maybe he'd thrown away some anger with the lamp. "No, when Jason started pulling his bullshit, I left home. The fighting. All I know is what I hear from my mom." He looked away.

"Anybody want to harm your father, Matt?"

Matt shook his head quickly as if he was trying to shake off a fly.

"Been home lately? Check on things?"

"Not since Jason moved in a year ago. Didn't really want to be near the psycho."

That statement didn't fit with Rose's recollection. I must've made a face because he asked, "What?"

"Your aunt says she saw you recently."

Matt said, "Whatever. Look, I gotta go to work." He averted his eyes.

"You mentioned the pushers were not local."

"Española. Go figure."

No surprise, Española. The city's population neared twelve thousand people but suffered a drug overdose death rate six times the national average, the nation's worst. "You remember or hear any more, call me."

Pecos exhaled, looked at his watch, stood, then said, "Man, I gotta go."

"I'll find them, Matt. I will find them." My stakes in this murder were no different than Matt's. Juan was a brother for the better part of my life.

Matt nodded, wiped his face with a sleeve. He followed me out, slammed the front door, then hopped into his vehicle.

Matt and I drove off in opposite directions. As the distance from Albuquerque increased, Matt's credibility decreased. Matt was distraught at his father's passing, but he asked no questions about the death. He seemed distressed at first but recovered quickly. Too quickly. I wondered if and what he was holding back.

My suspicions were the product of a cynicism I've developed over my life as a Marine and a cop. I had no evidence to suspect Matt except a feeling and that he owned an expensive truck. That could mean a lot of things. Or nothing. I tucked my doubts away. For now.

Morning traffic north on I-25 dragged the trip out and confirmed my reasons for not living in the city, any city.

Beyond Bernalillo, the traffic thinned and I floored it. No pueblo car, this. I was probably the only pueblo cop who had no official car. The pueblo's budget never included one.

I preferred it that way. They paid for gas, but this ride was mine. The growl of the engine and the whine of the Jeep's

28

big tires improved my spirits. I shifted to third gear and let the pipes blow. The rumbling glass packs made my world right.

Chapter 6

At my desk, a pile of paperwork I'd been putting off
waited. As I waded through it, I replayed the visit with Matt.
He seemed truly shocked, but who wouldn't be. It did not go
unnoticed that Matt never asked me how his mother was doing.
And he had memory problems over his last home visit.
Disbelief gnawed at the back of my brain, but my gut said to
withhold judgment.

The phone rang. "You down in Albuquerque talking to
Matt Pecos?" asked Special Agent Crutchman.

"Thought all your spy drones were in Afghanistan." It
hadn't been two hours since I interviewed Pecos.

"Don't get smart, Romero. You have no jurisdiction
and you're pushing up against interference."

"I have every right to inform next of kin, something
you fucked up. That's cold, Crutchman."

"I don't like rez cops telling me how to do my job."

I steamed, waited for the pressure to blow off. "Another
comment like that and I'll let every rez cop between here and
Oklahoma know of your appreciation of them. Better yet, I'll
take it to the SAC." I knew the Special Agent-in-Charge. She
considered me a pain-in-the-ass and would probably kiss it off,
but Crutchman, new to the field office, had no idea what she
would do.

"You won't get another warning, Romero."

"Either will you." I followed with a cheerful, "Have a
nice day!" I slammed the handset. Crutchman could take issue
with my supposed threats until he figured out the SAC didn't
give a shit what I said.

No, I wasn't staying away from this case. Someone had
killed my friend and his son on my reservation. I would not
stop probing just because some fed said so.

My personal line rang again. The same computer voice
said, "If you are Peter Romero, please press one..." I hung up.

In the past, I needed money fast. A neighbor's horse I
loved, Crowd Killer, had become available for sale by his
previous owner. By the time I found out, the horse was halfway

30

out of the barn on his way to Texas. Since my personal life was turning to shit, I couldn't stand to lose another living thing that would have anything to do with me. I put up my car for a loan from a payday service that called day and night if you missed a payment.

The bill collectors were on my ass. Harassment by phone and threatening letters interrupted my days and nights because I'd missed a couple of payments while laid off. No amount of discussion with a human being—I'd actually found one at BandelierQuickLoan—could persuade the collectors to lay off. I considered hiring a lawyer but that would take money I didn't have. I considered shooting the phone, but I didn't have enough money to replace it.

The talk with Matt had opened leads that required attention. I needed follow-up on the question of his last visit to the family but, in a pueblo like this, you have to question in a very circumspect way. Word gets around and may return to bite. As a Marine, I'd often throw verbal hand grenades and survey the destruction, but that wouldn't work here, so I had to figure another approach. For now, I had other tips to follow.

One lead pointed to Española, sixty miles north. Some road time and a few questions might turn up something. Sure, the FBI warned me away but they'd always done that, and I always managed to escape their wrath, not to mention, charges. To me, evading the constraints of the system has always been an art form.

Driving north, the collection activities of BandelierQuickLoan soured my mood. Fortunately, driving my Jeep had a way of making a bad day nicer. I flew on Interstate 25, then eased around Santa Fe traffic on the bypass, and rolled Highway 85 to Española. Traffic proved heavy in town because this day was the annual Lowrider Fest, a celebration of Chicano culture and showing off the hydraulically-athletic cars.

The Fest parking lot at the Española Plaza Convento was full but I made a quick tour of the area checking for the Hummer with Colorado plates that had cruised my rez.

Chances of spotting the H3 were zero-to-none but luck plays big in any investigation.

I parked near the plaza's entrance then walked around the place. In addition to classic and lowrider cars, there were bands, *Los Niños de Santa Fe* lined up to perform a dance set, food vendors cooked, and artisans sold goods at the periphery. Giggles and squeals emanated from bouncy houses. All under a clear sky and hot sun. It was a beautiful day to enjoy New Mexico culture.

Lowriders on display were eye candy for car nuts, me included. At least a hundred cars, every age, make, and American model. Ford LTD's and Galaxies; Chevy Impalas and Bel Airs; Lincoln Continentals and Cadillac DeVilles had gathered in colors resembling Halloween candy. Candy apple red, lightning blue, neon lime, iridescent magenta, dazzling gold. And colors of Indians: Inca and Aztec gold, forest green, sky blue, dusky purple. Sparkling flaked colors, pearled colors, and chrome wherever metal showed. And murals, too: Madonna with the baby Jesus, Jesus on the cross, Jesus in tears. Laughing floral skulls, Katrinas, Aztec women, Hispanic women, Chicana women, buxom women, naked women. A few crying Elvises, too. Lowrider paintjobs have always been over the top, and this was the cream spilling over the brim.

Between band sets, speakers boomed recordings of lowrider favorites: Divine Sound's "What People do for Money", Debbie Deb's "When I Hear Music", and *"Sabor A Mi"* by El Chicano.

A voice interrupted the music to announce, in Spanish and English, the lowrider jumping contest would start in thirty minutes.

When the band started playing again, I scanned the crowd. The combo, a seven-member group included guitars, a sax, flute, keyboards, and a hot percussionist. The crowd screamed when the group launched into War's "Why Can't We Be Friends" followed by "Cisco Kid" and "The World is a Ghetto." Relieved at finding no hostile faces, I walked over to the displays.

Lowriders are not just cars, they are lifestyles, social medium, expressions of the owner. There's an extensive social network built around them. A parking lot full of lowriders and music was an instant town plaza. This was a prime place to ask questions, and not because these people were involved in drugs and murder. The opposite is true. This tight community knew the kind of people to avoid. The kind I was looking for.

Spectators strolled up and down the rows admiring the cars and talking with the owners. I kept an eye on them. Some folks around this town knew me and not in a friendly way. In the past, I'd been on cases that ended with sentences for a few of the locals and running into their kin could be awkward, painful, or worse.

People seemed to be enjoying themselves and I wished I could, but I was on the job. I walked up and down the rows, then stood in front of a 1984, bagged and body-dropped Fleetwood Caddy with shaved door handles, windshield squirters, rain gutters, and gas door. This ride sported a chromed chain steering wheel, plush leather interior, and a dazzling candy red paint job that must have cost over twenty-five grand on its own. I walked around it and looked for the owner but couldn't find him.

While keeping an eye out for the owner of the H3, I wandered by a '95 gray Chevy Silverado with off-white leather and custom suede interior. Every visible mechanical part was chromed: wheels, shocks, hydraulics, axles, engine. The truck's bed was crammed with pinstriped hydraulic equipment. What little space remained in the bed displayed trophies proving this show truck could jump. A small sign in front advertised for sale.

"You sellin'?" I asked the owner, a local wearing a short-sleeve black t-shirt that displayed the seal of Chicano Nation, *Aztlan.*

He beamed and said, "Done with it. Old lady says I need another one." He laughed and launched into the details of the construction of the love of his life. I could keep up with most of the minutiae because I had built my own Jeep from junk. I feigned interest and waited for an opening to redirect the conversation to what I wanted.

As he became lost in his life, heat rose on my face. I could feel someone's eyes burning on me. I crossed my arms and turned to the side and pretended to listen while I scanned the crowd. No one seemed to pay any attention to me. I turned back to my lecturer who appeared to be cooing to his engine.

The sense of being scrutinized returned and I kept my head turned to my one-man tour guide while looking around under my eyebrows. This time I spotted a bearded man staring at me from behind a juiced low-low Impala jumping in front of a cheering crowd. The man appeared, disappeared, reappeared behind the front end of the Chevy as it bounced up, stalled at the top, and then slammed to the ground only to bounce up again. He vanished as soon as our eyes locked.

I circled to get a better look while trying to appear aimless. It didn't work because when I regained sight of him, he stood by three full-bearded men looking straight at me.

This is where I weighed options. Option Easy: turn and walk away. Option Smart: stand my ground and glare like a pissed brahma. Option Stupid: confront the four men by jumping in with both feet.

My old Marine Corps drill instructor reappeared in my head. Whenever he materialized, I was in for it. "You got one option and only one, Marine," he said, his hot breath on my face. "Move it!" my DI barked, the sensation real enough to ring in my ears.

Bravado and brains don't always mix, so I shit-canned my good sense, and puffed myself up while ignoring the feeling my five-ten height was not that impressive. I walked over to the group of hostiles and asked, "I know you?"

One man—had to be *the* man—showed missing teeth. "Who the fuck're you?"

I gave them the up and down, made a show of it. Each of his group wore the same sort of garb: blue jeans, black Nike skateboard shoes, t-shirts boasting Thrasher or Redemption. They watched my eyes. I said, "From around here?"

"Who the fuck're you?" Same guy, same question.

"Watch your language. Lotta kids here."

His lips, nearly hidden behind his beard, split into a smile. I took it as an invitation to put a fist in it.

Before I could, a voice from behind me said, "Ah, Romero. *Estado buscando para usted, cabrón.*"

34

I turned. Six enormous Hispanic males salivated over me like Wolf. My new-found enemies from Colorado would have to take hind-tit to the locals.

Chapter 7

The bangers were led by Ángel "Wookie" Gutierrez who was doing the talking. I'd put him behind bars many years ago, as well as his brother. Father, too, come to think of it. Wookie was blue with tats beneath a thick layer of arm hair, cue ball-headed, squat and roundish low-centered body. Prison-yard muscle rippled under the fat.

"*Que casualidad*, findin' you here, *vato*," he said loud enough for his homies, and the Coloradan boarders, and the surrounding lowriders to hear.

While watching others, it turned out, I was watched. I should've picked up on it earlier. But while I was focusing too much on finding informants and the Colorado boarders, I'd neglected my rear.

Wookie knew everybody who had done time most everywhere in the state. And everybody knew Wookie. For him, finding me was easy. Even in a crowd this size. People hurried away with their wives and children. The crowded parking lot emptied in seconds, leaving empty car displays.

Wookie smiled showing teeth, alpha dog at the head of his pack. "Long time, homes."

His voice sounded friendly, but I knew better. No doubt, he referred to his hard time in Vacaville after the local sheriff, the FBI, and I nailed him pulling a couple for-hire murders for an LA gang. I was surprised to see him out in the world.

Wookie scrutinized me up and down, then the Colorado snowboarders, then me, maybe deciding who he wanted to hurt first. To the Coloradans he said, "You *pinche chingaderos* still here?"

The boarders looked at Wookie, then at me, then at the bangers. I expected them to play cool, but they obviously knew Wookie. They hustled to a black H3 parked behind the crowd and laid rubber out of the parking lot. Wookie smirked.

Being alone with Wookie Gutierrez is not what I had in mind when I started this investigation, especially alone with Wookie and six huge cholos. He closed in, heating my face with red chilé breath, "Tell me why I shouldn't kill you now, *cabrón?"*

Any answer would be the wrong one, so I stayed silent.

"You owe me, Romero. You owe me time. Time in seg and the yard, man. For my brother and father, too. *Entiendes?"*

I understood; understood I had to get out of here or take my chances. I had some defensive moves, but not for six men ready for me to make them. Everyone but Wookie was packing, too.

"What do you want, Wookie?"

"For a long time, all I wanted was your heart, man. I planned it out, dreamt about it, man. Drew a picture of it on my cell. I could taste it. That's how much I wanted it." He drew an arm across his face, wiping my imagined blood from his lips.

"And now?" I readied without moving. Adrenalin surged through me, causing my legs to shake. I clenched my fists. If this was my day to die, a few of these assholes would join me.

He grabbed for a hip pocket. Wookie was famous in these parts for his knife work. The rush of self-preservation kicked me in the ass, and I lunged at him, but instead met a boot in my stomach from a man to his right. I ate dirt. His men laughed.

"*¡Cállate!* Wookie said. The gang shut up. "Take it easy, Romero. I got somethin' to show you. It's cool. Chill, homes."

I stood. Spit dirt. Wiped my face with an arm. He handed me a photograph of a little girl. The photo shook in my fingers.

A three-year-old smiled out from the picture, raven-haired and clothed in a fluffy pink dress. Love and innocence radiated from her beaming face.

Wookie pointed at the photo. "That's Ximena. Yeah, Ximena. I talk to her; she listens to me. That's what *ximena* means."

His daughter. "Beautiful like her mama," I said. I'd seen Wookie's ex at trial.

"Ella es tu Salvador."

37

"What?" Wookie's thick Spanglish accent was tough to understand.

"She's your savior 'because I only want her, now. Not you. She's *mi bebé*, and I want to love her like she love me."

"Okay," I said, voice flat and non-committal. I was not sure which way this was going, and my stomach signaled it didn't either. I swallowed a bad taste.

"*Sí, mijo*. You are the great *investigador*. Everybody knows." Wookie opened his eyes wide. No way in hell he meant it, despite the promotion from bastard to son. "I'm goin' straight and she is my family, *mi inspiración* to stay straight. Gonna send her to college, man."

"What do you want from me, Wookie." My adrenaline was inching down and I wanted out of here before I crashed or he decided to kill me.

"She's missing," he said.

"Who?"

"My daughter, *pendejo*." He pinched his eyebrows.

My status had dropped to stupid. This would not end well.

"Find her," he said.

"Call your ex."

Wookie smiled. "*Esta muerta.*"

The deadpan statement was ominous. To ask Wookie how his ex got to be dead would not help my position. "Call the police then."

Wookie elevated his head. "How's that gonna play out, *cabrón?*"

He had a point. Wookie Gutierrez had spent all his life in trouble before he went to Vacaville. The son of a Rio Arriba County deputy had been killed years before, but the body and critical evidence had never surfaced. Gutierrez was never indicted, but everyone in town knew he played a leading role. Wookie never took pains to deny it either, in fact, he had the deceased's name tattooed on his forearm. Law enforcement officers in this part of New Mexico wanted Wookie's blood and he knew it. That's why he didn't pack iron. No, going to the cops would not help find Wookie's child.

"I got no jurisdiction off the rez."

38

Wookie seemed incredulous. After all, I had arrested his ass years ago.

"Fuck that shit. You find her. I pay plenty," he said.

"I don't think I can help you, bro." I caught myself looking for a door, but in this open parking lot there was no escape.

Wookie showed teeth. *"Cabrón,* I don't *ask* nobody." His crew spread out. I could probably make it through three, four of them before they shot or stabbed me, but those were not encouraging odds. For what it was worth, I threw my baddest testosterone eye.

It didn't work. Wookie's face wore the dead, indifferent glare of a predator. I took a step back and straightened up.

"Nothin' I can do, man." I held up my hands, turned, and walked away expecting a bullet. His eyes stung hard on my neck as I walked, but I preferred the stare. I also knew Wookie would not accept my refusal and I would see him later.

When I got to where I'd parked, my Jeep was gone. My beautiful '53 custom that I'd poured my heart into back in the day. Damn near broke an arm putting in the Chevy V-8. My dad shit when he found out how much money I'd put into just the paint job.

I shook my fist at no one. "Jesus H. Christ," I said.

My face heated as I shot glances around the lot. Maybe I'd parked it somewhere else. Maybe someone was playing a joke. No such luck.

Wookie and three of his thugs cruised by in a '64 Impala SS Rag Top, gloss black and blasting "Lowrider" by War. The cholos scowled, each face showing how much they'd hate to be anyone else. The others followed in a low-low '67 pearled-cream Impala four-door, booming "Jeep Ass Niguh" by Masta Ace. The cars dipped and jumped like Weasel then sped off.

I looked for a rock to throw, but the lot was as clean as their tricked-out Chevys. I stood there like a fool, my face aching from grinding teeth.

Chapter 8

The Lowrider Fest parking lot repopulated as I walked away. People who live near psychos like Wookie develop a sort of danger-detecting radar like Squirrel. And, like Squirrel, they know when to run and when to come together again.

Now I was without wheels. Wookie must've known I would do anything for my car. The image of it being driven by some scumbag grated. I shuddered at the image of my Jeep rigged low-low and scraping sparks off the pavement. I walked to the south end of Española. My legs weakened like a newborn calf, but I headed out on the long walk home.

I was hungry, but I couldn't cook for shit. The thought of me fumbling around in Costancia's kitchen on my own reminded me of the divorce papers still sitting on my desk. I scolded myself for surrendering to self-pity, but that made me feel worse.

In some places, Indians have a hard time catching a ride on the highway, but around here, most everyone is Indian. I worked a thumb for ten minutes until someone stopped.

It was dusk, so I couldn't make out the color or detail on the pickup as it slowed and pulled off to the shoulder. The evening had started to cloud up and chill and I wasn't in the mood to be picky.

As luck would have it, the driver was not just any Indian, it was Clement Ouray Pokoh, the Southern Ute cop I'd mistakenly roughed up in front of my house. A man holding an AK-47 in your driveway is hard to forget.

"You hoofin' it?" he said, as I slid in.

"Startin' to think you're tailin' me."

"Looks that way to me, too." He pulled out into the traffic lanes of Highway 84.

"Seems like I run into you more than I need," I said.

Pokoh chuffed. "You need me, now."

"What gives, Pokoh?"

"You got some big head, Romero. You hold some kind of overblown image of yourself."

On our right, rolling hills hid the sun's remains. Orange and magenta clouds floated in a sea of blood pierced by green-

and yellow-striped shafts. Above the traffic noise, I thought I heard Coyote chuckling somewhere.

Traffic heading south was light. Pokoh's face looked aged in the approaching lights. I envisioned a prehistoric campfire flickering on his skin.

The ancients have always had a way of connecting to me if they wanted to and they were signaling something haunting about Pokoh now.

But what did any of that have to do with meeting him on this highway exactly when I needed a ride the most? I don't buy into coincidences and I didn't believe him. Before I could speak, he said, "What you want with Gutierrez?"

"Wookie wanted me. I was in Española huntin' for leads on murders at the pueblo, when he jacked me up and stole my car. How'd you know I talked to him?"

Pokoh pointed to a pair of binoculars hanging around his neck. Military and high tech. "What'd he want?" He looked at me and veered toward the centerline.

I pushed my boots against the floor. "His daughter."

"Daughter? No daughter. Not legally. She was fostered out a year ago."

"Oh?"

"There's more," Pokoh said. "His old lady went missing while he was in Vacaville."

"No other family?"

"Few are stupid enough to have Wookie in the family."

"Ever locate the ex-wife?"

Pokoh laughed. "Wookie plus missing ex-wife. Do the math."

"Figures. Then, why's he looking' for Ximena?"

"Don't know." Pokoh went quiet, then said, "I've been tailing his ass, figured him for the horse killings. Bad things going down around here usually have something to do with Wookie and it doesn't matter if he's in or out of prison. I was hoping you'd tell me why he wants the girl."

"Even if I knew, I couldn't tell." Sharing the details of my investigations was never a good idea. "So, you're connecting Wookie to the horses?" I asked, expecting him to violate my own rule.

41

He laughed while he said, "Fuck you, Romero."

Neither of us spoke during the remaining miles. He dropped me off at home under an ink dome perforated by ten thousand eyes of light. He looked at me a long minute and said, "You and I are gonna to come to an understanding."

He drove off before I could ask what he meant.

I was hungry, so I headed for our—my—kitchen. I averted my eyes from the divorce papers on my office desk. The refrigerator was empty except for two black lemons and some moldy cheese labelled with a name I'd never heard of. I found some wilted lettuce and threw it out. I looked for bread to make a cheese sandwich. After two inspections of every cabinet and drawer, I remembered I hadn't bought any bread. No car, so going to the store or out to eat was a non-starter. I could walk down the road to my neighbor Gilbert, a retired chef, but he was off somewhere in the Pacific with his new wife.

I ended up eating the mystery cheese while thinking about how the FBI had warned me off the Pecos family murders. Fuck them. The wave-off by Special Agent Crutchman only made me want the challenge more.

Burping stale cheese, sitting at the kitchen counter, I laid out the details on the Pecos murders; a double murder, brutal and senseless. Drug activity and theft was a potential motive. There was unusual traffic coming in and out of the pueblo by suspicious thugs with Colorado plates. And then there was the dead horses. Some had turned up here, others in Colorado. Colorado seemed to run through the case like an icy creek.

The potential connection in both cases interested me and presented an opportunity. I didn't want the horse case, but Palafox had made an offer. What if I worked a two-fer by looking for the horse thieves and the Pecos murders on the side?

What-ifs. I had a mind full of them including what if I did nothing? A vision of Juan Pecos surrounded by halo of dark blood shoved its way into my head. Juan was my friend. I had a duty to him. And my job as a cop was to chase what-ifs. If one didn't pan out, I would move on to the next.

The mystery cheese didn't agree with my stomach, so I got a glass of water to put out the fire. I walked to my office and punched in the number of Santa Fe County Security Consulting; the firm hired to get the bottom of the horse killings. It was late, but I would leave a message.

"Palafox."

Surprised to hear his voice, I said, "Sorry for the late call but is that offer to investigate your missing horses still open?" I stifled a burp.

Palafox paused. I could hear muffled talking off-phone at Palafox's end. "When can we talk?"

"I'll be there at noon tomorrow." I hung up and ran to the bathroom. My stomach had lost its battle with the mystery cheese.

Next morning, I smooth-talked a neighbor into a loaner and drove to Santa Fe near the New Mexico School for the Deaf on Cerrillos. Palafox's office was typical of the area; worn single story adobes undergoing gentrification. A secretary walked me to a private office. Some walls of the room, which looked like a former living area, were covered with old Indian weapons; part of an extensive bow and arrow collection. I couldn't resist examining a bow and imagine ancient hands the color of mine grasping it, prepared for battle. Other walls held professional certificates and pictures of Palafox shaking hands with Clintons and Bushes.

The man walked in, paid no mind to pleasantries, and started our conversation in the middle by saying, "I got questions, Romero. First, is motive. Strange to steal expensive horses then kill them. Makes no sense to me."

"Money's not the motive. What's the next?" I asked.

"Opportunity. Can't get a handle on how they do it. We got good cover on the ranch, but they still steal them, anyway. And Colorado, that's the third question. With the exception of the horse you found, carcasses have ended up in southern Colorado."

"What about the theory that the thieves have it in for the owner of the ranch? I understand he's a Saudi."

Palafox nodded. "We're working that angle. Nothing yet."

"So, you think I find the answers better than your own people?"

"Special Agent Jean Reel recommends you. I've known her for years. We worked together on White House detail. She's solid. If she likes you, I like you."

"Why not go to the FBI, then? This is a multi-state crime."

He snorted. "Why don't we bring in the New Mexico Fire and Police Pipes and Drums while we're at it?"

"But why all the secrecy? These are horses, not children."

"The owner is why. The owner of these horses is a discrete man-of-means and conducts his affairs out of the public limelight. He is adamant that his private business never makes the paper. Agent Reel says you'd understand the need for strict confidentiality."

"I got another case. Murder. I gotta work that, too."

"Okay, you do what you gotta do, but never forget you're working for me. Here's a retainer for expenses." He stared at me deadpan, waiting for my response. I grabbed the check and casually glanced at it. I gulped at the numbers, my monthly salary times six.

As I stared at the check, the dead bodies of Juan and Jason formed before me, their blank eyes imploring mine. Couldn't say if it was guilt or integrity that made me mumble out a half-truth, "I'm obligated to the murder case."

Palafox continued to stare. Silent as Owl. When I was ready to cave, he said, "Okay, Romero, do what you gotta do on the side, but I want results. Fast."

I said, "Yeah. I need a car. Jeep's out of commission." Not entirely a lie, but I wasn't about to admit my car was stolen.

"I look like Avis to you?" he asked. More silence. I waited for a *fuck you*. "I'll have a truck at your place tomorrow."

I left wondering how far I'd pissed him off and how hard it would come back to bite me.

44

Chapter 9

The next morning, a new silver Chevy Silverado HD 3500 6.6L Duramax Turbo-Diesel V8 sat out front. A note from Palafox gave his number and invited a call if I wanted anything else. What else was there?

It took thirty minutes to figure out all the buttons in the truck's cab. I hurried into the house when the police line rang. I picked up and a voice droned, "If you are Peter Ro—" I hung up.

I grabbed my overnight bag from the bedroom, a .357 Magnum S&W Model 686 revolver with a 4-inch barrel and a couple of speed loaders from the safe and locked the house. I hopped into the truck, adjusted the seat and mirrors, then headed off to Colorado.

The big truck gobbled up I-25, then US-285. When I passed Española, I felt a pang for my stolen Jeep. The '53 was more pet than truck. I missed it like a trusted companion and rage swelled as I thought of it being in the hands of some punk.

I punched the gas thinking of Wookie's demand I find his fostered-out child. I took US-84 and 64 to Navajo City, then north across the Colorado state line toward Ignacio, the home of the Southern Ute Tribe.

In Colorado, natural gas piping and holding tanks grew like oversized cactus. The green structures failed to blend with the rolling woodlands that defined flowered meadows. A crew of two attended one of the well pumps. Their white pickup sported a circle-shaped, two-feathers logo on the door.

To the north, snow-painted peaks of the San Juan Range sparkled like diamonds. I squinted in the bright sun. Piñon and juniper occupied most rocky ridges. In the flat areas, knee-high blue grama and wheatgrass covered the rocky soil. In this high country, I could see fifty breathtaking miles to the south and west. The ancestors were right: when Old Spider Woman created all things, she started here.

In Ignacio, a town so small it made Santa Fe look like New York, I found and parked at the Southern Ute headquarters; a modern red brick one-story named after a man named Burch. I stood in the parking area to stretch and enjoy the view of the San Juan Range. A glass entry sported a fancy logo of two feathers surrounding the name of the occupants, Red Pine Production Company. In the lobby, Pokoh leaned on a counter shooting the shit with a cute receptionist, a cup of coffee in his hand.

"Bout time you got here," he said.

"You knew I was comin'?"

He didn't answer as he led me past a sign that announced the Southern Ute Department of Justice and Regulatory. Pokoh motioned me into a good size office with a wooden desk, two chairs and a nice picture window view of an outbuilding. They say you can tell a person's influence from the size of their workspace. Pokoh had juice.

An assortment of baskets, pouches, stones, twigs, animal skins, bird wings, bones, pipes, and masks cluttered the place. Pokoh's office was reminiscent of the cluttered homes of some of my own tribe's elders, people still possessing powers of the old ways. Growing up we knew better, dismissed them when our grandmothers would bring them into our homes when we were sick. These ancient ones spoke to gods we hadn't witnessed.

They tried to teach us, the old ones. As we grew older, some of us reached back to embrace the old ways and the connections to the earth, life, and community. Some of us learned to just accept there was magic where we couldn't see it. Some of us never learned a thing. I wondered if the Ute children were the same. I also wondered if this was how Pokoh knew I was coming.

Pokoh sat behind his desk.

I sat in the only chair without something on it. I asked, "You a...what, a healer?" He couldn't be anything else with this assortment of ancient remedies, "or law enforcement?"

Pokoh took a seat behind his desk. "I deal with matters of the spirit. I'm a spiritual guide. It's in the family. Like a calling, you know. Law enforcement puts bread on the table."

"So, healing's like a side-job?" Ancient medicine is serious business and I regretted saying it as soon as it left my lips.

He inclined his head like Wolf sizing up an intruder. "This is no side job." There was bite behind the words. "Some people call me a shaman, but that don't mean much today. What people don't get, even many in my tribe I'm sorry to say, is the real meaning of the word. People can't see beyond the name *Shaman* to the sacred energy drawn from many aspects of the physical world, the mind, and the soul. A quality that emerges from all sorts of places to envelope us. No, people today just don't get it. You, neither."

I couldn't disagree with him. Not completely, but I have felt that sacred energy more than once.

Pokoh stood up, like he was going to salute. "We Utes are the oldest residents of Colorado and have lived here since the beginning of time. Our language is Shoshonean. We are ancestors of the Paiute, Goshute, Shoshone, Comanche, and Chemehuevi. Our power once extended throughout the great basin and our territories ran from Oregon to New Mexico.

"We and our cousins possessed a strong set of central values in a highly-developed society. But now, things are changing. And not for good." His smile had dropped as he spoke. "What makes it worse, we're sittin' on an ocean of natural gas. We're pulling seventy billion cubic feet of out of the ground every year. That doesn't include our leases in the Gulf of Mexico or Texas.

"So, nobody really gives a shit about the past. Nobody. The modern world pollutes our culture with its artificial values. Outsiders remake our pride and traditions, then claim them as their own. False shamans springing up everywhere with never-ending lies. To those of us who care, our traditions are no longer recognizable. The old ways gonna be gone soon, somebody don't do something."

"All our people have sad stories to tell, but I'm here to talk about horses." Me and my mouth. It's not a good idea to insult a source of information. I held my palms up in surrender.

"Yeah, you don't know shit," said Pokoh, still pissed.

"Look, I'm sorry I punched you in front of my house and I'm sorry if I insulted your calling," I said. Apologizing was something I didn't do often, but I needed Pokoh's help. "Come on, man. I drove up here 'cause you're on the case."

47

"Rumor has you're working private. I don't give a shit about private."

"On rez authority, too," I lied. "A murder."

"Whose?"

"Two men, father and son at the pueblo, had their throats slit in their beds."

"That's cold. Any leads."

"Working the idea the perps come from this area."

Pokoh stared at me, for minutes it seemed. "We had a similar murder two weeks ago. Similar M.O. A Mexican man. No leads, though." He turned his chair and looked out the window. "So, why you want to see where the horses were killed?"

I explained my arrangement with Palafox.

Pokoh stood. "Let's go."

We hopped into his truck, the same beat up '72 Chevy C10 I'd seen before and headed south along CO-172. The alpine air was clear and cool.

Pokoh said, "Altogether, we found three dead Arabians up here. All shot in the head at night. Weird thing is, there was no attempt to hide the carcasses. All three was dumped alongside the 172 in full view of traffic. First I figured they were a bunch of dumb shits just being dicks."

"And now?"

"Well, I combed the area and they was very careful about covering their tracks. No footprints, no tire tracks, no expended shells. Clean crime scene. No cans, bottles, or cigarette butts, so no DNA. Each dump site was at a road curve or cut that blocked view from most angles. Asked around the area. No strange trucks or trailers. No unusual noises."

"Locals?" I asked.

"Well, they seem to know the layout of the highways and traffic patterns to make sure they won't be interrupted or seen from a distance."

Pokoh said, " 'S'what I think. All three horses were found next to the road or partly on it, so no tire tracks or footprints."

We passed a hand-painted sign next to the road that said *This Land Was Your Land*.

48

"What's that about?"

Pokoh chuffed. "Sagebrush Rebellion, they call it. Utah, Nevada, here, Idaho, Wyoming, wherever you see big plots of BLM land. Assholes say they're riding a wave of citizen anger and claim to be locals. But the lying bastards are fronting flatlanders wantin' money-makers like grazing, oil, gas, mining. People with political connections are demanding return of federal land to state control. Return to the state, can you believe that shit? How 'bout returning it to the people that lived here in the first fuckin' place?"

"You need to quit holdin' it in, you know. Let it all out. Express yourself."

Pokoh laughed.

As we travelled, we passed several eighteen-wheeled tankers, each with the white two-feather logo I'd noticed before. "I'm seein' a lot of that two-feather insignia."

"Right, that's the emblem of Red Pine Production. Owned by Southern Utes, like everything else."

"Oh?"

"Big time. One of the most productive natural gas fields in the country right here. Plus, we Utes got gas leases in Texas, Wyoming, and the Gulf of Mexico. Got real estate near San Diego." Pokoh slapped the steering wheel. "Fuckin' traffic, too," he said while passing a slow-moving tanker.

"What's that written between the feathers?" I asked.

"Where?"

"Between the two feathers on the truck's door. A word in, what, Ute? *Queogand*. What's it mean?"

"*Queogand?* Bear. It means bear. Each truck has a name that symbolizes our past. Bear's a big deal in Ute legends. Better believe it."

When we passed another tanker, I asked the same question. "What's *Teahshooggoosh?*"

Pokoh said, "Deer. Deer is a survivor. Like us Indians, right?"

We passed two others, Coyote, *Yeodze*, and Wolf, *Shinab*, before we pulled over at a curve in the road where eight-foot berms hid the road from outside view. Pokoh handed me a pair of disposable shoe covers to wear. I put them on over my boots.

I stepped out of the truck and walked over to a stain on the edge of the highway. I pointed to the spot. "Blood?"

"Yup. The mare, *Rababa*. Pregnant, you know. Damn shame. Found two others down the road about a half mile. Same kind of place like this, but different days. I'll show you when we're done here."

The site was a perfect dump. The road curved through low hills and blocked all but the closest eyes. The nearest farmhouse, about a half mile away, was out of view. I walked south about three hundred yards but found nothing of interest. Ignacio Sheriff's CSI unit had picked over the place and footprints were everywhere. Pokoh leaned up against his pickup, arms folded, like he'd found all the evidence and I was wasting his time.

Since this crime scene had no human victim, the possibility that detective work may have been sloppy was strong. After returning and heading north past the blood stains, I spotted blue in the grass. "Look at this."

Pokoh trotted over. He picked up the blue cloth with a pair of tweezers and held it up to the bright sun. He seemed a little embarrassed when he said, "Good eye. Yeah, part of a hospital bootie, looks like. No marks or tags so we're down to about what, five million suspects?"

I said, "Also explains why there are no unique footprints."

"Only thing it proves is these perps is pros." Pokoh shook his head.

I stepped close to the scrap to study it. "There's a stain on it. Mud, maybe. Might be enough for analysis."

"I'll send it in," he said. He pulled an envelope out of his pocket and stuffed the bootie scrap in, sealed and marked the envelope. "Let's go, I got two more places to show you."

We headed to the truck. Pokoh hopped in behind the wheel and locked his seat belt when I did.

He turned to me. "I got this theory of what's going on."

"Shoot," I said.

"Well, I been asking around. Knocking on doors, hitting the bars, you know. Funny how people talk when you buy their beer."

I said, "Drunks can talk bullshit." I was an expert on the subject. I'd played the part back in the day.

"So, I'm talking to this sheepherder, guy named Rafi Maestrejuan. He jabbers a load of bullshit for ten minutes, then he brags he's got a secret. Don't tell no one, he says, but before I agree, he just blurts it out," Pokoh said.

He leaned in to start the engine, pumped the accelerator twice, waited, then turned the key. "Got to do it just right, it's touchy as hell," he said, chuckling. The engine sputtered, then coughed to a standstill. "Now we got to wait some to restart the engine, besides, you and me gotta talk."

A loud snap and the windshield spidered around a small hole. Pokoh's head jerked back, forward, then crashed into the steering wheel with a crack. Warm blood splattered over me and ran down the cab's back wall.

I threw open the door, dove to the ground and rolled. I scrambled behind the truck, tried to catch my breath and bearings. I caught enough air to feed my sprinting heart as I searched for the shooter. The shot had come from the front and at a distance, but the road-side berms hid the trigger man. The only way I could get a view was to crawl to the top of the mound. It wasn't a good plan until I had some idea where he was. A rifleman that good required a healthy dose of respect and fear.

Worse, I was unarmed, with my S&W sitting in my truck.

Pokoh had a Glock. I crawled around to the driver's side of the pickup and opened the door. If Pokoh had not been strapped in, he would have fallen on me, the poor bastard. I reached around his waist; the smell of copper strong enough to make my nose itch.

Pokoh wore a holster on his right side and I fumble-fucked with its safety strap, slippery with blood. The dead man did not cooperate, leaning into my arm as I tried to pull out his weapon

Stones clicked behind me. I pulled harder at the pistol, nearly dislodging the body from the front seat. A rock rolled down the embankment. I spun, dropped to the dirt on my ass. I pointed the Glock, adrenaline shakes destroying my aim.

Deer stood at the top of the rise staring at me with his huge eyes, his ears following sound independently and waiting for me to say something. Unable to speak or move, I stared through the quivering gun sight at the reddish-brown creature. His rack branched four feet across and reached up two feet above his head. The dark V-shaped markings on his forehead pointed to his twitchy nose.

Deer senses danger like Dog smells meat, so I lowered the Glock and relaxed. If the buck wasn't nervous, I shouldn't be. The sniper was gone. The animal sniffed at some scrub, then walked away.

Rubber legs made climbing up the berm difficult. I hoped to get a view of a distant getaway vehicle, but nothing betrayed the killer's exit. I called 911.

"Officer down," I said.

Exhausted, I collapsed on the hillside above the truck. Through the windshield, the noon sun glittered in the red splash covering the rear cab wall, Pokoh's body and what was left of his head. The urge to check his pulse swelled, but I suppressed it, the habit and my hope for him, pointless.

The poor man never saw it coming.

Neither did I. My chest emptied except for the despair every cop feels at the loss of a brother professional. I descended into self-pity.

But I was the lucky one.

Chapter 10

Within fifteen minutes, the road filled with black and gold SUVs from the Southern Ute Reservation Police Department and white Fords from the Ignacio police. Eventually, the La Plata County Sheriff showed, and even the Durango PD, fifty miles distant, joined. Cruisers, SUVs, and pickups flashed red and blue. Techs in clean, white suits and light blue booties swarmed everywhere stretching yellow police tape. Only the FBI, BIA, and Santa Fe Symphony Orchestra and Chorus were missing.

I felt pretty useless and wanted to leave but I was the eyewitness to an unseen shot from an undetermined location and the sole survivor of an anonymous shooter. Fuck me.

What held my attention, though, was the last thing Pokoh said, *You and me gotta talk.*

You and me gotta talk was the only thing he left me with.

The cops talked quietly in groups by skin—red, brown, or white—but the noise level increased when the subject of jurisdiction arose. The sheriff must've won because a deputy came over to my hillside-seat first. "You the witness?" he asked.

"Yeah." My head banged like ceremonial drums. The shot to Pokoh's head brought flashbacks from my days in the Corps. My adrenaline-fueled senses readied for the next battle, unknown, unseen, but inevitable.

The deputy sported a high-and-tight haircut under his cap, stood six feet, slight paunch despite the fact he looked like he could handle himself.

"Deputy Frank Jones," he said, then he asked me for identification. I handed over my Cochiti police ID. He looked at both sides, then asked, "A little out of your jurisdiction, son."

"I'm moonlighting on a horse-rustling case." No need to bring up the Pecos murders right now.

"For who?"

I didn't like the question or the way he said it. Why did he care? I said, "Santa Fe County Security Consulting." My voice flat and dead.

"You got a license to practice in Colorado?"

"New Mexico." Not quite true. I'd obtained one when released from active duty, but I let it lapse when I got the pueblo job.

"You need a license to practice in Colorado."

"Right."

"What happened, here?" he asked, thumbing over his shoulder at Pokoh's pickup.

"I only know the ending." I told him what I knew about the shooting. I was tempted to talk about seeing Deer, but that wasn't going to help.

"Don't leave the county before checking with me, Romero." He walked off. My face burned from the interview. If that was homicide investigation in Colorado, then this was the best state to kill someone.

Next, it was an Ignacio police officer who approached. He asked questions. I answered. Durango PD next. He asked more questions and offered nothing new.

I rubbed my face, sticky with the remnants of Pokoh's life. I'd heard his last breath, was present when his spirit crossed to the other world. I should have said *to hell with it* and gone home. This case was much bigger than I had imagined.

A vision of the headshot into Pokoh should have warned me off this case. Instead, it pulled me in deeper. Pokoh, a Ute, was not of my people, but our blood was one before time began. Now, the blood on my hands reunited our spirits.

I was not unsympathetic to the others, but when two Southern Ute officers stepped up, I choked up. These guys knew Pokoh better than me and I understood what it meant to lose a comrade-in-arms.

I asked the Ute cops if they suspected a motive. My interrogator shook his head.

"Who had it out for Pokoh?" I asked. They exchanged glances but said nothing.

"I'm investigating a double murder at my pueblo. I need your help."

"We got nothing on the wire about murders out of New Mexico. Aren't you out of your jurisdiction, Romero?"

So much for brothers-in-blood.

With no further role at the crime scene, I hitched a ride to Pokoh's office, picked up the loaner truck, then drove to a dumpy, sleepy-bear motel in Durango, mostly out of caution. I had no idea who the sniper was, and I didn't want to glance over my shoulder the whole time I was driving around here. If he had his sights on me, he was gonna have to work to find me.

After I checked into my room under a false name, I sat on the bed and called Palafox in Santa Fe. I told him my source of information for the horse-killer case was sniped a few hours ago.

"Jesus, man. You okay?" Palafox asked.

"Little shook, nothing much." Nothing I would admit to. I told him what little I knew about the shooting.

"I'll work it from this end," Palafox said. "Anything else?"

"Before he died, Pokoh gave me a name. I'll track him down see what I can find."

"What's the name, I'll look it up."

"Rafi Maestrejuan. A sheepherder. That's all I know. Name sounds Basque."

Off phone, keys chattered.

"Uh. Fortunately, he's got an uncommon name. Yep, that's him. From Bilbao, Spain. Here on a work visa. Wait. Yup, it expired four months, ago. Uh, otherwise no felonies, but coupla misdemeanors; DUI and bestiality with sheep."

"What, he screwed the victim in a car?" A church laugh bubbled up. Then I broke into uncontrolled laughter.

Palafox cackled, tried to speak through a horselaugh. "Listen to this. The victim's name was Dolly. In court, the perp apologized and asked for a pardon."

"You mean a Dolly pardon?" I barely got it out between gasps.

Palafox dropped the phone.

I could barely breathe, but I said, "He promise to marry Dolly?" I struggled to get the words out between heaves. I

wiped my eyes and tried to calm down. "Got an address for
Maestrejuan?"

"No physical address listed. Got a sister in Climax," he
said, in between hysterical wheezing. "Oh, God. I'm sorry.
I'm sorry," he gasped. "I can't help it." He paused, then spoke
between deep breaths. "All I got is a PO box. Man, you made
my day. Good hunting."

An enduring image of Pokoh's shattered head coupled
with hysterical laughter had drained the energy out of me and I
collapsed on the bed.

Rest would not come easily. My brain assembled and
disassembled every last moment before Pokoh's death.
Goddammit, there was nothing to add. Nothing before the shot,
not even a flash. There was life, then death. Only nothingness
followed.

As so often happens, my Marine Corps drill instructor
appeared in my head. He entered over thirty years ago and
never left. "You here to feel sorry for yourself, son?"

"Sir, no sir!" I said automatically.

"You have nothing better to do than feel sorry for
yourself?"

"Sir, no sir!"

"Get out on the street and do what a cop does!" he said,
then disappeared.

I never questioned why or when or even how my drill
instructor appeared, but I when I needed him, he showed.
When he showed, I listened.

Through the window, bands of orange clouds were
suspended in deep blue skies. I somehow managed to sleep
through the night as tortured as I was. Monsters and healers
paraded through my dreams and I'd fought and embraced them
all. I struggled out of bed, exhausted and as stiff as wood.

A double dose of motel coffee put my focus under
control. I ate at a place across the street before following my
only lead, Rafi Maestrejuan. Since Maestrejuan was a
sheepherder, he would be difficult to find. Sheepherders stay
close to their charges in *campitos* - mini trailers with no
bathroom, shower, or running water. They work for peanuts for

56

ranchers on a contract basis and could be anywhere on hundreds of thousands of mountain acres.

I drank coffee until ten, then called the Western Range Association in Salt Lake City. I talked to the executive director who said he wouldn't know where Maestrejuan worked, but he knew the Rocking Double Bar Ranch had been hiring. I drove to the La Plata County offices in Durango and searched for Rocking Double Bar ownership. The current owner was Freedom Calls, a Delaware corporation. The agent of record was a Donald LaBarge who, as luck would have it, lived locally.

The LaBarge address sat on the edge of town within hearing distance of the antique Durango and Silverton Narrow Gage railroad. There, an older ranch house needing paint nestled between low, wooded hills. Assorted auto parts decorated the acreage. I parked and knocked on the door.

"Who the hell are you?" asked a powerfully built man, dark hair, about five-ten. He looked me up and down like I just killed his favorite ram and was wearing it as a coat.

"I'm looking for a man named Rafi Maestrejuan."

LaBarge, or so I figured, snorted. "Ain't got no goddamn time for no Injun looking for no spic," he said, slamming the door.

"And a good day to you, sir," I said to the door. I'm no stranger to insulting behavior and wouldn't let that white trash ruin my day.

On the way to my motel, I had a stroke of luck. I knew the Rocking Double Bar property was in this area. Pokoh had mentioned he found Maestrejuan in a bar and there, on the right side of the road, was a bar. A sign said The Quaking A, but from the decrepit trucks parked in front, the peeling paint and missing shingles, I wasn't sure if the name referred to the neighboring aspens or its customers.

Finding the sheepherder here was a long shot. I suddenly thought of Pokoh and shook the idea away.

The Quaking A sported a single bar on one side that fronted about twenty stools. Two pool tables dominated the other side and six four-tops occupied the middle. Three high barred windows let in light that depressed more than illuminated. The place smelled like beer passed through who knows how many distressed kidneys. It was only three in the afternoon and a half-dozen men drank like they worked at it, smoked silently at the bar. I'd been kicked out of better places than this, when I used to drink.

My order for a cola earned stink-eye from the bartender but he served up. I sipped, waited for my presence to blend in, if that was possible. I flipped my braid over my shoulder and waited. Asking questions in a joint like this where the inhabitants are hostile can end up having to dodge fists and elbows real fast. I scanned the room under my eyebrows.

Ten minutes later, a cowboy walked in and sat two stools down. We traded glances through the back mirror. Finally, I asked, "Just bought a spread up the road and I'm wantin' to hire some herders. Know anybody lookin' for work?"

The man got up, put some coins into the jukebox. My answer was an ear-splitting version of Johnny Russell's "Rednecks, White Socks and Blue Ribbon Beer" followed by "Friends in Low Places" by Garth Brooks. During the third song my ears pulsed with lyrics that begin with the singer saying the Confederate stars and bars T-shirt he wore only meant he was a Skynyrd fan. The bartender and patrons glared at me. Some started to grow nasty grins. This was no sheepherder or Indian bar. I left.

A mile out of Durango, I spotted another bar. The last pissed me off, but I had a job to do. Inside, the odor of stale beer and ammonia wafted past. All redneck dives looked the same: bar, juke, tables, pool setup, maybe a dance floor, glowing Coors and PBR signs. Nasty patrons. I backed out quickly.

The third place was a fake alpine-style structure slumped off the road outside the city limits. I waited for an oncoming tanker truck to pass before I pulled into the gravel parking lot.

I sat at the bar. This dump summoned bad memories: headaches, vomit, lost keys, nights away. Mad wife. I didn't miss the life.

Two seats away, an Indian with a hatchet nose, kept eyeing me. I nodded. He glanced at his empty glass. I turned to his reflection in the mirror. Dive bar etiquette discourages direct eye contact.

"Lookin for Rafi Maestrejuan. Works at the Rocking Double Bar," I said to the bartender. I badged him making sure it was too fast to read. He turned and made busy with a beer tap.

The guy two seats away tapped his glass on the bar louder than he needed to. The barkeep turned and looked at the Indian, then me. "Beer," I said, pointing to the man. I dropped a twenty on the bar. The bartender rolled his eyes and served up.

The Indian lit up. I nodded. Buying a beer for a stranger was a cheap way to mine for information. In these dumps, everyone pretends to mind their own business. Truth is, everyone knows most everybody and most everything. Answers tend to flow at the same rate as the beer.

We both said nothing, and I stared at a group of shelves holding bottles above the sink and below the mounted head of a buck that reminded me of the animal that had appeared at Pokoh's murder. Even the mount seemed to be watching me. I mused over why Deer appeared then and what he wanted from me.

When the bartender took a load of empties out back, I asked the Indian which baseball team he liked.

"Fútbol," he said in clearly pronounced Spanish, South American for sure, Peruvian to my ear. Peruvians have replaced the Basque as migrant flock-tenders throughout most of the West.

Adhering to etiquette, we both kept our eyes on the back wall. "I hear United is doin' all right this year," I said in New Mexican Spanish.

The man launched into a monologue of soccer until I was sorry I brought it up.

When the bartender returned, the man shut up, finished his beer, and rushed out the door without so much as a nod. So much for my information-seeking tactics. My plan crashed with the slamming of the bar door.

59

After finishing my cola, I stepped outside. Halfway to my truck, my bar buddy stepped out from behind the side of a bailing wire coil and a Bondo pickup and gave detailed directions to Maestrejuan's *campito*.

In Spanish, I asked why he was telling me now.

The man shook his head. *"Usted no es un policía blanco, señor."* Not a white policeman.

The Peruvian hopped into his pickup, made three attempts at starting the truck, then drove off, trailing a cloud stinking of rotten eggs.

Chapter 11

The Peruvian left me scratching my head. Hate crimes against Indians anywhere are common enough. Some merchants cheat us, rednecks attack us for sport. There are even people out there who want to kill us, and some policemen don't take crimes against us seriously. That seemed to be the case when Pokoh was shot. Maybe that's why the Peruvian would talk only to me, an Indian.

Thoroughly frustrated, I headed northeast on Florida Road, then south on the 234, through pine-flecked hills that surround the city of Durango. Then down to the Old Orchard Farm on the left, just like the Peruvian told me. After a few bad guesses, I found a dirt road that crossed the Florida River. The road opened to wooded country that spent more time rising or falling than staying flat. The road cut between hills and headed south, then turned left onto a track that showed promise, until it turned into a game trail of ruts, rocks and cliffs.

Turning around required backing up on an unstable hillside. The mountainside towered on one side while the other side vanished into one-hundred-foot drop-offs. While driving ass up, I slid sideways on loose scree toward the precipice, tires spinning. My heart dropped into my stomach until the dual rear tires dug in and I stopped.

I stepped out to check my position and discovered the passenger-side outer tire kissing thin air while the inner had stopped on a rock, the only solid one on the hill. I sat down for a few minutes to calm my nerves, then dragged myself behind the wheel, moving as softly as I could despite puffing like an old man. I gently rolled the truck forward, steering a hard left until I hit safer ground. Down trail, the truck started another sideways slide towards oblivion just to re-energize my heart to beat.

Two miles in, the hills provided a natural oval-shaped bowl a couple of miles long with a grassy, open-area perfect for grazing sheep. Far off, a flock dappled white on green under a blue sky. The *campito* lay a mile off to the east.

As I drove in, it became clear the sheep were spread out. Coyote spends all day and night finding ways to grab his

61

next meal and the flock had opened themselves to him. Sheep should be clumped and under the protection of dogs, but there were no dogs. Every herder has canine guards. A good dog would be barking by now.

Rafi should've come out of the trailer when he heard my truck. I stopped and waited. Nothing moved. Close up, the white *campito* seemed barely bigger than the man it was supposed to bed.

Clothes had been thrown outside of the trailer. I grabbed my Smith & Wesson from under the seat. I stepped out of the truck but stayed behind the door. "Rafi?" I asked. Not too loud, either. "Rafi Maestrejuan?" A light wind answered. A rank, pungent odor mixed with a tinge of sickening sweetness that smelled like nothing else. Death occupied the trailer.

The smell of the dead is something I've never become accustomed to. Someday, somewhere, our own discarded bodies will be oozing that same awful stench. Maybe that's why death, common and universal, is so personal. Every death is too much our own.

Nothing signaled immediate danger, but the situation still demanded caution. Above, Buzzard drafted on-high, his wing tips splayed like fingers.

Holding my handkerchief to my nose, I opened the trailer door. A man lay on his side on the trailer's single bunk. The corpse's dark skin suggested Mediterranean ancestry and that led me to believe it was Rafi's, but I had no idea what the man had looked like when alive. He'd been shot and left for dead. Bled out fast, judging from the size of the stain on the bed and floor. The smell from the bloated body finally overpowered my senses, so I stepped away.

The place had been tossed; clothing ripped, dishes broken. The killers, four, judging from the boot prints, had destroyed the man's belongings, as poor and spare as they were. This was not a robbery gone bad. These sick fuckers had an agenda. Disgust heated my face.

I stuck my Smith and Wesson in my belt and searched the campsite. Twenty yards out curled a big Turkish Akbash male, probably a hundred pounds when alive. The medium-length, white coat hadn't yet been ravaged by scavengers, but the dog's black lips remained pulled back in death with teeth exposed in a valiant defense of his wards. This display of loyalty by this dog inspired and disturbed me.

The bloated carcass seemed mostly intact with only a few tentative buzzard bites. The canine had been poisoned, probably baited by female scent. Uphill, a dead vulture lay like a discarded feather duster. The bird's carcass bolstered my theory that the perps used some fast-acting toxin to kill the dog, and subsequentially the hungry scavenger.

Fifty yards uphill, I found another Akbash, a female, in the same bloated condition. She had not gone as fast, though. The lure of female scent didn't work on her.

Caked blood on white fur and a crushed skull told a different story. The poor bitch had been beaten to death, but she had gotten a piece of the assailant. The dog had locked jaws on a piece of blue cloth. The same type of cloth found where Pokoh was shot, a medical bootie shoe cover. "Good girl," I said.

After thirty minutes of searching, I found nothing more. My phone showed no bars, so I continued up the hill to find a signal. At the top, a three-foot-wide hiking trail ran east and north. The mountains were full of trails like this and the abundance of boot marks showed it well-used.

But this one was different: it offered more of the unmistakable smell of death. My chest tightened as I followed my nose to a pair of swollen corpses, skin split and turning black in places. Buzzard had enjoyed his work, bones protruding from the bodies. Shredded skin hung from exposed ribs.

The victims were in their early twenties, both Asian. One, a female dressed in hiking boots, shorts and hooded jacket. Her companion, a male, wore jeans and a Fort Lewis sweatshirt, a local college. Both were shot in the face. Gray, purple, and black mush oozed from a gaping hole at the rear of each skull.

Brown-black scavengers with wrinkled red heads sat in the surrounding trees and gossiped through their white beaks. No doubt Buzzard resented my intrusion. I sympathized and wanted to exit the scene, but I now had an intense, growing need to close this case. I wanted these killers who were capable of unspeakable brutality, wanted them so bad my jaw ached.

My phone showed three bars. "Reporting a triple homicide," I told 911. Blood rushing through my ears made the response sound distant. I spoke louder, gave them my location and as many details as they wanted.

On my return to the *campito*, I placed my S&W under the truck seat. I was licensed to carry in New Mexico. Colorado honored that permit, but I didn't want to complicate things with investigators I did not know.

Within twenty minutes, a herd of vehicles from numerous jurisdictions crowded around the *campito*. I got the same half-assed questions as I did when Pokoh was shot. All of La Plata County Sheriff's Deputy Frank Jones's questions were demeaning, but the one that set me on edge went, "You making this a habit, Romero?"

"What?"

"Seems like I get a report lately, you're calling it in. First Pokoh, now these three."

"I been in town day and a half. What are you talkin' about, Deputy?"

Surprised by Jones' attitude ambush, I matched him grin for nasty grin.

Jones closed in, his spit hot on my face, his coffee breath sour. He lowered his voice to a hiss. "You carrying, Romero?"

"I'm licensed in New Mexico. Makes it legal here."

Jones squinted, frowned, walked away. "Don't leave the county, Romero."

Jones was ticked at me and I didn't know why. I wasn't going to ask him. I was out of my home territory. I had no people in Colorado, no support, no juice. I had to pick my battles carefully because if I lost, no one would come to pick up the pieces.

At my motel in Durango, I steamed over Jones' attitude. I couldn't catch his act and it bugged me until I got bored with it. I had other things to think about.

The various crimes showed no pattern, but I was sure they were connected. Call it native intuition. Call it pig-headedness. I just couldn't let the idea go. Dead horses dumped here and there, two people murdered back home, four killed in Colorado. I was stumped.

It's Criminology 101. M.O.M; motive, opportunity, means. Motive is the thread that starts to weave the crime. Find the motive and the cover-up unravels like a cheap sweater.

People think of Colorado as a hip place, populated by millennials of the liberal-and-active set who spend most of their time biking, hiking, and skiing the Rockies—when they're not making big bucks at hi-tech start-ups or craft breweries. True enough in Denver, but there's another angry side goose-stepping around the outskirts. A dirty secret. North of Denver, a white supremacist group adopted a highway and got a mile of road to clean and a big sign to promote their hate agenda. A neo-Nazi parolee murdered the state's prison chief a few years ago. Colorado's famous beer family were hard-righters who sat on boards with a former KKK leader, apartheid supporters, and ultra-right Christian groups calling for the execution of homosexuals, adulterers and blasphemers. I don't know who they consider a blasphemer, but I know hate.

No investigator worth a shit should favor any one motive, but one haunted me. I've lived through this kind of hate and I sensed it here: the reception I got in the bars, the overly violent murders and pointed destruction of Rafi's belongings. Everything I'd seen till now smelled of it. The dead horses were owned by a Saudi citizen. Rafi was Basque. The two kids killed on the trail were Asians. The men killed on my reservation, Juan and Jason Pecos, were Indians. Hate is a far-too common motive. There could be other motives, of course, and I wasn't dismissing any possibility, but this one left a lingering taste in my mouth.

By the time I returned to the motel, the sun had set. I hit the bed without dinner. It may have taken all of three minutes to go to sleep even though my head pounded so bad I wanted to never wake up.

Chapter 12

A headache and dry mouth reminded me of one of the reasons I didn't drink anymore. My bed was a mess with blankets and the sheets on the floor, damp when I picked them up.

Deer walked through my dreams all night, grazing, watching me. The same buck that appeared when Pokoh was murdered, his rack unmistakable. He stared at me, begging me to understand him. I reached out, but he darted away. I ran but he sprinted. I woke up panting and feeling like I'd run a marathon. I never found out what he wanted to tell me. After a hot shower, I gasped when I looked at the clock: noon. I gobbled a granola bar, hopped into the pickup, and headed for the La Plata County Sherriff's Office in Durango, a place hostile to me. Deputy Jones had made that clear.

My soon-to-be-ex-wife, Costancia, always said I went out of my way to look for trouble, and, unfortunately for our marriage, she was right. She often claimed I was nuts, too. Couldn't disagree with that, especially since my plan today was to provoke Jones. I didn't trust him. Jones seemed to have an agenda and I was going to find out what it was.

I planned to ask for the case file of Pokoh's murder. The case was open and that meant copies could not be issued, a standard procedure most everywhere. But, the act of asking would raise a red flag. I was hoping that would be enough to flush out the bastard. Pheasant hides in the grass until stepped on.

The Turner Drive complex in Durango consisted of one-story cement structures that included the county lockup. Gloom emanated from the place despite a brilliant sun set against an azure, high-country sky.

When I asked the records clerk for the files on the Pokoh case, I got the expected answer.

"The case is still open, and records are not available to the public until closed," he said, pointing to a sign on the wall that explained the policy. He walked off saying, "Can't do it anyway. Server's down. Geek's coming from Denver. Give it a few days."

On the way out, Deputy Frank Jones talked to a uniform in the hall acting like he didn't notice me. A quick squint betrayed him.

Pheasant flushed. Game on.

After a short drive and a drive-thru hamburger, I returned to my motel, and passed time by shelling out twenty-five bucks for a walking tour of Durango. The town's history was rife with Old West gunfights, whorehouses, and hangings. I found myself enjoying it but that wasn't my reason for doing it. I hoped my wandering would lead Jones—assuming he was watching—to believe I was an unaware, easy mark.

Back at the motel, I waited until the sun peeked beneath the low clouds. If they were coming for me, they would come for me after dark. I readied myself the best I could. My pistol, a comfort under my belt, reminded me that this day could end ugly.

At last light, I bunched up blankets and pillows to mimic a sleeping form on my bed before I left the room. I hugged walls and shadows towards a neighboring building. The single-story, cement-block affair with a turreted, flat roof and brick chimney, offered a vantage point to the door of my room if I could get on the roof. The fading light through a low window revealed boxes and blue tarps covered in dust inside.

With a hard kick to the rear door, I was inside. No alarm sounded nor did visible wiring disclose a silent alarm. The place smelled musty and unused. An inside stairway led to an asphalt-covered roof. I sat against the base of a chimney where no obstructions interrupted my view of the street, the motel's parking lot, or my room.

Vehicles passed in numbers during rush hour. At seven-thirty, the street settled into its nightly routine with moderate traffic and few pedestrians. The temperature dropped soon after the sun but nerves, not chill, sent a shiver down my spine. The hours passed slowly. At ten, a dark '71 International Harvester Travelall passed, slowed, then drove off. It returned four times, twenty minutes apart.

67

Roof-sitting on a cold night waiting for trouble gave me time to think. The lack of evidence in both cases, the horse killings and the Pecos's deaths, had rendered my investigation stillborn. I would not impress Palafox when I reported with zip.

At two in the morning, a dark Ford F-150 drove into the parking lot and stopped behind my Chevy in a rattling idle. I froze and suppressed a cough from diesel fumes drifting up to my hideout.

Two black-hooded men, one tall, the other stout, climbed out and gently clicked the doors shut. The pickup k-turned in the motel parking lot and paused behind my truck. Streetlights flashed on metal.

Below me, they walked quickly to my room, the tall one with pistol raised in his left hand. I pulled mine, held it close.

The men stood at either side of the door, tall one on the left, to my room and scoped the surroundings. The tall man looked toward my hideout. I melted into the chimney. They nodded at each other and kicked in the door. Flashes popped behind the window curtains until the men bolted from the room. The tall one, threw thumbs up in my direction before they both hopped in the truck.

Thumbs up? I whirled.

The man pointed his pistol directly at me and fired. I shot twice. A street-lit badge pinned to a khaki shirt dropped with a thud. The acrid bite of propellant filled my nose. I spit dust caused by his bullet when it had grazed the chimney two inches from my head.

I sprinted to the body. A shocked expression contorted Jones's face as blood blossomed through his shirt. Apparently, he'd not seen me siting pressed against the chimney. I reached down to close his vacant eyes, the only token of respect he'd get from me.

Jones had earned the bullets, but I felt no pride of victory. This wasn't my plan. This wasn't inviting trouble, this was summoning the fucking apocalypse.

I jumped at the sirens and searched for the quickest way down.

On the ground, I bolted for my truck, jumped in, backed, shifted, stomped the gas. The shooters were gone, but the motel manager ran in pajamas toward my room with a pistol. He fired at me but missed. I stomped it, picked up speed and fishtailed onto Florida Road when I came to it.

Goddamn. Killing a cop in a capital punishment state is a stupid thing to do. I tried to keep my breath under the range of hyperventilation and kept telling myself I did what I had to do. Over and over. I kept my eye on the rearview as I pressed pedal toward the Ute reservation.

Nearing the rez, twists in the road came quicker and the road narrowed in the headlights, but I kept a heavy foot.

Deer stood motionless in the middle of the road. Wide, green eyes stared at me from a gray face.

I jerked the wheel and the pickup became airborne . The cab exploded into a coffin of inflated airbags. Then black.

The seatbelt held but the chest strap pressed against my windpipe, gagging me. The Chevy had landed nose-down and on its right side off the highway. I fat-fingered the buckle until it let go. I slid over the center console to the passenger door. I struggled to a standing position, feet on the passenger door panel, the center console pressing against my stomach.

My crowded standing position limited my ability to reach up, but I found the driver's door handle and pushed until my ribcage punished my effort with a sharp, breath-robbing stab. The Silverado's door weighed a ton. The door slammed shut twice when I pushed it upward from below. I gulped air, then shoved it again. At last, it stayed, pointing straight up into the night. My chest fired nerve shots as I used the steering column for leverage to haul myself through the door frame and over the edge of the chassis to the ground. I landed on my shoulders, then sat on cold stones to take inventory of my parts. Everything I counted hurt. Thank the gods, my neck was not broken.

Above me, the left front tire spun slowly, rubber and cord splayed like torn rags. Sirens approached at high speed and drowned out the engine's ticking.

I squatted next to the wreckage, ready to die by cop.

Chapter 13

The truck had landed in a ditch facing south alongside
Florida Road. I tried to stand but couldn't find the strength to
keep my feet under me and flopped onto my butt. I saw stars
and hoped they were real ones. Sirens grew louder.

The ancient ones had songs to sing when death was
near. I couldn't remember any I'd heard so I sang whatever I
could.

"I'm about to die. Fuck youuuuu," I sang. "Try to catch
meeee. I'm not your...son of bitch!"

Dizzy and out of words, I pulled myself up, using the
chassis for leverage. I raised my legs one at a time to see if
they worked. My ankle shot pain up and down my right leg. It
hurt like hell, but not enough to be broken. I held onto the
frame a few long minutes before I tried walking. My ankle
screamed in protest. I locked my jaw and put one foot in front
of the other.

Flashing lights neared as sirens warbled and whooped. I
froze. Lights brightened the ground where I stood, then left me
in the shadows. The sounds followed the red and blue lights
into the night. Eight cars by my count.

Florida Road loomed above me. Deer had caused me to
run off the road. I don't know if that maneuver was intended or
just a natural, buck-in-the-headlights stunt. My truck had
bounced over the guardrail leaving no broken posts or twisted
rails. The lack of damage and the roadbed's sloping sides
combined to hide the Chevy's wreckage from view. I thanked
every god that came to mind.

Using the road to find shelter was out of the question,
but the land on either side of the road looked like rough
country. Even in the dark, I could see the trees and brush were
dense. And, this high country was full of rapid streams, more
than a few beaver dam marshes, rocky meadows and boulders
the size of buildings. The journey was gonna be rough-going.

Green eyes stared at me blankly. Deer trotted into the
bushes, then poked his head out like a pet dog begging for me
to follow. The animal watched unmoved as I stiff-legged
toward him like an old man.

70

My head started to spin. I wrapped my arms around my chest, the movement sending pain through my ribcage, and I sensed the dazed beginnings of shock. I needed shelter. Cold mountain nights can kill. Deer put me in this position, but I would have to take my chances with him, now.

Rafi Maestrejuan's *campito* lay over the ridge up ahead. I flashed on the sheepherder's corpse and the dead dogs. It was a three-mile trip and the air smelled of snow. I had no options, the cold could kill faster than the cops if I didn't get moving.

The sheepherder's camp seemed a good place to hide because only a crazy person would return to the scene of the crime to camp out. By now, the police had processed the scene, taken photos and evidence, cleared out, and lost all interest in the *campito*. Or so I hoped.

The moon teased the horizon behind me. Soon it would provide some light.

We pushed through roadside brush and set out for the *campito*. Acting like he knew the way, Deer led, but kept distance. I followed, having laid out my trust like a beaver trap: one wrong move and then—what? After all, Deer had saved me from getting arrested or shot by the cops by causing the wreck and hiding me in the ditch but what he had planned for me, next?

As we walked, Deer looked back towards me and side-to-side frequently with an expression I took as concern.

"I'm okay," I said.

Deer startled and leapt into the brush. The scrub rustled, then quieted. I stood still, waiting, then starting walking again. A knot swelled in my stomach filling the hollow in my chest. If Deer had wanted to help me, I'd blown it.

The new moon lit my way. I tripped over roots and rocks as I walked. I don't know how many times I fell. Out of the corner of my eye, I spotted Deer. Inspired by his reappearance, I paced on legs painful but limber enough to make ground and kept my mouth shut. Stepping in water along the way upped the ante and threatened hypothermia. I had to find the *campito* or freeze. In the distance, the white peaks of the San Juan Range sliced skyward like ancient hatchet heads.

71

In an hour, I came upon a familiar meadow. Down canyon, the *campito's* white shell reflected the moonlight. I gave everything to get there. When I finally made it to the trailer, Deer trotted off into the night.

The police had strung yellow tape around the trailer and had taken Rafi's body and bloody bedding. I rummaged around, found some smelly clothing to wear instead of my wet ones. I crapped out on the *campito's* plywood platform bed.

Lights blinded me. Someone yelled, "Don't move!"

Four hands grabbed my arms and dragged me out of the trailer onto the ground. Someone recited my rights while another cuffed me. The plasti-cuffs dug into my wrists, but I was too confused to complain. I mumbled something. Didn't know what. I had no feeling in my legs.

A man leaned in close. His onion breath mixed with the smell of the valley's sweet grass. "What are you doing here?"

"Got an ID?" I asked. I had no idea who I was talking to. These men had taken me by surprise, and I was expecting questions about the cop I'd shot.

"I'll ask the questions. This is a crime scene. What are you doing here?

"Camping. What's it look like?" I said.

A knee pressed down and my arms were pulled up by the wrists. Lightning shot up my spine. "Okay, okay. I'm private, looking into horse rustling."

A hand pulled my wallet from my back pocket.

"PI? ID says you're a rez cop. Some kind of weird-ass investigation, you at a sheepherder's camp looking for horse rustlers."

"Better *per diem*." Up went my arms. Pain seared my shoulders. "I got a lead. What the fuck?"

"You have a weapon?"

I'd lost my Smith and Wesson in the truck. Or near it. Or under it. "No."

"Who's your employer?"

I lifted my head, tried to get a view of my interrogator. Up went my arms. "Tommy Palafox, Santa Fe County Security Consulting," I half screamed, half-croaked it out.

"What's his interest, Romero?"

"No fucking clue! He signs my paycheck. I don't give a shit about his interest."

My arms jerked up again. "Okay, okay. Jesus." My hip joints sparked, and my legs started to burn. "Palafox hired me to track down horse killers. Blue List Arabians."

The speaker and the man pressing me to the ground talked in hushed tones. All I heard from the conversation were the words "Palafox" and "dickhead". My opinion of Palafox went way up.

My interrogator walked away and made a call. He mentioned Palafox, then said, "Yes sir."

He returned, to me, he said, "You skated on this one, asshole."

The man on my back cut my plasti-cuffs. The blood flowed to my fingers, pricking needles all the way to my neck. "Get up," he said.

On my feet, I got a view of the men and their cruiser for the first time, a late-model Ford Interceptor SUV, La Plata County Sheriff displayed in gold letters, gold curving highway stripes in black. The deputy wore black trousers, khaki long-sleeve shirt with a logo shoulder patch. A black ball cap covered light-colored hair. His badge, reflecting the cruiser's headlights, flashed Ramirez.

"Where's your vehicle?" Ramirez asked.

I rubbed my wrists and waited for the bomb. The cop killer bomb. My stomach fluttered and my fingertips went numb. I focused on recalling any clues I might have left at the crash scene when it hit: my gun.

"Stolen." I grimaced, hoping to distract him.

"So, I'll find it listed in the stolen vehicle notice, huh?" He said walking away.

"No cell reception," I said, using the best excuse I could think of.

Ramirez payed no attention. The two men jumped into the Ford and rolled away, light bar flashing. I went to the trailer pretending to hit the rack but readied to get the hell out. The records clerk in Durango had said the servers were down and Ramirez may have not been aware of the police shooting at this point, but he would soon enough and return.

After changing into my own damp clothing, I waited ten minutes, then high-tailed to the trail at the top of the hill where I had found the murdered students the day before. I made for the summit, my knees and bad ankle sparking fire to my hips. My brain race-tracked everything I knew about the case. Little and damn little.

Chapter 14

The cold air helped calm my brain as I shuffled along the high-country trail with a twinge in my right foot. The wreck injured my ankle and now, when I needed all my strength, pain caused the big toe to drag.

The deputies could be back at any time, so I kept moving. In the moonlight, snowflakes blinked like fireflies.

Still damp from my cross-country walk to the *campito*, I picked up the pace to gain body heat.

I pulled out my cell; the one thing I hadn't lost in the truck rollover. No bars, no service.

I was Southeast of Durango on the Southern Ute Reservation. I knew that much. No lights betrayed the location of homes or barns and the moon hid behind clouds. The dark void caused my stomach to roll and my heart to thump. Dizziness blurred the trail and I couldn't swallow the sour taste in my mouth.

Up ahead, a pair of eyes glowed among the trees. I hoped those yellow orbs belonged to Coyote; an animal too small to attack a full-grown man. Colorado had been conducting a reintroduction of Wolf, however, and my fears were confirmed when the moon peered through the clouds and revealed a large gray form.

Wolf's yellow tracking collar meant Colorado Parks and Wildlife knew his location but by the time they thought to look for him, I'd be lunch. I hoped my casual stroll would somehow lessen my appeal. Wolf stared. Wet drops of drool hung off his canines.

Another pair of gold orbs appeared and looked straight through me. Attacks on humans by Wolf in North America are rare, but the pitiless eyes of this predator showed no hunger for statistics.

The eyes kept pace. A third set of glowing spheres tracked my movements, then two more sets appeared. Animals that do not fear man, command fear. Now, six pairs of eyes glowed unblinking, unfeeling, intent, hungry. Their intelligence called to me, Don't fight us. It's no use. Become one with us, brother. It will end quickly.

My only weapon was a cell phone with no service. Only stunted trees grew at this altitude, so escape up a pine was not possible. The night hid rocks to throw or sticks for stabbing. I broke into a trot. A foolish move: as I sped up, so did they. Wolf trotted beside me. Confident. In charge. In control.

The biggest loped easily while I forced a limping trot. He may have been the alpha male because the rest of his pack hung inside the tree line. He matched my pace naturally, a hungry smile on his gleaming teeth.

Wolf dropped behind me, a position I feared because I couldn't see him. But, I could feel his hot breath on my legs, and I imagined fangs dripping with blood until jaws clamped on my calf and threw me off my feet.

My fall must've broken his grip, but I ended on my face, then rolled over and sat up. The pack surrounded me with six snarling snouts, all within biting distance. I tried to rise, but one, with matted slobber smeared to his tracking collar, made a grab for my leg. A quick kick caused him to back off. He lunged. I countered with a boot square to his jaw. He dropped and stopped moving.

A third grabbed my right arm. I jabbed with a left, missed, then reached for his collar. He jerked me off my ass and dragged me across the trail. I rolled, kicked him away, and sat up. A fourth bit at my leg. I kicked, he dodged and lunged, again. I booted him, he swerved. Another seized my left sleeve. I pulled my arms inward. She let go.

My tormentor to the right had jaw-locked onto my forearm. He yelped and released when I jabbed a finger hard into his eye. At the same time, I grabbed his tracking collar, drug him to my chest, cradled his head while holding his snout closed with my free hand and twisted hard until his neck snapped with a dull crack. He collapsed.

The remaining pack members regrouped then launched at me in a simultaneous assault. Four sets of growling, snapping jaws and claws ripped my clothes and dug into my skin. I punched at fur, flailed at razor-toothed mouths. I seized another by the collar, but he pulled loose. I rolled, sprang to my feet. The pack backed off, exhausted, but with eyes fixed in instinctive hate.

Blood warmed my legs and arms. Dark patches staining my ripped jeans. Wolf might take me down, but the fuckers would have to work for it. I intended to die well.

And *Tsichtinako*, the Creator Spider Woman, had something for me. Her ancient energy fired my limbs, pulsed my heart with the momentum of long-ago, fire-lit drums. Pain vanished. Her power infused my mind with clarity, my heart with purpose, and my body with the strength of my ancestors.

No longer a man alone, I craved Wolf's blood as much as he wanted mine. I became like my attacker, raised my head to *Tsichtinako's* home in the stars and roared with a rage that came deep from my people's past.

Then, I attacked.

The pack struck back. Jaws grabbed at my arms, bit at my legs, tugged me to the ground in a snarling, snapping mass of fury.

I twisted, kicked, got my legs under me, and rose. One-by-one, the animals flew off and hit the ground like sandbags, only to attack again. I bellowed louder, grabbed fur and collar. In my frenzy the hundred-pound canines were weightless. No matter how many I threw off, though, as soon as they hit the ground they recovered and returned.

We fought until *Tsichtinako's* spirit deserted me. My power, my fear, and future floated away like ice in a spring river. Wolf yanked me down and the entire pack jumped on me. The furred warrior's hot saliva, mixed with my own blood, stung my face.

This was my day to die. I was ready.

Chapter 15

A blinding light clouded my view, but I could make out flowers, tropical flowers, everywhere. This was not such a bad place to be dead.

"You ain't as dead as you look," the flowers said.

All I could manage was, "Uh."

The blossoms belonged to a Hawaiian shirt worn by a behemoth. The big man looked Ute with chocolate skin and straight black hair pilled past his shoulders like mine. On his round face, he bore the hooked nose and keen, stern stare of Eagle.

My head throbbed, so I was alive, at least. I closed my eyes in thanks, then blinked open. The man waved a syringe. He rubbed a cotton swab on my upper arm, raised the needle and aimed in.

"Whoa," I said. "The hell's going on?" I pulled my arm to my side. It hurt to move. The skin on my arms and legs stung like it had been stretched. Every muscle I had ached.

"Profuse bleeding, for one thing. Shock. Multiple animal bites." He readied to stab with the needle. "Rabies make you happy?"

"Wait a minute. Who the hell are you and what makes you think you can poke me with that thing? You know how to use that thing?"

"Name's Walker. Twenty-eight years United States Navy, Master Chief Corpsman, retired. You better hope to hell I know how to use this needle. Shot more Marines than the Japanese Army."

"You sure, Chief?"

"Call me Oso, and I'm sure any symptoms show before this shot, you gonna die. Found two dead wolves on the trail. Got 'em in for testing, but it don't take no DVM to recognize the symptoms. No sir, spent four years at the Camp Lejeune Zoonosis Clinic."

When I tried to sit up, I got a stab in my forearm for the effort.

Oso pushed me down. "Take it easy, man. Don't pull out that IV."

78

"IV?"

He looked at the monitor next to me. "You're doing better, now, but I dragged your ass in here so dehydrated and short of blood, I could a sold you for chemicals. Probably don't remember the twenty stitches I put in your arms and legs, either. You had a temp so bad I coulda fried an egg on your forehead. Faded in and out half a dozen times. Babbling and making no sense."

"I need water."

"First, you're gonna get this shot." He jabbed.

"Damn," I said. "How many people you use that nail on?"

"For a Jarhead, you're some kind of a weenie."

"How—"

"Eagle, globe, and anchor tattooed on your left shoulder." Oso swabbed the puncture, turned, placed the syringe and cotton on a metal table against the rear wall. "Let me guess. San Diego. MCRD. Boot camp graduation. You got drunk and tattooed. Get screwed, too?" He laughed, snapped off his gloves

"How'd you find me?"

Oso smiled, said, "Just drove up to go to work an' heard howling and screaming, figured something was after the neighbor's sheep. You got some set of lungs, for damn sure." He lifted his chin. "You're not from here. Where?" he asked, still facing the wall, but eyeing me in a mirror.

"Cochiti Pueblo."

"Why're you on this reservation in the middle of the night playing with wolves?"

"Lookin' for horse killers."

"While chasin' wolves in a snowstorm? Don't think so." He turned, loomed over me like a tank. "So...you shot a cop?"

"What're you talkin' about?"

"Most people don't lie while hallucinating." Oso said, smiling. "Deputy Jones?"

"I? Who—?" My head started spinning.

"TV down the hall."

"Right." I pictured the Jones scene: a shadowy figure, a shot pulled off by instinct. I should've given it another second, scared up doubt instead of a gut reaction. I'd killed a man. Sure, I protected myself; it's what I had to do. And, I've killed before. In the line of duty, too, if you're not too strict on the definition of *duty*. It's part of the job description if you're not too precise about that, either. Problem is, some things you never forget, and the memory lurks inside. Killing is wrong but I live with it. Shot a kid once and can't get it out of my head despite the fact he had a gun on me. Jones, the bastard, is another story. His men tried to kill me in my bed, and he had his gun out when I shot him. It can be too easy to take a life, but it's easier to lose your own.

Must've been exhaustion, dehydration, lack of food, or just plain shock that pushed up bile up my throat. I threw up.

"Times like this, not feeling love for the job," Oso said, cleaning me up. "Vaccine can be a little rough at first, but rabies, hydrophobia, is an agonizing way to die. Difficulty swallowing and panic when presented with liquids. Water causes excruciating spasms of throat muscles. Symptoms include paralysis, paranoia, hallucinations, and death. Thank me later."

"What now, Oso?" I dreaded the answer and swallowed the acid taste in my mouth.

"You gonna be okay but now ya' gotta rest and hydrate." He busied himself with an instrument tray. From my viewpoint, he moved a little funny, reminding me of a standing grizzly. A big man aptly named.

"When they comin'?"

"Who?" He picked up the tray and headed for the door.

"The cops?"

He turned. "Cops? You come in hallucinating, saying what don't make sense? Never called the cops before. Why now?" He winked and closed the door behind him. "Jones was a prick," he growled through the door.

Despite his comments, I couldn't count on Oso's promise to not call the police. I just met the man and had no background on him. The reservation was huge, and it was just too convenient that I ended up within hearing distance of this hospital.

Enough of that. I had killers to find. I pulled the IV from my arm and the electrodes from my chest. Electronics beeped and, no doubt, alerted nurses down the hall. I hobbled to a closet and put on my torn clothes. Every move gave rebirth to Wolf's bite, especially when I pulled at my boots. I leaned against a wall, exhausted. I asked Spider Woman for strength, but no answer inspired me. I held no disappointment, for she bestows gifts at *her* will, not mine. I took several deep breaths and headed for the door. It was locked.

Irritating at best. I had to get out of this place, but I was trapped in a hall of mirrors inside a shooting gallery. Everywhere, an image of myself aimed in at me.

I could've punched my fist through the door but fear of what lay on the other side held me back.

Chapter 16

The room rocked as I moved, and my confusion made my balance more uncertain. I sat on the bed to steady myself.

Then there was this thing with Wolf. I was the pack's dinner until I developed that unreal strength. Now, I wasn't sure if the power was a calling or a warning. The spirits had called before. I had vague memories of travelling through time and seeing things that happened long ago. Sometimes my ancestors spoke to me but the force that called also blanked out almost every memory of all that had happened., I could never remember enough to understand what or why. This collection of vague half-memories drove me crazy. If I'd been able to explain them to Costancia, perhaps I would still be married.

To give my equilibrium a chance to recover, I lay down, fought sleep, and lost. In my dreams, Wolf charged me. Cougar stared with menacing eyes, daring me to shoot. I ran without getting anywhere while Coyote trotted next to me laughing. Deer ran back and forth in fright.

The snick of a key in the door jerked me to life. Oso loomed into the space. He displaced so much air, my ears popped.

"You got trouble," Oso said.

"Trouble? Maybe someday I'll tell you what trouble is." My Jeep had been stolen, my investigation into the deaths of Juan and Jason Pecos atrophied, if not ended. I'd been rousted by the FBI for interfering in their investigation. My sole ally, Clement Pokoh, had been killed in front of me, my lead witness, the sheepherder, killed along with his dogs and two innocents. I'd gotten nowhere tracking down horse killers, the job I was being paid to do. Oh yeah, I'd killed a cop. "You gonna tell me where I am, Oso?"

He shot a glance at the bedside monitors, noticed I was dressed. "You blew every alarm in the building and you're not going to get far in your condition."

"I got to get out."

"Trouble is what you got. More than you know."

I offered my palms. I couldn't imagine more trouble than I was in. "Gotta hear it."

Oso shook his head. "Tribal Rangers of the Wildlife Advisory Board is out for yer ass."

"They can stand in line. What're Wildlife Tribal Rangers, some kinda conservationist cowboys?"

Oso's eye widened, then narrowed. "I need to repeat myself?" He rubbed his chin, fueled a bonfire behind his eyes. "Listen, Romero. The wolves. These guys say you fucked up the prime federal grant program on the rez."

"Jesus, man. They attacked me." I upped the volume.

"Wildlife is a big deal here, Romero. Hard for me to keep you under wraps with this going on."

I stood tall as I could. "Under wraps? What're you talkin" about, Oso?"

Oso peered down, matched me mean for mean. "You got certain, let's call them, public relations issues down in Durango. Now you've got the fish and game people jumping up and down."

The man gave off a wet animal smell. I retreated to the other side of the room and turned back to him. "What?"

"Ya killed two of their wolves."

"You didn't mention the lab work?"

The big man said, "They didn't give a shit. They're going to the FWCO." Oso had dark sweat rings under his arms. His odor saturated the room. "Fish and Wildlife Conservation Office. The feds."

I paced back and forth, the small room limiting my travel to a few steps. I imagined being handed over to sheriff's men, envisioned them marching me to a hidden place and killing me. "How many times I gotta ask? Why you keepin' me here?" My voice pitched up as my stomach tightened.

"Grab your shit, you got an appointment." He turned, slammed the door behind him.

Oso's hit-and-run tactics—run in, drop a bomb, run out—raised my blood pressure enough to pop stitches. The room grew hot and stuffy. Again, I confirmed the space had no vents big enough to crawl through and no windows to jump out of.

The door burst open. Oso and another man a big as him barged in, grabbed my arms, and pulled me down a hallway.

"Jesus man, what the fuck?" I said, running to stay on my feet. My strength had not returned, and my wounds stabbed like switchblades. "Slow down. I got stitches, man."

"Pussy," was the reply as we pushed through a door.

Outside, a few stars asserted themselves in the sun's final glow. I must've been out of it all day. They dragged me to a Chevy pickup that hadn't seen paint in years, then shouldered me on to a bench seat smelling of dog urine. The big man with no name equaled Oso in size, so at five-ten, I must've looked like a child sitting between them. No Name's boots, railcars more like, were too fancy, horn-back alligator tail cut with inlay top, for some gorilla off the street:.

The tires spit gravel as I asked, "Where you takin' me?" I reconsidered why I wanted out of the hospital room in the first place.

"This place will be jumping with feds in no time."

"Last time I saw a fed, he didn't mention my notoriety," I said.

Oso looked at me, then back at the road. "Romero, believe me, you're the talk of the town. More people talking about you than Rihanna. They got Be-On-the-Lookouts to every local, state and federal agency from here to St Louis. You got more BOLOs than a Montana silversmith." He chuckled.

No Name chuffed. "That's good." The man's laconic way and thick braid to his waist pegged him as Lakota.

"Where we goin' in such a hurry?"

"Tell you when we get there." Oso clamped his jaw and produced a can't-stop-me look. He piloted the truck like a Dale Earnhardt wannabe attacking every pothole he could find.

The junk heap emitted a steady rattle of loose parts, springs, and tires. I noticed Oso avoided hard-surfaced highways, and from his habit of glancing side-to-side, the cops, too.

"Where we goin'?"

I coughed when No Name elbowed my ribs. I rubbed my chest and kept my mouth shut.

We arrived at a hillside and Oso parked under a tree. "Follow me," he said.

Like I had a choice. We were on the Southern Ute reservation, but the moon's failure to appear hid direction. I hadn't been cuffed but accepted I wasn't going anywhere by myself.

The smell of spruce and fir flooded our path. Oso took shorter steps than he should've, a bad back, maybe. No Name followed. I puffed but the air drew easy, so I guessed our altitude above seven thousand feet. Broken scree in a canyon with steep sides made footing shaky and each sliding step echoed back. Cliff walls narrowed the star field to a slit. The Big Dipper could've led me to spot the North Star, but black walls hid the view. I was sweating despite the cold mountain night and my gut quivered as the rock closed in. I questioned what waited at the end of this trail.

At the end of the canyon, a forty-foot trailer parked between trees. I don't know how Oso found it in the dark. They led me to a door. I pulled back.

"Relax. You'll want to see who's in here," Oso said.

"What is this?" I asked.

Oso shook his head. "You'll figure it out."

Red lights lit the interior, slide-outs made the compartment wider, and people with FBI stenciled on their backs populated chairs in front of monitors along the length of the vehicle. At various stations, TV talking heads mouthed in silence over breaking news banners. From the far end, voices came from a room with a table. I could see backs of heads, little else.

"Hello, Peter," said Jean Reel from a dark corner. "What brings y'all here?" she asked in her prep school and Okie mix.

My stomach fluttered.

FBI Special Agent Jean Reel wore cammies and had gathered her raven hair in a bun. Camouflage utilities were designed to disguise the human form, but in Reel's case the task failed. Her high cheek bones highlighted a Cherokee heritage, her black eyes held me prisoner. Her lips...well.

Yeah, I had a thing for her. We'd worked together before. We had to work close. Maybe too close. Costancia caught wind of it way back. Nothing had happened with Reel, but now, as an almost-divorced man, I wouldn't have minded revisiting the idea.

My disorientation gave way to awkwardness. I tried to say hello but gave up and smiled. I wanted to pull her to me, crush her in my arms, but offered a hand instead. Seeing her at work, when I really wanted to see all of her, made an already complicated situation frustrating as hell.

She displayed an odd look, asking, Aren't we formal? She held out her hand. Electricity shot up my arm at her touch. The spark was still there. So were the complications. She knew why I was here. I didn't.

Oso snickered, inspected the ceiling with hands clasped behind his back in innocence.

"We have work to do," she said, turned and walked off.

To Oso, I said, "You—" I returned my eyes to Reel. She had a way of moving that a uniform couldn't hide. The command post's surroundings faded away. I didn't care where we were as long as she were around.

Oso broke the spell when he asked, "Me?"

"You in on this?" I looked around the command center. "What's goin' on?" I turned to ask No Name the same question, but he'd disappeared.

"Reel asked me to ensure your presence." He followed me down the corridor toward the conference room. A half-dozen agents sat at folding tables along the way. The walls absorbed their voices. Tripod easels holding large paper pads leaned against walls. Some showed writing and charts, others had pictures taped to them.

I couldn't read the captions, partly because of the low light, mostly because a slow anger blurred my vision. I'd been set up. I'd been set up by Oso with a bullshit story about the Ute Wildlife Tribal Rangers' charges over the dead wolves.

My face heated and I must've looked angry because agents at the conference table gathered their papers and left the room when we entered. Oso and I waited as Reel studied a

86

stack of documents a foot high oblivious to our presence. Her dogged intensity was one of the things I admired about her.

"How'd you find me?" I asked.

Reel looked up. "Oh, we just followed trouble and there you were," she said, smiling with more teeth than sincerity. "Please, sit." She patted the adjacent chair, but I sat in the next one. No way I could maintain my self-righteous anger so close to her.

Oso sat quietly. I could have sworn he sniffed the air.

"I've got something for you." I held my temper. Always the professional, Reel had a tough side and, if approached the wrong way, could attack. I had been bitten enough in the past few days.

She said, "We've uncovered groups who have their fingers in extortion, drugs, and terrorism operating out of Durango. We're working it, hard."

"That gets you a dozen monitors, satellite phones, cameras, and a bunch of flat screens?"

She rose from her chair and walked to the far side of the room. At a tripod holding large sheets of paper, she turned over the first page, then stopped. "Peter, you need to treat everything I'm going to tell you as classified."

"Sure you want to give me that kind of info?"

"Meaning?"

"You're using me, Jean."

Reel glanced at Oso who then rushed out of the room.

"You walked right into this, Officer Romero. I didn't know you were up here until you, uh, established an impressive notoriety, let's call it, around Durango." She paused. "Now, I'm recruiting your help to find suspects in the case you are about to be briefed on."

"What? Jean, I have my own work. I'm on a retainer to find horse killers, and I'm investigating murders of two men on my pueblo. No way—"

"Too late, Peter. You placed yourself right in the middle of this case with the murders of Clement Pokoh and the sheep herder Rafi Maestrejuan.

"Bullshit. I reported the murders. That's all I did."

87

"Fine, but there's a problem. Rumors have it someone shot Deputy Frank Jones at a Durango motel. Know anything about that?"

My head spun like I'd fallen into a deep well and treaded water understanding no help would come. They had one witness for sure, the motel clerk. They had my registration at the motel. The locals had my wrecked truck, by now, too. My anger at being roped into this situation shifted to self-preservation. "I want a lawyer."

"Calm down. I'm treating those rumors as just that…for the moment."

My heart pulsed against my ribs. She had a slam dunk case. Nothing but net. Despite our past and the life-ring she just threw, she was a federal agent. Her eyes showed stubborn determination, but they held empathy, too. I'd known her for years, seen her work, watched her clear the toughest cases and I appreciated, needed, her willingness to cut corners for me. If she was using me, our past overruled my indignation at being setup.

Reel raised her voice above the low hum of activity in the command center.

"Peter, I'm not the one you have to answer to. These rumors also say law enforcement officers were involved and it's reasonable they might want to finish the job. So, I think you'll agree your best interests include sticking close to us." She stared her black eyes into mine. "If you believe those rumors, that is."

She had a point.

"Everything depends on the locals' investigation and we'll be following that closely." Her expression left no doubt in my mind that she had the ball, bat, and glove. The whole damn diamond.

Sucking it up, I said, "Pitch."

Her smile was relieved. "Here's what we've uncovered so far." She pulled up a page of the tripod's pad and revealed a bullet list handprinted in marker. She picked up a collapsible pointer, pulled it out to three feet.

Without looking at the board, she briefed her assignment, a RICO investigation. The Racketeer Influenced

and Corrupt Organizations Act was designed to go after the
Mafia, but in this case the FBI used it to target a local
consortium engaged in police corruption, extortion, bribery,
and dealing in controlled substances in Southern Colorado.

She explained the immediate purpose of this illegal
grouping was to disrupt the groundbreaking for a new hospital.
Recently, the Southern Ute's business organization, Red Pine,
had donated reservation land for a hospital near Durango. The
city would break ground at a ceremony in one week.

"That gives you a RICO investigation?" I asked.

"Oh yes, we have a full-blown conspiracy. Here is a list
of players." She flipped the chart to another item on the list
written in neat block letters. She stabbed her pointer at the red
bullets.

"We have four local groups involved.

First, traditionalist Utes oppose the construction
because they feel it threatens their cultural values. As you well
know, it's not uncommon for tribe members to oppose
development for traditional and spiritual reasons, but this group
has resorted to violence in the past. Now, they are planning a
demonstration at the groundbreaking ceremony. We've had
difficulty identifying current participants."

The pointer again. "But, a local, right-wing cell of
twenty-five, called *Clear Chivington*, who advocate an
immediate return of all federal lands to local communities, is
planning to counter the Ute demonstration. The great-grandson
of one of Colonel John Chivington's officers heads this group.
He is on the Terrorist Screening Center surveillance list. This
organization has a history of racial violence and we have
evidence they plan an armed confrontation."

During the American Civil War, violence broke out in
Colorado Territory. Constant tit-for-tat fighting led to the Sand
Creek Massacre in November 1864. Colonel J. M. Chivington
and his Colorado Militia attacked a quiet village of Arapaho
and Cheyenne, killing mostly women and children. Once back
home in Denver, the victors gloated. Chivington's unprovoked
Indian massacre was motivated by his need for notoriety and
nothing more; a slaughter that was used by both sides as
justification for violence ever since.

"But's that not all the players." She continued. "The Mexican cartels have interest in this event. The Chivingtons' weapons are funded by a clique of snowboarders from Breckenridge headed by a nephew of a high-ranking Sinaloa operative. Their motive is to create a violent distraction to their drug operations. We have them under surveillance and know they're planning to move a large quantity of fentanyl while law enforcement is engaged at the hospital groundbreaking hostilities."

"Ooh. Bad stuff." My interest grew. So, these were the assholes at the Española lowrider show. "I suspect these people are involved in two murders at my pueblo. I'd be interested in what you've found."

She paused, studied her chart, pointed to another bullet. "The reason this investigation has such high interest in the Bureau is we've identified a cluster of law enforcement officers also involved within the La Plata County Sherriff's Office in Durango, formerly headed by a Deputy Jones, who is now deceased." She looked at me, made a big deal of marking an X over his name with her pointer.

"We believe these deputies are in the pocket of the snowboarders and act as security for guns and drug-running. They are not above murder to protect their interests. Your own experience may be an example of that."

An image of my own attempted assassination and near death at the hand of Deputy Jones flashed before me. I changed the subject. "Chivs, punks, cops, and Utes," I said.

She paused, looked puzzled. "What?"

"Chivs, punks, cops, and Utes. Got a ring to it. Sounds like the name of a law firm."

Reel gave me an eye-roll and a half-grin.

It seemed improbable extremists, cops, and drug dealers could work in concert. Regardless, somewhere in this collection of thugs were leads into my own investigations. "What more can you tell me?"

She nodded. "We think it's going to go down this way; after the land and hospital donation was announced, a consortium formed due to their perceived common interests."

She flipped a page on her chart, pointed to a line titled *Scenario*. "On the day of the groundbreaking ceremony, the Utes plan to picket. They've already announced that fact. The Chivingtons will counter-protest. Each of these factions have access to firearms provided by the snowboarders' money. Tempers and firearms. You know what'll happen."

"And the sheriff?"

She pointed to a bullet paragraph. "They may be conspicuously absent or conveniently late to the action. Some of them will be off running escort for the movement of the fentanyl."

"Escort? Why not just look the other way?" I asked.

"We hear another cartel is planning to highjack the cargo. We're talking an impressive amount of drugs, here," she said. "Potential for many casualties."

"A lot of players," I said.

"Yes and a lot of money and tight lips. We don't suspect the sheriff himself but he's blind, deaf, and dumb to what's going on under him. Been in office too long, if you ask me."

She collapsed her pointer to the size of a pencil. "Once again Peter, I need to emphasize the secrecy required. No one outside of this RV has knowledge of the nature of this investigation."

"Oso and No Name?"

"Both men are on my staff."

"Sweet operation, but where do I come in? You got a connection to my horse killer case or the murders at my pueblo?"

"For now, I want you work with me undercover and identify the Utes who are involved in this conspiracy."

Reel had no authority over me, and I had no legal obligation to her. I straightened in my chair. "You don't have any Indian agents who can do that?"

"I have access to as many Native American agents as I need." She walked over to her chair and sat down.

Swiveling in my chair, I said, "Why me?"

Her expression told she knew more than she would say. "I know what you can do."

91

"You must think I can become invisible, or something."
I said, teasing her.

"I only have one week to prepare. I trust you and need
you."

From where I was sitting, she sounded almost
affectionate. I let that sit for a while. "True, but I'm not
unknown in town."

"Stay on the reservation Peter. The sheriff has no
jurisdiction here, but I do." She stood. "I have complete faith in
you.

Oso stepped into the room on cue.

"You'll work with Oso," she said.

She grabbed a thick binder off a shelf, handed it to me.
"Memorize this. If you need support, call." She hurried out of
the trailer.

She stopped when I shouted after her. "What if I said
no?" She started walking again. "No, goddammit!" But she
was gone.

Oso said, "Just like a woman."

"What?"

"Won't take no for an answer." His laugh went from
guffaw to poorly hidden church-giggle.

Jean was right. She only had to look for trouble to find
me. And now, I had as much trouble as I could find: Jean Reel.

Chapter 17

I steamed as I looked through a black ring binder over an inch thick. Mugshots of Indian men were arranged six to a page. More than a few looked angry, some were clearly underaged. Some photos were booking shots, some were taken with the subject unaware. I paged through it until everyone looked alike. "How in hell I'm supposed to memorize this?"

Oso shook his head, said, "You're not. We're gonna dance. C'mon."

"Hell of a time for a party," I said.

Oso led me out of the trailer. No Name, who'd been outside smoking, followed as we headed up the narrow path to the truck.

Oso chuckled. "Big with the talk, back there. No! No, goddammit! Hah!"

"Fuck you, Oso." Truth was I never wanted to disappoint Reel. She knew more about me than I did. And my motivations were selfish; she was my best hope for beating a cop-killer rap.

"She wants me to ID Traditional Utes who could cause trouble at the hospital groundbreaking."

"Troublemakers? Piece of cake, we'll just ask around."

"Subtle," I said.

I glanced back at Reel's mobile command center, a gray-on-gray Pierce forty-footer with Federal Bureau of Investigation lettered in yellow on the side. The rig had a firetruck cab with an expandable body and had enough antennas to communicate with every law enforcement agency in Colorado, New Mexico, and DC, if need be. A big truck for a big operation.

Oso drove back the way we came, me in the middle, my stitches reliving the pain. "How 'bout finding a smooth part of the road?"

"Sure," said Oso.

No Name chuffed.

Oso aimed for the potholes. As we bumped along, the truck squawking like geese, I replayed the actors in Reel's investigation. Chivs: white supremacists with a your-land-is-my-land agenda. Punks: cartel-connected boarders. Corrupt cops paid to look the other way, and kill, if necessary. Traditionalist Utes who opposed development on their sacred land no matter the cause.

I know what you can do, she said. I questioned her confidence in me but accepted it more happily than I wanted to admit.

Sun reflected off the white peaks of the San Juans to the north confirming my location on the Southern Ute reservation. I wasn't sure what I was doing here but at least I knew where I was.

I finally accepted that escape from Reel's project wasn't optional. Every cop around here with quick tempers and hair-triggers was looking for me so I was safer on the rez. Reel's tasks should keep me alive until I could figure what to do about the dead-cop rap. Weighing options is easy when there are none.

"Wanna know where we're going?" Oso asked. I didn't answer. He was going to tell me anyway. "Utes. At the Sun Dance going on right now. We call it, 'standing thirsty', *tagu-wuni*. Each dancer goes for four days without food or water, then dances to gain spiritual power from the Great Spirit."

"Oh," I said.

"Bear Dance is my favorite." He laughed then said, "Marks the beginning of spring, rejuvenates the tribe, you know? Given to us by Bear after hibernation. New year, new cycle. Traditionally, it's done before the Sun Dance. Pretty cool concept, ya think?"

Oso plowed through a succession of ruts and potholes that made me wince.

"The Sun Dance outlawed long ago," I said.

At one time, the ritual was feared by whites throughout the West for its brutality and as a prelude to rebellion. Meant as a sacrifice to honor Mother Earth, some of the Sun Dance practices could be hard to watch. Participants would dance around a pole to which they were fastened by ropes with hooks piercing their chest muscles. Often, skin and sinew were pulled six inches or more away from the body.

"People are trying to bring the ceremony back," Oso said. "Respect for the old ways, you know. A lot of Traditionals think the tribe is going to hell, so they want to bring back the old ways, show more respect for the spirits and the land. They don't like gas pipes desecrating the rez, you know?" He nodded.

My own reservation could use a little of that kind of desecration. And income. "You gotta tell me, Oso, how come you don't know these people, already?"

"Twenty-eight years in the Navy didn't bring me around Southern Colorado much. We got a whole generation in the tribe I haven't even laid eyes on." His voice caught when he said it.

"So, we gonna stare at these people for four days?"

"Just one day. Don't get your hopes up." Oso grew silent as we drove into the Sky Ute Fairgrounds outside Ignacio. He entered through a back way, keeping an eye out. "Can't be too careful," he said.

The fairgrounds consisted of an RV park full of all manner of vehicles, three horse barns. an indoor arena for equestrian events, ceremonies and tribal gatherings, and an outdoor grandstand facing a racetrack. All new. The Los Piños River flowed to the east, and Ignacio bordered the west.

We parked in a sea of cars and trucks next to the indoor arena. Inside, seats were full of Utes and some whites, I guessed a thousand people. Since 2003, most tribes no longer allowed non-Natives to attend the sacred ceremony and seeing the sprinkling of whites surprised me. The sound of whistles filled the barn and bells jingled to the steps of a dozen feathered and sweating bodies. To get a better view, we sat in an upper row of the grandstand.

On the dirt floor, highly decorated dancers stomped, hopped, strutted, twirled, twisted, and bounced to a drumbeat booming over loudspeakers. The dancers wore their finest feathers of red, yellow, blue, and white fanned to half circles down their backs, full circles on their arms, and behind their heads. The drummers, eight to a drum, beat and chanted a shrill song in Uto-Aztecan, a language I didn't understand.

95

The sight, the sound, the energy swelled my heart with pride. I have seen many such ceremonies throughout the Southwest and each time I have marveled. These dances, like the cultures that produced them, have withstood the test of time, natural catastrophe, discrimination, and genocide. Today's Indians value their endless capacity for survival.

We scanned for people who could be violent extremists. Spectators milled about while drummers and dancers stood aside until they were called to perform. Everyone seemed focused on contributing to the communal prayer the ceremony was meant to deliver.

Oso elbowed me, rubbed his neck, talked so I could barely hear him. "Don't look when I say this. Over there, against the far wall, behind a woman in jeans and white hat."

I waited, shot a glance at the man, medium height, black braids, tats peaking above the collar of a checkered short-sleeve, a wide belt, jeans and boots. "Yeah. Hard lookin' dude, late forties, early fifties? Nasty scowl."

"Younger than he looks. Posey Trujillo, member of Colorado AIM. Trouble follows him like an STD. Known him most of his life but he's not the kid I knew. Tours with Delta Force in the Gulf fucked him up. Spent time at Cañon City. Poster boy for PTSD."

No Name stared at Trujillo like he knew him.

"So?" I had my own issues with PTSD, and I knew what the American Indian Movement was, too: an assembly aimed to right wrongs against Indians. Fair enough, but in a few cases, good intentions backed by righteous outrage has led to murder.

Oso said, "Trujillo gets people excited when they don't need to be. Seen trouble around here? Bet your next paycheck he was mixed up in it."

Trujillo moved about the arena while I kept an eye on him from the grandstand. I made eye contact with no one in the crowd. If people looked at me, I glanced away. Trujillo talked to a teen by the concession stand, then stood in line, bought a drink. He left it on the counter to talk to another man. He wandered around the arena paying little attention to the dancers, spending his time scouting, then talking to various men, all of them late teens or early twenties with quick eyes and waist-length black hair.

No Name and Oso remained seated when I left the grandstand.

"Good plan," I said. No Name was not Ute and would draw attention. Oso's size and tobacco-colored horn-back alligator boots would not be overlooked.

I followed Trujillo around as he talked to young men. The noise of the crowd, pounding drums, and whistles drowned out most of Trujillo's voice, but I got the gist of what he was saying. Trujillo impressed me as an opportunist of discontent. Each member of the group wore a serious expression as the older man laid out the true way. Hormones pumped up their broad shoulders and filled muscled arms with a jittery energy as they listened. As I step closer to hear, listeners edged away in spite of my feigned attention to the whirling floor show. When Trujillo gave me the stink eye, I turned my back and strolled away.

The increasing drum tempo signaled a climactic point in the ceremony. Singers pitched up in octave and volume, Utes in feathered and frilled buckskin whirled to the beat. Sweat drenched their clothing. The spectators quieted as the song grew. The color, sound, and movement mesmerized me. I imagined a time long ago when such ceremonies preceded war, celebrated victory, or gave thanks to Mother Earth.

When I refocused, Trujillo's crowd had vanished. I spotted one of the young Utes in Trujillo's awe leave the building. I followed. Outside, young men had gathered again with the evangelist at the center.

As I tried to pick up Trujillo's words, he eye-locked me. I tapped a man near me, asked for a cigarette. I've never smoked but I had to come up with something. The man pulled out a pack from his breast pocket, shook one out, offered a light. I inhaled. It took all I had to suppress a cough. I took another puff, blew out. Trujillo lost interest in me.

The Trujillo's group talked while I continued smoking. Trujillo looked my way again. Just then, a member of his crowd walked to one of the portable toilets lined up like plastic, blue teepees near the parking lot. I followed and waited in line. Trujillo's glare heated my neck.

The portable became available. Inside, I sat wondering how watching participants at the Sun Dance would help us find any militants until a disembodied voice from the portable next to me said, "You heard Trujillo, right?"

"Couldn't hear shit," another said.

"Tonight. County Road 324, the farm. Eleven sharp. The whole Capote clan."

The reply came back, "Epic, man. Got it."

My interest already piqued, skyrocketed when the first man said, "Bring guns."

When returned to the seats, I told Oso what I'd overheard in the portable. He said, "Sounds like a bunch a crap." He nudged No Name who managed a grin.

"Think about it, Oso. Who else would say things like that if they didn't mean something by it?"

"Capote clan is mountain people. Lot of hunters in that clan."

"We got a month before the season starts." I flipped my braid to the front.

"What's the chances of you shittin' next to one of the guys we're lookin' for?" He growled, turned his attention to the arena floor.

I didn't like being blown off like that. As dancers whirled, and howled on the arena floor, I, again, questioned my reasons for letting Reel shove this assignment up my ass. This was taking time away from finding horse killers and murderers and, at least, finding them came with a paycheck.

"Okay." Oso jarred me out of my thoughts, "You might have something there, something to think about. Maybe."

"No shit," I said. A small victory. "Stake out County Road 324. Tonight."

When a performer dropped to the ground, I lost the attention of both Oso and No Name. Some officials ran into the arena and dragged the man off, trailing his heels in the dirt. We continued to watch the dancers all afternoon without speaking. We discovered nothing new and saw no one else we recognized as trouble. Reliving the port-a-potty conversation in my head, my gut told me we would find all the trouble we needed tonight.

Chapter 18

We had dinner at El Amigo, a place near the center of Ignacio, a small home repurposed as a restaurant. Serapes, sombreros, and paper flowers decorated the walls.

Oso and I sat at a booth while No Name smoked outside keeping watch for deputies on the prowl. Being out in public for the first time since the police shooting made me nervous. I wanted a strong drink to calm my nerves, but I had faced that devil years ago and settled for water. I ordered the nightly special combo: taco, tamale, a little burrito, and enchilada smothered in red chilé sauce with beans and rice.

As a native New Mexican, I generally look down on all other forms of Mexican food as tasteless, but this was good. The peppers were wimpy, but I cleaned the plate and devoured the *sopapillas* with sage honey like they were the last on Earth.

Bloated from dinner was not the best start for a stakeout but we headed off anyway as the low sun fanned the sky with yellow and scarlet rays that stained the clouds like cotton candy.

"Man, would ya look at that," Oso said, as he drove.

The man's infatuation with the evening's beauty was intense and out of character. The truck swerved as we were nearly side-swiped by a two-feathered logo tanker blowing past us.

By eight, we had travelled east for four miles on State Highway 151 to a flat plain with scattered farms and low, pine-covered hills in the distance. We turned south on Rd-324. Scattered natural gas pumps and tanks proclaimed proof of the Ute's underground wealth.

We found a dirt offshoot leading up an arroyo hiding pockets of snow from the sun and followed it until we parked behind a wind-break about a half mile out. We had a good view of the road and waited for people driving south. The truck's clock said 8:45. The event was not scheduled until eleven, but we had no idea what to expect and could take no chances of missing anyone coming to this party.

Coyote yipped off somewhere at the last hint of sun. The smell of dust hung over the road. When the sunlight turned purple, the temperature dropped. I didn't have a jacket, so I sat in the truck shivering. At least, the cold kept me awake.

Nine o'clock and waiting. I watched stars grow by the thousands and shooting stars pull tails behind them. When the moon rose in a blaze of white light, I swore I could have touched it. The smell of sweet pine drifted our way.

A stone click. I froze. Another. I held a finger to my lips, but Oso and No Name had already alerted, eyes quick and wide. In the sideview mirror, a dark shape moved toward the truck from the rear. We'd been discovered. No one moved.

Soon, Deer stared in the window at me. His eyes reflected moonlight, until he turned away. The animal paused to glanced back as he strolled off.

Oso elbowed me." Anyone you know?"

This animal had been following me since Pokoh was shot and I had yet to understand why. "No."

Being surprised by Deer was distressing. "We bring firearms to this rodeo?" I asked.

Oso held out his palms. "Nah. These are my people. Supposed to ID them. That's it."

Reel had shown me mugshots of Utes she suspected of being involved. Between the three of us, we'd be able to pick out some of them back at her command post once we were done here. That was my plan, a plan with some holes. "Okay, we observe these guys up close and they spot us. Then what?"

"So? We tell 'em we're supporters, ask to join up." Oso looked at me like I should've figured that out myself.

"A hug-fest just like that? A little cozy, don't you think?" I asked. Keeping hidden from view was a better plan. "And the younger ones who don't know you?"

"You worry too much." Oso's mood had gone sour and he almost growled at me. It seemed he hadn't bought into this stakeout.

"It's your show," I said, not meaning it. I was going to get what we came for, regardless. Reel had put her neck on the block by shielding me from the sheriff who was looking for Deputy Jones's killer. Her ongoing conspiracy investigation

101

would inevitably expose law enforcement involvement in the assassination attempt against me. Until her inquiry was completed, no way in hell would I disappoint her. Staying alive was pretty good motivation, too.

But I began to question Oso's commitment. Reel must've had confidence in him; she put him in charge of me, whatever that meant, so I leaned towards trusting him myself. A growing doubt told me something else was going on.

At nine-thirty, a truck towing a cattle trailer rumbled by. It's sudden, loud introduction got my heart moving, but it turned out to be a false alarm. More waiting. Owl and some bats proved the area rich with wildlife and provided the only reward for our surveillance.

Ten o'clock. An hour to go and still no traffic. Coyote howled far off.

Oso answered with a wail of his own. He appeared bigger, as if the howling had added fifty pounds to his bulk. Oso's face reddened and exhaled hard. His body exuded an odor more animal than human. I stared at him.

Oso lowered his eyebrows. "Just staying close to my roots."

I was about to ask what he meant when the dirt road suddenly became as crowded as a Denver freeway. A convoy of pickups and sedans passed. I counted a couple trucks bearing the two-feathered logo. Nineteen heads total.

"Show time," I said. My watch glowed ten-thirty under a straight up moon.

Oso sat sullenly; corners of his mouth pulled down.

No Name said, "Alright."

The Lakota's enthusiasm made me wince.

We gave the travelers distance before pulling on to the road, then followed with headlights off. The convoy turned right a half-mile south and we followed down a dark farm road until light glowed from behind a hill. We pulled off into a stand of trees and hoofed over a small, wooded hill that climbed steeply, levelled off, then ascended again. On the far side, farm lights coned the ground in front of dark buildings.

102

A stream of red lights moved towards one of the buildings, an old Grange Hall. Other buildings included a barn and a ranch house that, even in the dim light, had seen better days.

The convoy parked and engines stopped. Doors opened and riders stepped out. Someone pulled a drum, four feet in diameter, out of a truck. Headlights and kicked up dust gave the drum skin a mystical glow as if to announce its purpose at the sacred ceremony. Two men carried it inside. Men gathered, bottles passed, people laughed and talked, but their words were too heavy for the breeze to carry them our way. I made out silhouettes of rifle barrels. Coyote rebroadcast his presence with a long, soulful howl from far away.

The drums started at eleven sharp. Utes crowded into the Grange meeting hall. Compared to my count of the convoy, two were missing. Only seventeen of the nineteen men had entered the building. Two unknowns. Two surprises. I thought they were probably guards. I had to know where they were before we could identify the Utes safely. Apprehension squeezed my chest.

I finger-signed the count to Oso and No Name, then circled a hand in the air and pointed toward the house, then to my eyes, indicating I would circle the area to get a closer look. With a palm I signaled them to stay here.

Oso shook his head. I took off. They followed.

The dark waters of a pond mirrored the moon. The outbuildings, sheds, and junk autos reflected its light. I circled around the pond keeping distance from the building. Using a barn and corral to screen us, I led them behind a derelict RV. We waited in place while I scanned for the two guards, but neither sound nor shadow betrayed them. I turned my attention to the dance.

Drums pulsed from the house accompanied by shrill chanting in the same way as the dances earlier today. I slipped from behind the RV, crept toward the back of the hall, using stacks of irrigation pipes for cover, then hid in an orchard fifty feet from the building's windows.

The sound of bells, whistles, and drums came from the building, the tempo louder and faster. The dancers whooped and ululated as the pulse increased.

Photography was too risky, so, I needed to see inside to imprint these faces on my memory. I signaled and the three of us pressed up to the building. I peeked through one window; No Name took another.

No Name mouthed, "Aw, fuck!"

Four nearly naked men leaned against hooks piercing their chests. Taught ropes attached the hooks to the ceiling. The dancer's skin stretched six inches from their rib cages. Blood seeped from the wounds and dripped dark on the floor. The sight made me wince. The hooked men seemed in a trance while others, shirtless and bootless, danced around the supplicants to the sun, yelling encouragement in their Uto-Aztecan language.

The sight stunned me. I've always loved my culture's rituals, but this dance wasn't the benign prayer to Nature I was used to. This ceremony spoke to a warrior's thirst for sacrifice. I could not come to any other conclusion: the bleeding, sweating, glaze-eyed dancers meant violence.

"Hey! You motherfuckers doin'?" Someone yelled from behind a tree.

The man ran for the other side of the building towards the door, but I beat feet and tackled him before he made it. He grabbed for a gun at his hip. No Name ran up and stopped the man with a swift kick to the head. I grabbed the pistol and tucked it into my belt. No Name tied a bandanna across the man's mouth, then we dragged him away from the building. The bright moon allowed us to find bailing twine on the ground and we tied the gagged man like a calf.

In the scuffle, I hadn't noticed that Oso had disappeared. Or that the drums had fallen silent.

The sounds of yelling and running feet burst from the meeting house. No Name and I stood over our hostage in the orchard in an indefensible position and unarmed. The snick of many rifles dominated. "Let's get back to the hill," I said to No

Name, but he had gone, running toward the hill carrying our captive over his shoulder like a bag of beets.

We made the hill without being followed and crumpled behind a log. "Where's Oso?" I asked, puffing like an old dog.

No Name said, "Don't know."

Our hostage groaned.

"He okay?" I asked. The Ute prisoner was our only leverage. No Name had trussed him up so tightly the man had trouble breathing.

The big Lakota shrugged.

I'd expected our respite to be interrupted by a charge of armed and furious Utes. Instead, screams and rifle shots erupted on the other side of the Grange Hall. People ran to their vehicles. More shots. More screaming. Another roar. Engines ignited and car doors slammed. Trucks sped from the parking area. Those that backed out hit other vehicles but didn't stop. One hit a tree, then sped away. A pickup, with lights off, hit a running man and kept on. A second thumped twice over the fallen man without stopping. At least three men ran down the road on foot.

"Something scared the shit outta them," No Name said.

The sight of armed men running in panic was pathetic. These young pretenders wanted to bring back the old ways and running in fear was not a Ute warrior's way.

The .38 pressed under my belt. I said, "Keep an eye on our hostage," before heading for the meeting house. Halfway, I realized No Name crept close behind me, anyway. I motioned him back to the hostage with my barrel. He replied with a middle finger. We retraced our steps aware that whatever was big enough to scare away these wanna-be warriors could still be near.

We moved slowly, taking advantage of the sparse cover. A brilliant moon lit the way but did not aid our secrecy. We reached the meeting house, pressed up against the siding and scanned through the window. Four dancers leaned against hooks imbedded in their chests, backs bowed, arms splayed in a swaying crucifixion dripping with blood. The room was

otherwise empty except for the drum, and a pile of abandoned
shirts and boots.

No man is my enemy when helpless. In the kitchen, I
found a knife and cut the ropes while No Name supported the
men's weight. We lay the unconscious Utes on the ground, one
by one.

I pressed my head to the chest of a kid who couldn't
have been sixteen.

No Name checked another's pulse, a kid of nineteen
years, and said, "Resurrection. Rebirth. Honor the past."

The color of the third participant had returned to his
face. No Name attended to the fourth man, shook his head, but
before he could speak, a loud groan came from the orchard. I
ran outside toward it. No Name followed. Oso was sitting
against the base of a tree.

"What happened?" I asked.

"I'm okay," he said. "Dizzy."

No Name tried to help Oso to his feet, but Oso said,
"Give me a few minutes."

A quick scan of the area verified we were alone. I
turned to head back and stumbled over a body lying in a
shallow ditch.

Gripping the pistol at my side, I said, "Hey, buddy."
His features were hidden in the dark, but I could see his eyes
were open. He did not answer or move, so I pulled his legs,
limp and unresisting, until the moon light revealed detail.

"Oh man," I said, stepping back. A series of four
parallel slashes identified an assailant that possessed enormous
paws, an eight-inch spread with claws as big as cigars. They
had ripped his face, tore his clothing, and slashed open his gut.
His intestines trailed off toward the far side of the orchard.

I listened as my pulse red-lined and my knees quivered.
Nothing interrupted the quiet night, the monster, if still near,
had to have been as stealthy as a cat. A breeze hissed through
the trees. Something thumped in the orchard and I froze. The
pissy little .38 in my hand felt useless.

I rushed back to No Name who had Oso up and
walking.

106

Noise came from the meeting house as we manhandled Oso up the hill to our former hide. I suspected some of the Ute dancers might've returned. Oso dragged his feet. No Name and I pulled, pushed, and cajoled Oso, lubricating the progress with foul language. No Name propped up Oso's right arm while I suffocated in Oso's left arm pit. At the top of the hill, we found our hostage where we'd left him and cut him loose. I helped him stand until blood returned to his legs, then he ran like Rabbit to the Grange Hall, taking off in the remaining truck.

My watch said two in-the-morning as the moon set. Through the pines, I had a good view of the place and kept watch for movement. No telling if the Utes would get their act together and return. Maybe the four we'd cut down had recovered enough to confront us. They could be watching now, for all I knew.

Our attempt at gathering intelligence on the Ute group had failed in an unimaginable way. We had to get out of here.

Chapter 19

It took ten minutes to drag Oso to his pickup hidden at the bottom of the hill, then another five to get him into the front seat. Oso was in no condition to drive, so No Name hopped behind the wheel. Oso slouched between us.

I relaxed a little once we reached NM-15 heading towards the FBI trailer. I pushed Oso forward and to the left and fished out his cell phone from his back pocket. Damn, he was heavy. The limpness of his big frame worried me. I called 911. The men we'd cut down and those who'd been run over by their own people needed medical attention.

I said, "That body I found back there was mauled by Grizz."

Oso made no response as we drove and stared out of the windshield with lifeless eyes. I was worried about him. He had no visible wounds, but he looked to be in a trance. Given his bulk, I suspected a heart injury of some sort. He coughed and gasped for air.

"No Grizz in Colorado," No Name said. "Female, killed up there in '79. Last one." He pointed to my right where the snowy peaks of the San Juan Mountains glowed under the stars.

Experts say grizzlies have been driven from most of the lower 48 states, though some of the more resilient ones still held reign in the Yellowstone and Grand Teton National Park areas. I was sure they were wrong about Colorado. Hunters keep up on the grizzly population, because the last animal a huntsman wants to meet on a trail is *Ursus arctos horribilis*, emphasis on the *horribilis*.

Sightings have been reported for years, but none confirmed by Colorado Parks and Wildlife. The bears' numbers have expanded in Wyoming over the years, so it's likely some had migrated south to Colorado. A wildlife biologist friend photographed tracks last year, but Parks and Wildlife had not paid attention.

"P and W counts Grizz like they count Wolf," I said. "They're more worried about tourist-count than dangerous-animal-count. You see the wounds on those guys? You find

108

something else that makes a set of scratches that big, let me know."

No Name held his hands at ten and two, eyes glued to the road.

Oso moaned. A flicker of life had returned to his eyes, but his breath was labored.

I perked up. "You okay, Oso?"

"No," he said in a sandpaper rasp.

"What happened back there?" I asked.

"Don't know." He coughed, grimaced.

"Oso, I heard growling. I think it caused the gun play. Did you see anything?"

He worked at forming words, then said, "No."

"What were the Utes shooting at?"

Oso coughed. "Don't know."

This conversation and Oso's condition were going south. His deterioration worried me. "I want to know what happened."

Oso coughed again; this time deeper. Blood peppered the dash and ran down his chin.

"Get to a hospital. Push it," I said.

No Name stomped the pedal and the old truck wheezed, but didn't accelerate until it burped smoke, then lurched toward sixty. At seventy, the front wheels wobbled until No Name slowed.

We made it to the Ute emergency facility where I'd been confined earlier. No Name and I managed to haul Oso down to the pavement as the gurney arrived. With the help of two medics, we lifted him to the rolling bed and pushed him inside.

At the double doors to the operating theater, one of the medics pointed to the waiting room. We were the only people there beside the staff. My watch showed four-thirty in the morning.

One of the nurses, a Ute who looked like he'd been up for three days, walked over and said, "I'm sorry, but you can't stay here if you're armed."

"I have a permit."

"I need to see it unless you're in uniform."

Police on my pueblo were not issued uniforms. "It's on file." A statement mostly true. I'd filed it in the glove compartment of my Jeep, my stolen Jeep, ready to present when off my reservation.

"Show me, or you'll have to leave the building." He pointed to the nurses' station. "I could lose my job."

No Name devoted his attention to an old Western showing on the wall-mounted big screen. It was the kind of movie where the cowboys played guitar and the Indians died.

There were a hundred reasons why I wouldn't give up my gun without a fight and that corny movie reminded me of one of them. As an Indian, a Marine, and a cop I cannot shake the idea that someone who wants my pistol intends to kill me with it.

"Can't you reason with this guy?" I asked No Name.

No Name crossed his arms over his chest.

"You still packin'?" I asked.

No Name patted his holster. "Do it," he said, "You're safe here."

I handed my weapon over to the nurse who locked it in a safe.

When the TV movie finished, a doctor came out of the operating theater looking glum. The double doors whop-whopped to a close behind him. Blood sprinkled his scrubs.

Muscles jumped under my skin. I rubbed the nape of my neck, grabbed at my braid so I had something to hold on to.

"How is he, doc?" I said, my voice stressed tight. "One minute he was fine, the next, he was hurtin'."

"The gunshot wound to the thorax resulted in internal bleeding, pulmonary contusion, rib fracture, thoracic wall lacerations and sternal fracture. Some ventilatory problems, as well, but he's stable."

Oso must have caught one in the chest when the Ute dancers fired at Grizz. "He gonna make it?" I asked.

"Prognosis is guarded." The doctor turned, glanced around the room and sighed. "What a night it's been. Five with

110

animal wounds just came in and I have more coming. Excuse me." He turned to go.

"Grizzly?" I asked.

He disappeared behind the doors, saying, "Colorado has no grizzlies."

Oso's chances were decent, but not certain. "Oh, man," I said, rubbing my face with both hands.

No Name, as usual, remained impenetrable.

Chapter 20

My head weighed a hundred pounds and my neck ached after three hours of nodding off in a waiting room chair. My mouth tasted like powdered tar but didn't feel as rank as my worries for Oso.

The doctor emerged from the operating room's double doors with the corners of his mouth creasing upward. "He's improved. He's one tough man, but you should go home and get some sleep. You look worse than he does. Both of you." He disappeared behind the doors.

I took the good news and doctor's orders to heart. "Know a place to crash?" I asked No Name. He headed for the exit. He waited behind the wheel while I retrieved my pistol.

The twisting road gained elevation, narrowed to the width of the truck, then squeezed further, providing no room to turn around. Above, piney hills stretched upward and peaked five hundred feet higher. To the front and back, the road disappeared around rocky bends. After thirty minutes, we arrived at a small cabin near the base of a bluff just as the sun peeked over the hills. The building's dark, stained logs and asphalt roof contrasted with the blue-gray and pink-banded rock behind it. We hadn't passed another structure for the last five miles.

No Name pulled into the gravel driveway and stopped.

"Who owns this place?" I asked, opening the truck door.

"Sleep here," he said.

The entry opened when I gave the knob a twist. No Name drove off. "Little weak on passing information, ain'tcha?" I asked his dust.

Dog-tired, I checked out the cabin. The place was stark, only housing a couch and a splay-legged, wooden chair leaning against it, a stove occupying the left corner along with a table, and another broken chair. A bedroom contained a single bed, unmade, but inviting. The adjoining bathroom had no privacy. Cardboard boxes, the kind movers use, were stacked in corners unopened.

112

A wood-framed glass rectangle with navy felt backing contained a triangular-fold American flag, an array of Navy enlisted insignia, and a collection of ribbons, medals and marksmanship badges. A small engraved plate at the bottom of the frame honored HMCM Bertrand "Oso" Walker. Another wall mounted several framed citations, all praising Master Chief Petty Officer Walker for his performance of duty. The testimony and signatures from admirals and generals impressed me, but his house was a mess. How could a man who excelled under military spit and polish be such a slob?

Out back, a small stand of lodgepole pine and quaking aspen crowded the area between the cabin and the bluffs. Several trunks had been stripped of bark and snagged with fur. Branches were broken off up to six or seven feet high. They appeared to be rub trees. I pinched some of the fur off and rubbed it between my fingers. Bear.

A mixture of black bear, *Kuhaya* in my language, and grizzly tracks covered the ground. Scat-covered leaves littered the imprints of round pawprints of the black bear. Away from the house and visible fifteen feet away, the eight-inch paws of Grizz invoked a vision of the mass of *horribilis*. My .38 possessed meek stopping power and would only piss off an animal as large as this.

Kuhaya and Grizz had come and gone from the area, so why was this all here? Why would competitors—they ate the same things and even each other—pick a scratching spot in the same place? And why would shy, territorial animals like bears choose a rub so close to each other and human habitation?

Questions or not, I had to sleep. Inside, I locked the rear and front doors to block visitors, human or otherwise. Oso's place was messy but homey. Sleep hit me like a bucket of rocks.

"Get up."

"What the—" I patted around the bed for my pistol, expecting the worst.

No Name, man mountain, loomed over me. "Relax."

"You." Sleep had not released my wits. "What?"

113

"Let's go," No Name said, halfway out the front door.
"Now."

I pocketed my .38 and stumbled in a haze to the pickup.
When No Name floored Oso's pickup down the dirt road faster
than its curves allowed, an adrenalin jolt woke me up with a
shock. "Jesus, man."

No Name paid no attention to me as he leadfooted
through turns, narrows, and sidehill cuts toward San Juan high
country. Memories of Wolf howled in my stitches.

We passed former mining towns sporting wild-west
motifs for tourists and skiers. Along the highway, abandoned
mills and grayed skeletons of big-beam elevator headframes
crowded both sides of the highway. Rusted gears, ore buckets,
ore cars, cables, pipes, water tanks, and corrugated metal sheets
littered the ground. Mounds of rust and yellow-brown tailings
covered hillsides and meadows. Drooping field grass circled
dead, silver-stained ground in places. A yellow stream hugging
the motorway rushed away into the valley we'd come from.

One hundred fifty years of ecological abuse of such a
beautiful place would've brought tears to my eyes if No Name
hadn't broken into a four-wheel slide around a curve bordering
a hundred-foot drop. The old truck's lap belts did little to
prevent me from slamming against the door with each sliding
turn. I swallowed my stomach and crushed the handle and
wondered if I could survive a deliberate bailout through the
side window.

As the highway climbed, vegetation gave way to rock
and fields of summer snow. I spotted Mount Sneffels, figured
we were headed toward Red Mountain Pass on US-550 not far
from Ouray. In the distance, a natural gas tanker labored uphill
behind us. "Where we goin' in such a goddamn hurry?"

No Name said, "Found 'em."

For a second, I feared he meant the rock face dead
ahead, but he steered back on track. I asked, "Found who?"

"Chivs."

"Chivingtons?" Jean Reel had briefed me on the group
as well as the other conspirators she was investigating: Chivs,
punks, cops, and Utes. The alliance of four had nothing in
common except greed, the great unifier.

In 1864, Colonel John Chivington led his Denver thugs
to kill 150 Cheyenne and Arapahoe old men, women, and
children. The modern-day namesakes, part of the plot to disrupt
the Ute's hospital groundbreaking, were just haters and killers
hiding behind their snow-white agenda.

"You gonna tell me what's going on? My job is to ID
Ute Traditionalists. Why'd you track these people down?"

No Name looked at me, smiled, stopped the truck, and
hopped out from behind the wheel next to a track leading
uphill. He fiddled with the hubs of the front tires and twisted
them into four-wheel operation.

When he jumped back in, I cocked my .38. "You better
be on the level."

"You gonna like this," he said, with a smirk on his face.

He gunned the engine and four-wheeled up a track I
wouldn't take a horse. As we climbed, the engine whined in
low gear, while the rough terrain jerked me side to side. Each
time the truck's oil pan met a rock, I winced and imagined
sparks licking the gas tank.

We arrived at a cut in a peak close to a scrub cluster
that could hide the pickup. At this altitude, the sun blinded, and
each step required a double draw of air. Ahead, Bighorn stared
at me, flashed his rump, then disappeared over a boulder. Mats
of small purple flowers emerged from between jagged granite
cracks. Tortured, wind-burned pine and fir clumps leaned
easterly. Even plants struggled to live on this barren ground.

No Name pulled two rifles from behind the seat, jerked
them out of their scabbards.

"What's that for?" I asked, between pulls of air.

No Name scratched his nose, seemed to assess my
sanity, then handed me a bolt action .308 with a scope and
sling. He walked off.

I exhaled. I wasn't too happy holding an unfamiliar rifle
after shooting a cop, but No Name didn't leave me much
choice. I hurried after him, wheezing like grandma's washing
machine.

Near a precipice overlooking a lower plain, he
crouched, then lay prone. I did the same. He pointed to a log

115

cabin edging a pine forest 1,500 yards downhill. He shouldered
his rifle and peered through the scope. I raised to the sitting
position and used a hasty sling to steady my aim. I adjusted the
scope focus as I waited for my heartbeat to slow.

The scope was a good one and I got a close look at men
drinking beer outside the cabin. Some were armed with rifles,
some with sidearms. A few of them wore Civil War era
military-style gray coats.

"How'd you find these people?" I asked.

No Name offered up no answer. No surprise.

In a couple hours of watching, we learned little more
than the group, twenty-four men by my count, liked beer. I
began to wonder why we were here. I checked out the
surrounding area. Our eagle's perch offered an unobstructed
view of whatever it was we were waiting for.

A seventeen pickups parked in a dirt lot in front of the
cabin. I spotted six Harleys mixed in. Two of the trucks had
horse trailers attached. My heart pumped a little faster. Nothing
moved in either trailer, but even if I'd seen a horse, the distance
prohibited the clear identification of breed. The chance I'd
found my horse killers was an unwise leap of logic. But I
tucked it away in my mind.

I was about to ask No Name, why he'd tracked these
hoods, when a sable black '64 Impala SS Rag Top, pulled up to
the cabin. Four men rode inside. I recognized the car, I knew
the driver, too. The wait was worth it.

The Impala's horn sang the theme from "Grand Theft
Auto," a video game my son had become attached to years
back. A few people stood; most paid no attention to the
newcomer.

"How in hell did a car that low get up a bad road?" I
asked.

"Blacktop comes all the way up," said No Name.

A few men gathered by the driver's side as four cholos
stepped out of the Impala radiating gangbanger 'tude. The
driver moved into view. Ángel "Wookie" Gutierrez. Wookie's
appearance at the hideout of a violent gang was no surprise, he
knew where the money was.

"Damn," I said.

116

"Know them?"

"That prick stole my Jeep."

Wookie and his posse talked with the Chivingtons and drank for an hour. Through my scope, the conversation seemed civilized and calm. The fact that a group of racists would talk at length to a cholo meant something big and profitable was going down. They even shook hands. Wookie and his crew got back in the Impala and headed down the road, dipping and jumping out of sight.

"We gotta follow Wookie. That banger is in the middle of Reel's case," I said.

"No way." No Name shook his head.

"Why?"

He pointed to a rocky trail twisting below us. "Take thirty minutes to get there. Not gonna catch 'em."

Downslope, the trail had more hairpins than a hairdresser's styling kit. In this part of Colorado, motorways came in two variations, up or down. "Damn."

By now the snow caps and hillsides glowed gold in the late sun. The temperature dropped with the light.

"Let's go," I said. "Reel's gotta know what we've just seen." I trotted back toward the pickup, rifle strapped at my shoulder, No Name on my heels.

Shots rang out by the time we made it to the truck.

Chapter 21

At the cabin, flashes of light followed by a burst of
popping and snapping created a surreal light and sound show.
The cold mountain evening served up distinct shouts and
screams, even at this distance. I glanced at No Name. He
looked away.

Wind-borne guttural rumbles mixed with the cries
reminded me of last night's Sun Dance mayhem.

"We gotta see what's going on down there," I said to
No Name.

"No."

"You hear it?" I asked.

"Thought you was gonna see Reel."

In his face, I said, "As soon as we find out what's going
on down there."

No Name climbed into the truck. We drove back down
the road we'd used earlier, the ruts and potholes more
unexpected and treacherous in the low light. We made a few
hairpin turns, then parked in a thicket three hundred yards from
the cabin we'd stared at all day.

We watched from cover of the brush. I expected some
talk from the building, but none came. The idea of a silent
killer, Grizz maybe, waiting close by spooked me with visions
of disappearing behind his teeth in chunks.

Rifles at the ready, we crept toward the cabin stopping
every few yards to listen. Moans came from inside.

An infinity of stars lit the sky but their light provided
no warning for the body I tripped over as we approached the
building. The poor bastard was gutted, his backbone visible
through the gaping hole in his abdomen. The copper smell of
blood and rank stench of feces steamed from the body. No dead
man is my enemy, but I dismissed sadness over his fate. This
was no time to morn or even respect the dead. My icy cold
attitude, as feigned as it was necessary, spread tension to my
shoulders and ached in my arms.

Scrub pine trees dotted the approach to the log structure
and No Name and I used them as cover until we hugged the

118

side of the building. Someone groaned. The interior lights were on. A quick peek through the window showed men inside: two on the floor, and one sitting at a table in a dazed stare, blood pooling at his feet. I spotted a pair of boots and legs inside, their owner partially hidden under the window.

I checked my cell to call 911 but the screen showed black. No Name pulled his phone, gave thumbs up, and headed in a crouched run for the far tree line.

While he found a place to make the call, I checked on the wounded through the window. The man half-hidden beneath the window had not moved. The man at the table had dropped his head, arms splayed out front. One of the two on the floor had crawled to a couch. A blood trail marked his route. The other, on his knees, leaned against a chair and stared off somewhere, his jeans ripped and soaked dark with blood. Everyone I could see, alive or dead, was armed, but those I couldn't see bothered me the most.

I wanted backup. No Name and I needed to enter the building from different sides simultaneously to throw the occupants off guard. But he'd not returned, so I scouted the area keeping an eye out for more Chivingtons. Out front, I checked the Chivs' trucks and pocketed the keys I found in the ignition.

At the back window again, I waited. Time passed and I began to worry. No Name had either run off, sought a place with better reception, or bumped into a Chivington. Or Grizz.

I couldn't yell for him, so I scrambled to higher ground, a place he might have chosen for better reception. The surrounding area alternated dark and darker and blanketed all detail. Dread constricted my throat, making me cough. I covered my mouth; noise was the last thing I needed.

Maybe he'd gone to the truck. I cut across treeless ground toward the thicket where we'd parked. The truck was where we'd left it, but No Name was nowhere to be seen. I checked the ignition. No keys.

A snort and a grumble like ball bearings dropping on a bass drum. Then a deep, back-of-the-throat growl. I froze. Cold, wet droplets of sweat formed at the base of my spine. I scanned my surroundings.

Chuffs as loud as air brakes echoed against the hills. A growl as loud as a jet made me jump. I edged toward the truck, knowing the animal could hear my pounding heart and rapid breath. Every step took a lifetime. Sweat stung my eyes as I cursed my shaking legs.

Grizz's eyes glowed green from behind scrub, then vanished.

I jumped into the passenger seat and slammed the door. Grizz could sniff all he wanted, the smell of gasoline would disguise my adrenaline stink. I flashed the headlamps. I pounded the old truck's horn, but the fucking thing was dead. I exhaled, watched the cabin, and listened.

The truck rocked from a deafening impact on the driver's side. Glass showered my face. When I reached for my eyes, my rifle slipped to the floor. Shards protruded from the window frame like crystal canines.

A massive head exposing two-inch fangs shoved through the broken window, inching toward me. Grizz roared. I pressed against the passenger door ready to kick at the animal's muzzle until I was dead. Grizz retreated, then returned, paw reaching ahead of snapping jaws.

I scraped the rifle toward me with my foot. I grabbed it by the barrel, but the weapon's sling caught under the dash and caused the stock to drag against the floor mats. I struggled to extract the weapon and get the stock to my shoulder.

A massive paw, railroad spikes for claws, missed me by inches, then crashed against the steering wheel. As I pulled at the rifle, claws inched closer followed by nose, teeth, and eyes red with rage. Another swing missed and raked the dashboard. His violent thrashing pinned his shoulders for a split second. I jabbed at his eyes with stiff fingers. He yelped and jerked away.

The truck shook like a ragdoll as he tried to withdraw, but jagged shards of the window frame stabbed at his neck while he struggled. Blood coated the window frame and splashed on me. I pulled at the rifle to free it, but the tangled sling held fast. Grizz's earsplitting roar deafened me.

120

The shaking sprung the passenger door and I tumbled out like a bag of rocks, landing flat on my back. I rolled and took off toward the cabin.

Grizz roared and yelped, stuck in the truck window as I sprinted the three hundred yards to the cabin, fear my energizing partner.

The rear door was locked. I kicked the entry open, entered, slammed the door shut, then jammed the closest chair under the knob.

I backed against the wall, evaluating the opposition, calculating my chances. Fortunately, of the four men in the room, only one pair of eyes stared my way. A Chivington, a hater, eyes rolling, and delirious. A pool at his feet meant he probably didn't have long to live. I said, "Grizz's still out there."

"Who the fuck're you?" slurred the man. An empty Beam bottle lay next to him.

The other man on the couch hadn't raised his head since I barged in. The man at the table hadn't moved, neither had the man against the wall under the window. "Are they dead?" I asked.

"Fuck you, Injun."

A hall led off to my left and I listened for others in the building. "Anyone in the other rooms?"

"Your ass." He raised his weapon.

"You picked a bad time to act hostile. It's me or Grizz." My heart beat in my temples.

Click. Color bled from his face. He dropped the empty weapon.

"You don't look so good," I said, stifling my relief.

"My legs."

"I'll find a bandage," I said.

The two back bedrooms were empty but, I found stiff, filthy towels in a bathroom smelling of urine. The man's wounds were torn so deep I could see bone. I wrapped them as best I could.

He looked at me with curiosity. "You the one killed Deputy Jones?"

121

"That what you think?" I continued binding, applying pressure until he cringed.

"Fuck yeah, it's you, Injun. Ponytail, height, boots. All that shit."

I finished wrapping and tucked the towel ends. Blood began to seep through, and I doubted the rags would stop the bleeding. Unless the EMTs arrived soon, he would most likely bleed out.

He smiled. "Yeah, you're the guy. Awesome, dude." He chuckled then surrendered to a deep cough. He spit. "Yeah, Jones was an asshole," he said. "Got a cigarette?"

His demeanor was odd for a dying man. "You a cop?" I asked. He could've been a plant.

"Gotta be a cop to smoke?"

When something scratched at the door, I put up a hand. I inched toward the door.

The man slumped in a pool of blood at the table had not moved since I entered the room. I grabbed his AK-47, then I pulled out the mag, checked and slipped it back in, regretting the click. I stood by the doorway, rifle at the ready. It squeaked open.

The AK snicked when I cycled the charging handle. I put pressure on the trigger when a grunt came from behind the door. A hand slid from behind the door and gripped the edge. No Name's head squeezed in. "Let me in, man," he said. I removed the chair and he stepped in.

"Party's already started," I said.

"Big-ass bear come up when I was callin'. Climbed up a rock and he run off. Better reception up there, anyway. EMT's here in thirty minutes."

"Hey, Leslie, you got a cigarette?" asked the man on the couch.

"What's he doing here?" asked No Name.

"Know him?" I asked.

"Dillard Johnston. Dilbert's more like it. Flatlander from Limon. Busted his ass at playoffs back in the day. Fourteen zip. Fuckers had no defense and their special teams was more like special ed."

Johnston said, "You only scored twi—"

"Your running back couldn't hold a football shoved up his ass."

"Take it outside with Grizz, you wanna talk football," I said.

Johnston turned sheet white, slumped back on to the sofa. Leslie, No Name seemed more appropriate somehow, filled an empty beer bottle with water from the bathroom and gave it to Johnston. He pulled a cigarette from his breast pocket, lit it, gave him that, too. Johnston inhaled deeply, blew out, then coughed.

The deep rumble of an eighteen-wheeler echoed across the hills, sounds bouncing off the rocks. The noise could have come from miles away. Through the window, I studied the darkness. Sirens warbled, but this noise was close, not an echo. "We gotta get out of here," I said to Leslie No Name.

"What about him?" No Name asked, pointing to Johnston. The man's mouth slacked open, his breath rasped coarse and shallow. The cigarette had burned past his fingers, but he hadn't dropped it.

"Done all we can," I said. Sheriff's comin'.

The Lakota shook his head. "I'll badge 'em."

"I got better odds with Grizz than the sheriff," I said, showing the keys I'd taken from the Chiv's trucks, I said, "Out front."

Red and blue lights flashed far downhill as No Name and I hopped into a Ford F-150. I drove up the trail we'd taken before. As we rolled, the moonlight showed Oso's vehicle on its side, the 2,500-pound truck lacerated by claw marks.

Leslie No Name let out a grunt and dropped his jaw at the sight.

I drove on to find Reel. This was her case and she needed to know both Wookie and Grizz had put new faces on her investigation.

Chapter 22

Reel sat at the command center's conference table reading a stack of papers, when I told her about Wookie Gutierrez's appearance at the Chivs' hangout.

"Chivingtons?" Her face colored. "What were you doing near the Chivingtons?"

I'd just stepped in it.

"My investigation led me there," I said, seeing no reason to tell her that Leslie No Name, a member of her own staff, dragged me there. She wasn't about to fire me.

"I gave you explicit instructions to find members of the Southern Ute Tribe who may be involved in the upcoming demonstration against the hospital groundbreaking," she said, voice pitched. "That did not include the white supremacists."

"You know I go where evidence or suspicion leads me. You should be more interested in what Wookie is doin' than what I'm doing."

Reel kept her composure, but her frustration broadcast heat. I stepped back.

"Confine your investigation to the Utes from now on."

"That's not the way I work."

"Wrong, Officer Romero. That's the way you *will* work."

I wanted to say, Like hell I will, but a frontal assault on her never worked. I reverted to a time-tested tactic: tell her what she wanted to hear, then do as I damn well please.

"Yes, ma'am." I clicked my heels.

"Don't get smart with me, Peter."

I let off steam with a short huff. "There's another thing, besides Wookie. Grizz."

"Colorado has no grizzly—"

"Grizz mauled at least five men, maybe more, in the two camps."

She stared at me seeming to be without words. Might have been a first. Then she asked, "You have Oso look at the victims?"

"Oso's in the hospital."

"No, he checked himself out. The doctor called me livid, says he won't take responsibility for Oso's recovery."

My jaw dropped. "He was hurtin' bad when we took him in. Gunshot."

Reel shook her head. "Haven't heard from him. I'm worried, but I can't leave the command center. Check on him. I want you under his close supervision from now on."

How about I keep an eye on Oso? "Right."

"Thanks for the tip on Wookie," she said, when I walked out of the RV.

Oso's cabin lay in the hills and I headed there. I'd asked around for Leslie No Name, but he'd disappeared. No way I was going to wait for him. Reel had pissed me off by demanding I limit my investigation and that wasn't going to happen. I was glad to get away before I opened my big mouth and told her so.

Oso's self-checkout from the emergency room troubled me. The man had spent his entire career in healthcare. Too many things could happen with an unhealed wound. I knew better and he knew better.

The mountains and canyons offered general directions to Oso's place. The roads, though, zig-zagged in confusing ways due to the legacies of miners, loggers, and off-roaders. The canyon I travelled seemed familiar, but tracks crisscrossed and paralleled the one I drove. It didn't help that No Name had driven here the first time and I'd slept part of the way still groggy from all night in the emergency waiting room.

At a fork in the road, both ways looked equally familiar and strange, but the steep hills that backed Oso's place to the north made the choice obvious.

I drove to the right. After driving for a mile, I stepped out of the vehicle, pressed between the truck's front fender and a fifty-foot drop off, then scouted ahead. Each turn produced another. I walked a mile uphill until it became obvious I'd picked the wrong road and would have to back down the way I came.

As I walked back to the truck, I spotted Oso's cabin below me. By luck, the wrong road had put me at a spot

125

directly above by fifty yards, the place I'd intended. Reel wanted me to check on Oso and submit to his supervision. I wouldn't submit to anything, but I wanted to know how well he'd recovered from his gunshot wound.

A short, deep grunt caught my ear. I peered over the edge of the cliff. An Aspen shook, its branches quaking with no wind anywhere. At the base of the tree I spotted a brown form. Through the foliage, an animal scratched himself against a tree in Oso Walker's backyard.

Then, Oso walked out his back door. Before I could yell a warning, Grizz lumbered at him running like a draft horse. The brute stopped in front of Oso, stood on hind legs, then scooped him off the porch with massive paws. My heart sank, Oso was about to be killed in front of me.

I waited for screams. The poor bastard had no chance, the possibility of rescue fruitless. I shrank back from my overlook ready to run for the pickup I'd stolen last night. I pictured Grizz chasing me and attacking through the pickup's window and succeeding this time.

A roar swallowed a laugh from Oso's yard. Another laugh. I bent down and crept close on hands and knees to the edge. Grizz stood on hind legs, towering over Oso who seemed to be enjoying the experience. Oso raised his arms and made a circular arm movement. Grizz twirled. Oso laughed loudly and cheered at the eight-hundred-pound ballerina.

On signal, Grizz dropped to the ground and played dead. Then the man clapped. The beast pushed up to a sitting position, a gigantic teddy bear. Oso swung his arms overhead in a circle and Grizz rolled over and over while Oso laughed. Oso and Grizz hugged again, then both walked into the cabin.

I was dumbstruck. The way the man and Grizz interacted was remarkable. Like best friends. Like family. Now that I thought about it, Oso's ambling gait and gruff exterior was most bear-like. I was surprised I hadn't realized the connection before.

A picture of Oso and Grizz sitting inside and enjoying an afternoon coffee flashed before me, a vision no crazier than what I'd just witnessed. At least, it would explain the broken furniture in Oso's home. Now I understood why there were so many tracks around the cabin, and so many rub trees.

I wasn't sure if Oso could be some kind of animal trainer or a shaman with spiritual power over wildlife. I didn't imagine either being true, but I didn't picture what I had seen happening, either. One thing I did know was that this must be the same animal that attacked the Utes two days before and the Chivingtons yesterday.

Something grunted behind me. A black bear, *Kuhaya* my people call them, crouched between me and the pickup. I froze. This was the second time in as many days a damn bear snuck up on me. *Kuhaya* sported a brown muzzle and light markings on his chest over a cinnamon coat. Black bears are not as aggressive as Grizz, but this one eyed me with a mixture of fear and dislike. At two hundred pounds, the animal had twenty-five pounds on me, and an arsenal of teeth and claws that deserved respect.

Blacks are not normally belligerent, but *Kuhaya* swayed his head, huffed, popped his jaws, snorted, and clacked his teeth. Then, he lowered his head and laid back his ears, ready to attack.

Neither aspen nor pine offered shelter: the trees grew either below me at the foot of a cliff, or above me on the bluff. I had to stand my ground. Blacks often bluff, so I played the odds.

Kuhaya charged, but it was no bluff. In his eyes, he wanted blood. I waived my arms high to look bigger and yelled, but *Kuhaya* kept coming. I yelled again. I looked for a place with enough vegetation below to break my fall when I jumped off the cliff.

Someone yelled from the vicinity of Oso's cabin. *Kuhaya* veered to his left and threw himself down the cliff. I peered over the edge. The animal had not only survived but seemed unhurt as he ran off. Trees shook and bushes parted as the bruin crashed toward Oso's house.

I hurried for the truck.

My elders told me long ago that animals can act as role models and teachers, appearing and reappearing at will. I had experienced this in the past, but this time was different. One of these animals had attacked and killed humans.

"Animals have much to offer, and we must listen," Grandfather often said to me. As a child at his knee, I'd listen to him for as long as he would talk, snuggled up in an ancient blanket in a warm room smelling of piñon, the earth outside blanketed by snow. As I grew older, the more I understood his values.

But now, I didn't know if Oso was commanding these animals or if they were just protecting him, either way, the group was deadly. I reversed down the mountain. I had a lot of questions for Oso.

Chapter 23

The road widened and leveled, so I could turn around and head for Oso's cabin. In the distance, the sun painted snow-streaked peaks blinding-white. Chokecherry, box elder, and lodgepole pine lined my way. A slight breeze caused the Aspen leaves to quake as I inhaled the sweet butterscotch of ponderosa.

The engine began to smoke and cough. The heat gage had pegged, so I parked to the side, killed the ignition, and waited for it to cool. Backing down rough roads had taken its toll.

Both Grizz and *Kuhaya* were with Oso, now. I was uncertain what Oso's reaction would be if I showed unannounced, but damn certain what Grizz's response would be. Grizz reminded me of the Colorado legend, Old Mose, a 1500-pound grizzly that had an ambling gait that made it seem he just moseyed about. Legend had it that he walked through fences like matchsticks and killed a horse with one bite. The great "King of the Grizzlies" killed three men, and three bulls before he was taken down in 1904.

The engine cooled and it's ticking faded. I tried the ignition.

"Get out of the truck. Now." My eye focused on a black hole just over my left shoulder at the end of a long barrel. A squinting man at the end of the rifle held it steady. The rifleman stepped back, giving me room, but no time to curse myself for being so lax about my surroundings. I pulled the handle and opened the door. Slowly.

I had a foot out of the pickup when someone yelled, "Get on the ground."

"You gonna tell me what this is about?" I said, lowering myself to the ground. His scowl and M-16 were persuasive. I kept my eyes on him. Black hair hung past ripped shoulders. A black short-sleeved uniform barely contained his biceps.

"I need to see some ID," the cop in me said. I inhaled dust, coughed.

129

"Captain Hanlon, Tribal Rangers, Ute Natural Resource Enforcement Division, Justice and Regulatory." He patted his M-16. "This here's my ID. Put your hands out in front of you."

Four other uniformed men, armed, walked out of the bushes. One dropped a knee on my back, then pulled my arms behind me. He plasti-cuffed me, jerked me to my feet, then pulled my wallet from my rear pocket.

He threw the wallet to Hanlon who snatched it out of the air. Hanlon examined my ID, smiled. "Well, well. Peter Romero, uh, Officer Peter Romero, you are under arrest for violation of Title Thirteen Wildlife Code, Unlawful Taking or Possession of Wildlife." He recited my rights. "Do you understand?"

"No, I do not. What are you talking about?"

"You are suspected of killing two wolves, a protected species on this reservation."

"Is this some kinda joke?"

"Do you have a Title Thirteen permit to take or possess wolves?"

"No."

He huffed, "Let's go."

The ranger standing next to me grabbed my arm while the others kept their firearms at shoulder ready. "Where?" I asked.

"Processing, then Durango."

"Durango?"

"You're popular around here. Got a BOLO on the wire four days ago. Been tracking your ass and here you are. Lucky me. Only trouble is, Durango gets first whack at you. Charges for killing a cop beats wildlife charges. Same thing, you ask me."

One of the rangers whispered, "That the guy shot Jones?"

Someone laughed, "Yeah. Jones was a prick."

Hanlon threw stink-eye at his troops. "Knock it off. "

I broke free of my arm holders and ran for Oso's house. Handcuffed or not, I had a better chance with Oso and his two bruins than I did with the deputies in Durango. I gained yardage at first, but a deputy ran me down with a tackle that slid my face across gravel. He lifted me to my feet as I spit dirt.

They pushed me to a dark blue F-250 crew cab. A ranger shoved me into the back seat. Rangers climbed in back from both sides with me wedged in the middle. It was hard to breathe, much less move. Another sat in the front passenger side and turned to watch me. Hanlon drove. The acrid smell of sweat and stink of testosterone flooded the cab.

Salty, warm liquid ran over my lips. "My nose is bleeding," I said.

No one paid attention. Blood reddened my shirt, but that didn't bother me as much as knowing Durango's deputies would have their shot at me. "Look, I can prove I acted in self-defense against Jones." I lied. It was my word against the assassination squad.

Hanlon eyed me through the rear view. "What, Jones bite you, too?" The rangers laughed. I looked at them for some explanation, but they weren't offering any.

Ranger Hanlon drove to downtown Ignacio and stopped at a plain, single story on Goddard Avenue that housed the city hall, municipal court, and police department. They recited my rights, then locked me in a holding cell for twenty minutes until I stood in front of a desk sergeant with a handful of forms and an attitude. I answered questions with as few words as I could. The sergeant finished, nodded at Hanlon who walked me back to the truck handcuffed, shackled, and surrounded by Tribal Rangers. I got the impression a cop killer was the biggest bust they'd made in years.

We drove off for Durango, I felt like a steer being led to slaughter. My life ran before me in a circuit of endless seasons during the thirty-minute drive from Ignacio to Durango. As I looked back, I regretted only a few things.

Mainly, I regretted how I treated Costancia. She didn't deserve what I handed out. She deserved more respect, more maturity, more care. I wished I'd had it in me to appreciate her when I should've. I lamented not knowing her as deeply as she wanted, needed. I regretted that she'll always wish I had. At the same time, like a jerk, I regretted not taking a chance with

Reel. We were a team and I trusted her. That trust was what Costancia had craved the most.

I didn't regret killing Deputy Frank Jones. I did regret being stuck in this truck.

The La Plata County Jail in Durango was a two-story, yellow brick fortress built to repress and depress its occupants. Inside, they booked and processed me and read my rights, again. The word must have spread before my paperwork was completed, because a crowd of uniformed onlookers had gathered.

Some of the uniforms smirked, but my celebrity was not all laughs. Some sneered. A name tag, Lettau, the shithead who woke me in the middle of the night at the sheepherder's camp, seemed delighted to be hosting me in his jail. Had I not been handcuffed; I would have middle-fingered my thanks for his hospitality. The group's vibe was menacing, like the pack of wolves I'd been arrested for.

Lettau, who stood a head taller than me, and another deputy led me, shackled and shuffling, through a series of access cages and down a long cell-lined corridor.

"You da man!" a prisoner hooted from his cell.

"Right on, motherfucker!" said another.

"Blue lives ain't shit," a third said. "Jones was an asshole."

As I shuffled down the corridor, the sentiment for Jones, in and out of jail, seemed unanimous but offered little comfort. Unaccustomed in the role of hero to men I normally imprisoned, I only nodded at the catcalls and whistles.

My heartbeat spiked when I realized the cell they'd chosen for me was separate from the others. Lettau unshackled my legs using his left hand. A lefty, as was the tall assassin at my motel.

The deputies exited, locked the door, then uncuffed me through the meal tray port. Lettau made a finger pistol pointed at me. "Bang," he said. It was too easy to take that gesture as an admission he was involved in my attempted assassination.

I stared at the blank, gray door as the rhythm of boots on a cement floor receded, a door down the hall crashed shut, an electronic lock buzzed, another slam, another buzz. Silence.

"Nice little place ya got here."

I jumped, whirled, flattened my back against the door. Deer stood in front of me. It was no doubt the same deer I'd seen at Pokoh's shooting and later when I rolled my truck.

"You?" I asked.

"Do not trust him."

"Huh?"

"Oso. Who'd you think?" Deer twisted his head, his rack nearly touching both sides of the cell.

"I have no idea. I thought I'd find Arabian horse-killers and the perps who stabbed two men from my pueblo." I stared at the talking buck, unconvinced I wasn't hallucinating.

"I didn't think I'd meet a retired master chief of the Navy who is either a bear trainer, a shaman, or a bear. And most of all, I didn't expect to be locked up for killing goddamn wolves. You gotta believe it never occurred to me that I'll probably be murdered tonight." I regulated my voice and words to hide my uneasiness.

"Quit pacing. Your hysterics are unbecoming."

"Hysterics? By morning, I'm dead."

"Keep it up, you'll have a stroke first."

I inhaled, let it out slow. "Okay, okay. So, don't trust Oso. Why?"

Deer's eyes widened like he was ready to run. "You cannot recognize a *yee naaldlooshii?* A skinwalker?"

"No. No way." Some shaman can transform themselves into animals. Some call them shapeshifters. "Not Oso. No."

Deer threw his head back. "You, of all people."

I knew the campfire stories and legends. My former wife—still an uncomfortable description—was raised on the Navajo reservation and I'd been there countless times to visit family. Skinwalkers were a Navajo tradition and a worrying one at that.

I said, "I know what a skinwalker is. Like a witch, a bad witch, an animal like Wolf or Grizz, maybe a…Oh shit." Wolf's bites on my legs and arms tingled.

"Now it becomes clear?" Deer said.

133

"Oh, man." I sat on my bunk, put my head in my hands. "Okay, what's a skinwalker doing on this rez? I always thought they were Navajo."

"We Utes have them, too," Deer said. "Last year a security officer on the Uintah and Ouray Reservation spotted a huge creature with coal red eyes. He and another officer pursued but couldn't catch it.

"Utes and Navajos have been at odds for centuries. Things worsened during the 1800's, when we started selling Navajo children as slaves."

"We?" I asked.

"Later, my ancestors joined Kit Carson against the Navajo, who then cast a spell on our tribe. We sent medicine men to make amends, but the Navajo refused to lift the spell."

I heard a key in the door. A head appeared and said, "Who're you talking to?"

"Don't know." I spoke the truth.

He glanced around the cell, then at me. "Smart ass," the jailer said. He slammed the door.

I asked, "Who are you?"

"Don't change the subject," Deer's hooves clicked on the cement floor as he shifted weight. "I don't blame the Navajo, but it's time to end it." He snorted.

"Oso Walker? A retired Navy master chief corpsman is a skinwalker?" My brain was a demolition derby of theories crashing together trying to make sense, but just making junk. Crazy junk.

Rubbing my face, I said, "Okay, why the hospital groundbreaking?"

"A shared history of trouble makes more trouble easy."

"Mayhem at the hospital groundbreaking. Doesn't seem like much," I said.

"It will be when the shooting starts. Clearly, you don't understand what you've stepped into. You will soon." Deer misted away and I was alone.

Deer's words puzzled me. As an animal guide, Deer is ordinarily compassionate, kind, and empathetic. I didn't see that in this spirit. I saw other attributes. I saw a bad omen, a warning.

But I understood one thing from Deer's history lesson: the need for revenge never dies.

Chapter 24

Lights out on a hard bunk. A dark cell made the worst place for my last night. Death was supposed to come in bed with loved ones at your side. I expected instead, a staged jailbreak in the middle of the night that would certainly be my fate. My guess: a bullet dead center in the head from behind.

With eyes closed and breath deep, I reached out to my elders' ghosts. I had no prayer dust or sage to purify myself, no animal guide to follow. No drums, nor music. Only this black cell and the hiss of silence.

I slowed my heart, directed my mind to an ancient campfire on a cold night long before time. In its flame, I purged self-pity, strove for complete honesty until my thinking came clean and clear. My breathing stopped. I lifted upward in deep relaxation and floated to a place of no form or time.

Footsteps, toenails clicking on a cement floor, drifted my way. The steps grew louder, then stopped. Breathing. Not mine. Growling. Not mine, for sure. A brown mass moved—indistinct in form, clear in menace. Smells drifted toward me: the tell-tale stink of wet dog. The musk of Grizz. Rapid sniffing. A snort. A grunt.

I pushed myself up, then collapsed. I sucked air, blew hard to waken. A blue mist enveloped a feminine figure with both arms beckoning. A beautiful woman sang a mournful song, but not in a tongue I understood. "Come with me," she said. I couldn't move. The time had come to sing a death song, but I had none.

Light flooded the room. Reality intruded with a cell door crash, walls shining gray like ancient pottery. Three men shouldered into view, scowling, smelling of coffee and armpits. Hands on pistol butts. "Get up."

This was no dream. I got up.

Deputy Lettau head-motioned toward the cell door. I walked out. They didn't bother cuffing me, an invitation to make a break for it. I knew better but looked for a way out just the same. I walked a dead man's walk until we stopped at an

exit that led outside. A deputy held it open. Lettau motioned
for me to exit.

"No," I said.

Lettau pulled his pistol. "Outside, Romero."

"Shoot me here, Lettau." Blood is difficult to clean, and
harder to explain. Inside the building the fluid would
complicate the inmate death report.

Lettau's grin showed teeth. "Who gives a shit where?
This shoot's righteous. You killed Deputy Jones."

"Were you there?" I asked.

Lettau smiled, said, "Got your ass dead to rights."

If they had me dead to rights, why take the risk of
shooting me? I knew too much. Lettau's real interest was my
silence.

A door at the end of the hall opened. Everyone turned. I
delivered a front snap kick to Lettau's groin. He dropped. A
deputy grabbed me from behind in a sleeper choke hold. My
world blackened.

"What's going on here?" said a voice down the hall.
The choker released me. I sucked air.

The voice had come from a deputy who wore the rank
of sergeant. He looked me up and down while two men helped
Lettau stand. "Well, Lettau?" he asked.

Lettau's face washed ashen, and he said nothing

The others had nothing to say.

I rubbed my throat, an instinctive dose of survival
locked my jaw shut.

The sergeant looked at me, then at Lettau. "Why's he
not cuffed?" Then he gave the deputies a once over, said,
"Why are you armed in the cell block?"

Lettau opened his mouth to speak.

The sergeant said, "Can it. I want all three of you
standing in front of my desk first thing tomorrow." In Lettau's
face, he said, "You better have the right answers."

To me, he said, "With me."

I followed. With a quick glance back at the deputies, I
caught Lettau mouthing, "This isn't over."

The sergeant led me to an interrogation room, said,
"Wait in here."

The soundproofed room was as welcoming as my recent cell. Time passed. I went from near death by law enforcement to near death by anticipation. The door opened, the sergeant held out a hand and said, "He's all yours."

Jean Reel walked in. "Peter," she said.

My jaw must have dropped because she raised her eyebrows as she held out a pair of hand cuffs. She said, "Turn around, arms at your back."

"What?" I asked. Her face turned stern and I complied. Never a dull moment with her.

"Procedure," she said.

She cuffed me. Outside, a black SUV waited. She put me in the rear seat, then sat next to the driver.

Reel twisted and looked across the front seat at me. "Why do I spend most of my time pulling you out of trouble?"

"You protect and serve?" I asked

"Smart ass."

"Love your timing. How'd you spring me?"

She smiled, waved a hand in dismissal. "FISA warrant."

The FBI can go to the Foreign Intelligence Surveillance Court to get a warrant but they're not easy to come by. "Man, you got that kinda juice?"

"I told you from the beginning, the Director has personal interest. He went straight to the court. This case has widespread implications."

"Widespread? FISA? You mean foreign and you mean terrorism. What's that have to do with me?"

"You don't need to know, Peter."

No use pressing her for an answer, and it didn't take a genius to reckon this case had foreign interest. Natural gas draws big, sometimes bad, money. Federal regulations governing Indians are hopelessly complex and some reservation business enterprises take advantage by dealing directly and secretly with foreign interests for gas and oil leases and timber.

"So, you waltzed into the sheriff's office and flashed a warrant for my custody, and he let me go?"

138

"That's how it works," she said, her tone suggesting you-damn-well-know.

"Am I under arrest?"

"Yes, Peter, you are. The charges for shooting a law enforcement officer have been subordinated, not dismissed. Plus, you just picked up another charge for assaulting a law enforcement officer in jail."

"So, I'm on loan?"

"You could look at it that way. And the wolves, don't forget the wolves." She couldn't keep a straight face on that one.

"Funny," I said.

We drove until we arrived at her mobile command post in the woods. She led me to the conference room, still cuffed. She said something to the people in the room and they exited. She hung a placard that said classified on the outside knob and closed the door.

"Sit," she said.

A half-turn showed my cuffs. "Any chance?"

"Oh, sorry. A formality." She crossed behind me and unlocked the cuffs.

I rubbed my wrists and sat.

"Okay, Peter, tell me what you've found out," she said, sitting in a chair next to mine.

Before I could speak, her voice, smell, and beauty struck me dumb. I fell into her black eyes.

"Peter, you okay?"

"No," I said. An irrepressible sensation swept across me. Her eyes tugged and I lost control. Seduced by a combination of longstanding yearnings and love unbound, I cradled her face in my hands and pressed my lips to hers.

She kissed back. Good thing, I could have received a knee to the nuts. I pulled away.

Her black eyes glistened. "Peter?"

"I'm sorry. I was out of line." I let go.

"I don't believe you're sorry and out-of-line fails to describe it." She put her arms around my neck and kissed with an urgency that took my breath away.

139

We freed ourselves from our chairs. I laid her back on the table.

A knock on the door. We jumped up, grabbed our chairs, pretended to be seated all along.

Reel said, "What is it?" An arm pushed a stack of paper through the door. Reel grabbed it. The arm disappeared.

"Can we continue?" I asked between breaths.

"Later," she said, "Later, most definitely." She straightened her cammies, fluffed her hair. After a cooling down period, she said, "Okay, Peter, now tell me what you know."

Reel could return to work much faster than I. My heart had yet to slow.

There wasn't much new to tell her about the traditionalist Utes. I had already briefed her on them, the activities of Ute activist Posey Trujillo, and the secret meeting of the sun dancers at the farmhouse. I reported the appearance of gangbanger Wookie Gutierrez at the Chivington cabin and described how Grizz had ripped up both groups.

I briefed her on the events that bothered me most. Oso and his bruins. I told her what I'd observed. "So, Oso is either one hell of a trainer or he is not all together human, at least not all the time. There's more," I said.

"Why did I see that coming?" She dead-panned and I couldn't tell if she believed me. I imagined her about to call for the paddy wagon and shrink. Sometimes her Indian got lost in her FBI.

"Oso is a skinwalker." Her eyes widened and now I could see the Cherokee in them. "That's Navajo, Peter, and you know it. And, Oso passed a background check."

"This one's Ute. Background paperwork got a section on skinwalkers where you can just check a box?"

"We combed naval records and everything else. I have his DD-214 discharge certificate. Case closed."

"I'll bet I know where you didn't check."

She slapped a palm on the table. "Really, Peter?"

"Indianapolis. The pay center for military retirees."

"I told you I have his discharge."

"Faking paperwork is kid's stuff. Is Indianapolis payin' him?"

She had no answer for that but picked up the phone and called her security assistant, Dean, one of the agents working outside the conference room. "Check on Oso's retirement pay status. Indianapolis pay center. Yeah, I know, I know. Humor me."

We sat staring at each other while sexual vibes fluttered around the room like a trapped sparrow. I tried to ignore it and said, "How'd you know the deputies we're going to kill me?"

"You were the target and only witness to an attempted assassination. And you killed a cop. Your incarceration offered a slam dunk opportunity for those thugs."

"Fair enough. Your timing was perfect."

"Thank you."

"How'd you manage it?"

She swiveled in her chair to face me. She rolled her eyes, shook her head, then turned to her pile of papers. "Come on, Peter. Why don't I just tell you everything about my operation?" Her cynical humor was endearing, more like enticing, but I settled for the memory of her in my arms.

"It's a thought," I said. True, much of her investigation was classified and I had no security clearance. I sat with nothing more to say.

The phone rang. Reel answered. "No. Really? You sure? That's not what you told me the first time, Dean. We'll talk, later."

She hung up, slapped the table. Her face reddened and, for a moment, she couldn't speak.

"Master Chief Petty Officer Bertrand "Oso" Walker died of heart failure two months after retirement."

Chapter 25

"Oso is dead." She put her face in her hands. "Compromised. My whole operation is compromised." She rose from her chair, started to pace, working up a head of steam. I'd seen her angry before and didn't want to be in front of that train.

I said, "A faked death certificate is easy to pull off. Oso Walker was a stranger to his own tribe, so when he died there may not have been much social or official notice. Few, if any, people knew him or cared, for that matter."

"Shit. We *never* should have missed that." She shook her head, slapped the back of her chair. It spun, then faced her as if offering a seat.

Pointing to the chair, I said, "Good idea. Please sit." She sat, but I let her cool before saying, "Listen. If Oso, the skinwalker, is on a vendetta against the Utes, he has no real interest in your conspiracy case."

"No, Peter, the fact he's on my team at all is the problem. He's had access to classified information. No telling what he's done with it. If the Director gets word of this, I'm on a plane to Minot."

Many agents considered Minot, North Dakota, the worst duty station the FBI could offer. People ask and answer, Why Not Minot? Freezin's the reason. Agents go there to fade away and shiver out their time until retirement, or so the story goes.

"You're over-reacting, Jean. Classified exposure is the least of your worries. Have Dean call the pay center again and get them to send the death certificate, the real one. Might show how natural the death really was."

"Why, Peter? Why the pay center? Why not the Ute Council? Why not county or state agencies?"

"Then, you risk the wrong people find out you're lookin'. Besides, it's one of them that passed on the fake you relied on."

She rose from her chair. "If I can keep from killing him, I'll have Dean make the call."

142

"Go for it," I said. "We have to know what we're dealing with. What we've seen so far makes no sense."

A crescendo clicking of keyboards invaded the space when she opened the door, then faded with her closing it. Reel yelled. I imagined poor Dean trapped between monitors and status boards with no way to evade her anger. She returned and sat at her monitor, remained quiet. From time to time, she sorted paperwork.

I wanted that death certificate and had little doubt it would show up, so I kept quiet and pretended to read the status displays on the back wall.

Twenty awkward minutes later, Master Chief Petty Officer Bertrand Walker's certificate, the one held by the pay center, appeared on Reel's monitor. She read aloud, "Says here immediate cause was sudden cardiac arrest due to cardiomyopathy. Also says, no autopsy performed."

"Very interesting. Ever check his Navy health records to confirm he had a heart condition?" I asked.

Reel called Dean. She asked him for a summary of Walker's Navy medical records, waited for his answer, then put down the phone. "Dean says, if he had a heart problem on active duty, it is not reflected in his records. There is no mention of any heart condition, no record of a medical or physical evaluation board of any disability, no VA claim and he was not assigned disability retirement."

"Something stinks, here. He retires from the Navy and dies two months later? The guy was healthy." I asked. "We have a sudden death with no readily obvious cause and no autopsy. Had a case like that as an MP. Turns out the cause of death was too damn convenient for the person who signed it. Got a conviction, too. What does federal law say?"

"Follows state law. Let's see." Reel typed. "Okay, here it is, in Colorado an autopsy is required when death was sudden and happened to a person who was in apparent good health."

"Okay, red flag," I said. "Let's look at the certifier's signature on the real one and the fake one," she said. She brought up both certificates on her screen.

143

I bent down behind her to get a better look at the monitor. Her perfume, a woodsy blend of vanilla and coffee, went straight to my head, then my heart. I shook it off. "Right. Signature," I said. I heard a sigh, must've been mine. I caught a slight upturn at the corner of her mouth.

Each certificate on the screen was identical with the same signatures.

"Dr. Donald LaBarge, MD," Reel said.

"LaBarge ?"

"Know him?' she asked.

"LaBarge is manager of the Rocking Double Bar Ranch where I found the sheep herder Rafi Maestrejuan murdered. A real charmer. Hostile when I asked for Maestrejuan's whereabouts."

Reel worked at her keyboard. "Okay, I sent someone to have a talk with LaBarge. Tell me more about the ranch, Peter."

I put my head in my hands, rubbed my eyes. "Yeah, a Delaware corporation owns it. Strange name. Let me think. Freedom Calls. Yeah, that's it."

She typed; the monitor blinked. "Here we go. Owner of record, Freedom Calls. DBA name of Fraternal Action for Racial Equality or FARE, Inc., founded in 1978 and headquartered in Denver," she said.

She had access to databases much bigger than mine.

"Listen to this." She read, "FARE leaders have ties to white supremacist groups and have made many public inflammatory and racist statements. FARE's founders have expressed their goal that America must maintain a white majority at any cost."

"Any cost?" I asked. "Not sure I'd vote for that."

"You're about five hundred years too late."

She read on, "FARE is known to support groups favoring violence against non-whites."

"Sounds like they're talking about the Chivingtons. Wanna bet there's a link?"

"I wouldn't take that bet, but I'll find the connection," she said.

"What's an MD doing in a group like that?" I asked.

144

"Not that uncommon, I'm sorry to say. Let me check something else." Reel mumbled as she typed. Her eyes lit up. "Well, well. Seems that Doctor Donald LaBarge had his license revoked a year ago by the Colorado Medical Board." She tabbed to Oso Walker's death certificate. "Yup, had it jerked before he signed this off. And, there's more. LaBarge is under indictment for overprescribing painkillers, criminal sale of prescriptions, and falsifying records. Might connect him to those punks, the Colorado boarders and their Sinaloa sponsors."

I had a hard time with this line of thinking. "Okay. The certificates are the same and you can nail him on practicing without a license, but that does not answer the big question."

Reel looked up. "Go on."

I could've dived into those black eyes now, but she was the all-business Reel.

"Assume our Indian-hating friends are in some way responsible for the demise of the real Oso Walker and had LeBarge falsify his death certificate. Or, maybe the real Oso died naturally, and they took advantage. Doesn't matter.

What matters is, how did a skinwalker insert himself into a conspiracy to disrupt a hospital groundbreaking so he could seek revenge? Another thing, the Navajo beef with the Utes began in late thirteen hundred. Why seek retribution now?"

She smiled. "Well, that's your next assignment, Peter. Find out why. In the meantime, I'll try to figure how much damage he's done to my investigation."

"Am I under arrest?" My tone suggested a pleasant evening in a bedroom somewhere, but at the back of my mind, I had a bad feeling I was being jerked around.

She smiled in a way that quickened my pulse. "Let's call it supervised custody."

"Really? Then who is my, uh, supervisor?" I couldn't help but grin.

"You've been working with him all along. My assistant, Special Agent Leslie Ponsford."

It would have been less deflating had she tossed a hand grenade in my lap. I went from merely frustrated to thoroughly

145

pissed, but kept my mouth shut while pretending to find a bug on the command post's ceiling.

She called out the door and Special Agent Leslie Ponsford— No Name—took a seat at the conference table. No Name nodded in my direction.

Reel briefed him on what we'd learned about Donald LaBarge and his suspected falsification of the real Oso's death certificate. He maintained his silent demeanor but raised an eyebrow when Reel mentioned the skinwalker. "Say what?"

She said, "We suspect Oso is a skinwalker and killing Utes as a bear. Grizz, Peter calls him."

No Name's shrug emphasized the breadth of his shoulders. "Figures."

"What?" I asked.

"Ain't no Grizz in Colorado."

Reel started laughing, tried to hide it.

Everyone's a comedian. "Okay, what's the deal?" I asked.

"Special Agent Ponsford has been with the FBI for 10 years. Brown graduate. MS in Cybersecurity, right? And, yeah, a former Green Beret."

Ponsford chuckled, held out a hand. "Call me Les."

I took his hand, but my face heated. "Is there anything real about this investigation?" I pointed to Reel. "You're scammin', he's scammin', Oso's scammin'. What the fuck's going on?"

"Calm down, Peter," Reel said. "Nobody's scamming anyone. What we have is a very fluid situation."

I said, "I might just float out the door on your fluid situation."

"Okay, Peter, okay. Cool your heels. Sit and I'll explain everything," she said, with a mixed expression of worry and determination. "My operation, as I've told you, has very highly-placed interest, not only in our government, but in certain foreign governments as well. That gives special facets of this investigation a high classification and you do not have the clearance or need to know."

I said, "I don't need a clearance to know what my role in this investigation is or what part of this classified information is going to get me killed?"

"Try listening, Peter, something you don't always do well." My ex-wife said the same thing. I shut up. I'd already screwed up one relationship with my hot head and this one threatened to slide downhill.

"At first, this operation was multi-state graft and corruption, pure and simple. Our investigation has revealed so much more. I can't tell you everything, Peter, but I can give you an overview. As you know, we have four groups involved in a conspiracy to disrupt the groundbreaking for a new hospital."

"Right."

"Militant traditionalist Utes oppose the hospital, because they feel it threatens their traditional medicine and religion. They're planning a demonstration at the groundbreaking."

"Okay."

"The Chivingtons are planning to counter with armed violence, but's that not all the players.

A group of Breckenridge snowboarders is supporting the Chivs and the Utes with firearms to divert attention from their drug operations in the state.

Finally, the reason this investigation has such high interest in the Bureau is the Breckenridge snowboarders have small group of local law enforcement officers in their pocket."

"You've told me all that, and I've run into all of the players in the past week. Tell me something I don't know."

"You know everything you need to," she said. "But, now we have additional complication, the skinwalker."

She gave it a dramatic pause. "And, Peter, you are going to make Oso the skinwalker go poof."

I agreed Oso Walker, or whoever he really was, had to be stopped. But a skinwalker was still human. Part of the time, anyway.

"You want me to kill him?" The fact she had said it set me back, but it didn't surprise me.

147

As a Marine or cop, killing comes with the territory. Warriors kill, but never murder. Murder is committed in cold blood for no good reason. When a warrior kills, he is influenced by a moral code subject to the law. A true warrior kills not for self. His motive comes from a higher cause and supports a noble belief.

Reel's request stirred up the muck of nightmares; A confrontation with a tweeker teen in New Mexico and a strapped-up woman in Iraq. Never mind the kid was armed and one more sleepless night away from full psychosis. Makes no difference the woman was wearing an explosives belt, ready to die while taking a few U.S. Marines with her. I still wake drenched over both, reliving regret and possibilities I didn't take. Legal or not, some things never leave you.

"We need a minute," she said to Ponsford who took the hint and left the room. By the time he'd closed the door, she looked at me concern in her eyes.

We sat in a forced silence so deep, only the hum of the command post's generator penetrated the room. Here was the woman I had fallen for asking me to kill someone. What scared me was how she could sacrifice her soft side to her job so easily. Flirt to functionary, just like that. It made for an accordion relationship. Pulled in one minute, pushed away the next.

Was this the real Jean Reel before me? In the past, her Indian resilience and stamina led to a mutual understanding. We both knew what a cop needed to do. Now, my head whirled like newly corralled mustangs. I asked, "What's going on with you? You telling me you want someone dead?"

Tension lined her face. "Peter. I believe in you. I know what you can do. It's why you're here."

Her Cherokee had suddenly come through. She was appealing to my connection to the other world. My head pounded. I said, "Yes, sometimes spirits call me, but I can't summon them."

"You know how to deal with the spirits. Do what you have to do," she said. She cut off conversation by returning to the paperwork in front of her, then she turned back, and spoke

148

as if our previous discussion had never happened. "By the way, that truck you took from the Chivingtons? My techs went over it. Someone had gone to great lengths to clean it, but my people found traces of horse manure on the cab floor under the seat."

Reel back at work, her Cherokee gone. If her suggestions about killing the skinwalker bothered her, she masked them well.

"Lots of cowboys around here," I said, dead-faced. My turn to switch off the emotions.

"I sent the test results to the Arabian Horse Association Registry."

The registry had collected DNA for all foals for the past fifteen years. "And?"

"Conclusive match with one of the horses you were looking for. Truck's owner of record is Braydon Downing, head of the Chivingtons. He's a nurse at Mercy Regional in Durango. Was he there at the Chiv's cabin?" she asked.

I flashed the dead and dying men in the cabin. "Don't know. Only spoke to one Chiv, a Dillard Johnston, and he expired while I was there. The others died or bailed."

Fragments of hospital booties were found at the horse killing sites, but I didn't tell her. It was unprofessional to hold back but the horse killings were my investigation. I kept my mouth shut. We stared at each other for a long time.

"I'll pick Downing up. Your job is Oso Walker. And you need to know I put Lettau and his goons under surveillance this morning. They go after you again; my people will back you up." She rose from her chair with an armful of papers and rushed from the room.

"No, I'm going to find Downing myself. That's what I came up here for in the first damn place. I don't want anything to do with your investigation, anymore." If she heard me, she made no sign, hurried to her office and slammed the door. "I quit."

She called me special, claimed I had capabilities like no other. True or not, it emphasized the fact she was using me. Like a sap, I'd assumed we had a special relationship, one that would go somewhere. Turns out we were in different ballparks playing different games.

Reel returned to the conference room with an aide and No Name who crabbed down the command post's hallway to keep from touching both sides at once.

The aide talked softly and glanced at me as he spoke. Reel nodded, whispered things I could not hear, and didn't look in my direction. Fact of the matter was, I didn't want to hear what she had to say, so I headed for the door. No Name blocked the doorway by filling it. Finally, she dismissed the aide, then focused on me.

I put my arms across my chest and held a hand up. Whatever she was going to say, I didn't want to hear it.

She ignored me. "We have a police report that a bear attacked some people just off the Ute reservation. Sheriff units have responded. You and Ponsford get on it. Now."

Apparently, my body language didn't mean much to her.

Since members of the La Plata County Sheriff Department were trying to kill me, I didn't take the idea of being at the scene with them as good news. I ran a mental movie of Grizz on one side and deputies on the other with me in the middle figuring how not to die.

"No, I quit," I said.

Reel said, "Do I need to remind you, you're under arrest?" She left the room with a my-work-is-done-here look. "Dean's got your pistol."

"Sounds like we have our orders," said Special Agent Leslie Ponsford. The big Lakota pulled me aside, said, "Don't even think of quitting. I'll lock you up." His eyes said, After I fuck you up.

I looked him up and down, mostly up, and decided I had no way out. So, I decided to follow orders, even crazy ones, and the idea of being near Lettau or Grizz qualified as crazy. But, I was not going to die that day, not by Ponsford, Lettau, or Grizz.

No Name and I walked past a row of agents busy at their computers. At his desk, Dean made me sign for my .38. I asked him if he had a rifle because I was after Grizz.

"Aren't any grizzlies in Colorado," Dean said.

"Never mind," I said. All I wanted was out of the command center.

Heading for the pickup I'd stolen from the Chivs, I remembered Reel had impounded it as evidence. I asked, "You got wheels?"

No Name Ponsford pointed to a Dodge Charger, black on black with tinted windows.

"Seriously?"

He stood dumbfounded, said, "What? It's got an epic pursuit package."

"For a bear? You been watching reruns of the Dukes of Hazzard?"

"Who?"

"Never mind." Waylon Jennings lyrics ran through my head...*Just the good ol' boys...Never meanin' no harm....*

No Name walked out of sight. A vehicle started and No Name drove up in a late model Dodge Durango with four-wheel drive. He had somehow managed to squeeze his mass behind the wheel.

"Cute," I said hopping in. "Let's go find Grizz."

We headed toward Durango and the address where the attack took place. He glanced at me. "Don't care what you think of me, but Reel's setting you up."

I said nothing for miles while I tried to figure out how I was going to turn this around. Around me, forests of ponderosa and aspen evolved to juniper, then short grass prairie, scrub, and occasional prickly pear. As we travelled north, then westerly, large swaths of beetle-killed pine dyed distant slopes red.

"Think I didn't know that?"

151

Chapter 26

As we drove toward Durango, I remembered I'd known Reel for years and had worked several cases with her. She protected me behind the scenes and, I suspected, creatively violated the letter of the law on my behalf. Our relationship was one of mutual trust, though shaky now, never failed before and I would not, could not let that trust go.

I knew that I shared some of the blame for my predicament. Even though my sole involvement was reporting two crimes, I'd blundered into the middle of Reel's case.

Then there was the shooting of Deputy Jones while his men were trying to kill me. I hadn't admitted the exact nature of my participation, but based on my experience with her, I would have to trust her not to probe too deeply into the case.

At first, she said she was recruiting my help to find Indian suspects. Then, when I identified Oso Walker as an imposter and skinwalker, she claimed my insight would prove useful. I was pretty sure she didn't know what she was talking about. It's true that many times I've been visited by beings who have passed to the other side, but it wasn't something I was in control of. They visited me when they wanted, I didn't command them to come. It was laughable to think I had any power over them. I told her I had no fast-serve window to the spirits, and that didn't seem to bother her. So, like it or not, I was assigned to find Oso; the man, the spirit animal, or both.

No Name concentrated on the road and said, "Those sheriff's deputies are probably waiting for you, right now."

"Thanks. So, what else is new?" I stared out the windshield, but with renewed interest for details. If deputies were waiting for me, I wanted to see them first. "Your job's to protect me. Do your job."

"Not sure I buy this skinwalker story you're peddling," he said.

"You were there, Ponsford."

"What I saw was a grizzly bear."

"You remember a lot less than what I saw. Don't worry about it. Just take care of the deputies trying to kill me. That's something you can buy into, isn't it?" I didn't care who believed the skinwalker story except Reel.

No Name said, "How in hell are you going to find this bear?"

"My gut says he's gonna find us."

"Your gut should worry more about the deputies."

"Gonna let you worry about that. Protect and serve, right?"

"Fidelity, bravery, integrity."

"What?"

"FBI's motto. Fidelity, bravery, integrity." He looked at me like I was stupid.

I liked him better as No Name, a Lakota of few words.

We had a job to do and a slow burn heated my face and upper chest. I didn't want to wreck chances of our mission's success with my smartass remarks. Instead, I let the beauty of the distant snow-capped peaks sidetrack my anxiety.

Leaving the reservation, we cruised west on US-160. Farms checkered the rolling plains. West of Bayfield, red and blue light bars flashed just off the road to the south. No Name slowed.

In a utility lot with fenced-in natural gas equipment and several gas trailers with Red Pine logos, a half-dozen sheriff's Interceptors parked near three older pickups. A couple of blue-on-whites from Durango PD mixed in. From the road, I could see uniforms walking the scene, eyes on the ground. A man poured a thick substance into a depression, probably of Grizz's prints. Three men grouped in a discussion marked by occasional pointing and head shaking. A photographer worked the area from all angles.

"Drive up the road. We'll watch from that hill," I said, pointing to a ridgeline just north of the lot. A dirt road offered enough separation and cover to get us behind the scene without being observed. "Up there," I said. No Name turned left and drove up the road one-quarter mile.

Down the road, a man walked. I glanced back as we turned off the road, but he was too far away to see clearly. I

couldn't see what he was doing. I spotted a farmhouse nearby.
Maybe he lived there.

No Name's earlier comments casting doubt on the
existence of a skinwalker at first pissed me off, but now they
haunted me. I'd been close-up with Grizz, observed Oso and
Grizz together, acting like old friends.

Skinwalker. When I was in jail, Deer insisted Oso was a
skinwalker and I bought into it. Not sure I knew who the hell
Deer was, anyway. There was something that escaped me,
something that flickered at the edges of my mind. No matter
how I tried, the more I wondered, the less I knew.

We walked through fields of scattered white oak scrub,
pink wild rose, clumped black sedge, and grama grass. We
settled on a rise behind some scrub and watched police activity
at the crime scene.

Dark stains covered the scene of the attack in places.
The bloodied victims were being lifted by gurney to
ambulances idling outside the gaggle of patrol cruisers. Grizz
must've attacked these men in broad daylight. Looked like he
dented a few truck doors and busted some windshields while he
was at it.

Another ambulance departed the scene without a siren
and drove towards Durango at normal highway speed. The
passenger didn't need to get where he was going in a hurry.

The word, "grizzly" floated my way when the three
men huddled around some plaster molds laid out by the crime
scene techs below our hiding spot. One man whistled when he
spotted the bear's prints, others laughed a nervous guffaw.
Deputy Lettau was among those laughing. The conversation's
volume faded.

"Can't hear shit," I said.

No Name cupped his ear, hunched his shoulders, and
shook his head. I wanted to get closer but couldn't. They
wouldn't try to kill me with No Name and Durango PD as
witnesses, but this wasn't the time to test that theory. No need
to push buttons. Yet.

In a whisper, I said, "They don't know you. Drive down
and see what you can find out. As soon as they leave, I'll come

down to join you." No Name nodded. He knew the risks. Then he trotted in a low crouch back to the truck.

The sun shaded the mountain slopes when No Name pulled into the crime scene. He badged the uniforms and talked to the lead, Deputy Lettau. No Name, his enormous bulk a head taller than anyone there, examined the plaster casts, acted surprised at the size of them.

Near me, the sun highlighted a bare spot on the ground between clumps of grass. Sun and shadow defined the imprint of closely spaced, round toes. A front paw. Claw marks in the soil drew interlocking circles in the sand like an animal turning around. Rear foot impressions appeared to exceed eight inches in diameter. Grizz appeared to come through here on his way somewhere.

At the scene, the uniforms headed for their cruisers and drove off. Technicians packed up their gear and took off in their van. No Name and Lettau kept talking. And talking.

No way I was going to walk over there with Lettau present. The conversation continued, but the tone seemed light. I couldn't imagine anyone engaging in small talk with a prick like Lettau. It may have been No Name's personal method for extracting information. Charming it out of them when beating it out of them wouldn't do.

Three tow trucks pulled up, hooked up the victims' pickups, and dragged them down the highway.

The breezy, evening dusk blew No Name's words away. I strained to hear him when a sudden chuffing behind me froze me on the spot. I braced myself. I turned slowly to look for the source, expecting the worst. Nothing. I stayed put.

Grizz, I knew in my bones it was him, was close but the heavy brush hid the source. I heard his jaws chomp like the sound of boots in sucking mud. Teeth snapped and a low grumble filled the air.

Pistol cocked, aimed at the sound, I waited for Grizz's charge, my .38 revolver against the animal's thick skull was as effective as a pop gun against a tank. My only chances were lucky shots to the eye sockets or the back of the throat just before he killed me with one swat.

I considered running away from an animal capable of running down a quarter horse. Stay and die. Run and die.

Stones clicked, bushes rustled, branches snapped in the faded dusk. A head poked through the bushes.

"What are you doing?" No Name asked.

"Jesus, man, you scared the shit out of me." I tried to catch my breath, "Thought you was Grizz."

No Name held out both palms. "Could you put that pistol down? Romero, you got Grizz on the mind. Give it a break."

"Bullshit, I heard it. Chomping, teeth clacking, the whole deal. He was near where you're standing right now."

"You heard the truck, dammit."

"Don't tell me I didn't hear Grizz."

"Okay, you win. Now put the damn gun down."

No Name's image quivered like a mirage. Maybe I *was* hallucinating. I stuffed the .38 under my belt.

We headed back to the Dodge Durango. I kept a nervous eye. As doubt grew, I remained on full alert. I felt the tingle on the back of my neck like eyes burrowing in, but I could see little in the last light. Still, my instincts insisted someone, something was watching.

At the truck, No Name started up, headed for the highway.

"I want to check out that farmhouse off to the left." I pointed toward the area where a single light glimmered a half mile distant. "Over there. Down that road."

"What for?"

"Someone walked there earlier, I want to talk to him."

"I didn't see anybody." No Name shook his head but turned and drove toward the building. When we arrived, a farm light illuminated the building from a pole. Boards covered the windows and, even at night, peeling paint emphasized the building's lack of care. Tall weeds and dead branches added to the sad impression of neglect.

"You happy?" No Name asked me, annoyed. "There's nothing here."

No Name pissed me off, then something moved near the shadowed rear of the house. "See that?" I asked.

156

"No." he started the engine, made tracks for the highway.

"Where you going'?"

"I'm done with this bullshit, Romero. You're paranoid as hell. If there was a grizzly anywhere near here, you'd be dinner. Could've been a black bear. Could've been a fucking raccoon. They're all over the place. Get over it."

"Stop the truck, Pons'-whatever-the-fuck-your-name-is, you and me gonna come to an understanding." I pushed my face as close to him as the seat belt would allow.

Ponsford gave me a smile that mixed doubt with a bring-it attitude and braked. I got out and walked back to where I saw the movement, pistol arm cocked at the ready. My .38 pistol was in gross violation of Marine Corps Rule of Engagement Number Six: Do not show up to a fight with a handgun whose caliber does not start with a .4.

Ten thousand stars lit the Colorado sky, but the rear of the building lay in darkness. I waited for my eyes to adjust. I listened. Ponsford killed the engine, got out of the truck. I kept my eyes glued to the backyard. His footsteps travelled to the other side of the house, around it, then toward the back.

Loud sniffing and soft grunting came from shadows within shadows. I thought I caught a whiff of wet dog. Claws scratching in dry earth sent shivers up my back and heated my legs. This was no dog.

A circle of light appeared from the other side of the house, Ponsford behind it. He swept the beam across the ground and through the brush. A pair of green eyes glowed in the light from behind a mask. A raccoon scrambled into the scrub.

"You happy now, Jim Bridger?" asked Ponsford.

"Fuck you," I said, hoping my comeback didn't sound as lame to him as it did to me. I walked back to the truck.

Ponsford trailed, chuckling softly. "A racoo—"

The bushes exploded. A dark shape sent Ponsford flying before I had a chance to turn. The flashlight spiraled up and away. Grizz grabbed the man and shook him like a rag toy.

157

I rushed at Grizz, emptied my pistol into his head hoping to make the bear let go. The animal dropped the big man and snarled. I backed up, looked back at the truck, then at Grizz. Grizz looked at the truck and back at me. Eyes working me over, the beast lumbered toward me, confident and unstoppable.

Grizz stopped and snorted, stood on hind legs, glared down at me, seven feet of killing machine. He yelped, recoiled as if stung, then disappeared into the brush.

I ran to Ponsford. Kneeling. His left thigh was deeply punctured and torn. Through a tear in his pants, his right shin showed shredded skin, pink muscle, and white bone. Blood soaked both pant legs. His left arm, a shredded mass of tissue, splayed out at a weird angle.

I reached for my phone and called 911, then pulled off my shirt and wrapped the wound. Blood patterns darkened the cloth as soon as I tied it off.

Through lidded eyes, Ponsford said, "You're blue."

"Funny man." I swore at the ambulance to get here faster, before shock set in. I had no way to help him. "Just breathe. The EMT's are on the way."

Ponsford choked the words. "Blue."

"Okay, it's a little cold. We'll get through this. You're gonna be fine." I held his head in my arms. My blue arms. Blue. Blue as sky, blue as sapphire, blue as a fucking peacock.

No Name stiffened, went limp.

"Hey. Stay with me, buddy. Hang in there." I smacked his face. His eyes slitted. No Name had saved my life.

"Come on man, we got work to do!" I slapped him. Hard this time. I wanted to get his attention, take his mind off his wounds, piss him off, make him focus on me and not his injuries.

While my fingers checked for a pulse at his neck, a form emerged shapeless and ghost-like. It hovered above, then floated up and away. I yelled at him. "Wake up, damnit!"

Sirens grew louder. The sound boosted my energy. "Ambulance is almost here. Stay with me." I pushed his chest with both hands, blue hands, pumped hard, then inflated his lungs with my own air.

When my arms finally gave out, the ambulance pulled up and EMTs ran over. One pushed me out of the way. "Sorry, need room," he said, the man interested only in his patient. I moved back, grateful, exhausted, out of words. I had strength for only one word, "Grizz."

Another EMT, looking worried, handed me a blanket. I took it, my skin turning back to the color of caramel. My flesh. Indian flesh. I wrapped myself in the blanket and collapsed, too shocked to think about blue skin or what it meant.

The EMTs attended to No Name, the lead barking commands to his people. They bandaged his damaged legs and arm, heaved him on to a gurney, strapped him down, and pushed the rig toward the ambulance. I grabbed an EMT by the arm and told him No Name had the truck keys in his pocket. He fished them out with a gloved hand and handed them over.

In the back of the van, someone said, "clear". The sharp thud of a defibrillator followed, then the rear door slammed shut. The ambulance sped away, siren at full warble.

I walked toward the pickup. The silence was off-putting. I remained stumped by the temporary discoloration of my skin. Blue, my skin had been colored blue. Long ago, Grandfather told me the wearer of that color became strong, important. Blue meant power, wisdom, and confidence. Vast things were blue: the ocean, sky, or distant mountains. Things blue were beyond perception like the heavens.

Grandfather also said that the color blue was an invitation to become a person of power, instead of a victim. Grizz must've seen something in that color because he fled from it.

Spirits call only when they have messages to deliver and it is possible the blue was a message. I prayed it was and hurried to the Durango. A hospital visit to No Name was out of the question, but I had to tell Reel that he had been attacked and injured.

A La Plata County Ford Interceptor swooped in to block my path to the pickup.

"Fuck."

Deputy Lettau stepped out from behind the wheel and said, "Well, now. How did I get so lucky?"

Chapter 27

Lettau pushed me into the back of his cruiser, handcuffed and blindfolded, cracking my head on the doorframe in the process. The hard, backseat plastic insert did not give any comfort. Lettau chuckled to himself as he drove. We travelled highways. I tried to memorize every bump or change of road noise. The smooth surface revealed none, so I counted twists and turns, but every road in this part of Colorado snakes though valleys and hills. Only the downshifting of the automatic transmission told me we were headed uphill.

"Where you takin' me?"

"To your happy hunting ground, Injun." Lettau laughed.

He didn't understand my culture and I wasn't going to educate the prick. My final resting place, according to the ancients, was *Shipap*, a realm below, the place we inhabited before and after life on Earth.

I ignored him. Reel told me she had the renegade deputies under surveillance. I was certain the feds tailed us now, tracked our every move, waited in the bushes to arrest my abductor at the right moment, and catch Lettau with the goods—me—red-handed.

We followed a truck for some time. It sounded like a big diesel, when we finally passed it. The fact that a tuck would be driving in the middle of the night into the San Juans, a place remote and unpopulated, was strange, but I had other things to occupy my mind.

Lettau signaled arrival with a shower of gravel against the cruiser's underside as the road roughened with potholes and ruts. The deputy had not bothered to fasten my seat belt, so I slid around on the prisoner's insert until I lay down to stabilize myself by pressing my head and feet hard against the car's sides.

The door rattled softly, just a couple of clicks. On a sharp turn, I pushed with all I had. As I'd hoped, the lock released and spit me out headfirst. I landed hard against a cluster of scrub, then rolled to the ground.

Lettau braked and opened his door. He ran toward me through a cloud of dust glowing red. The fall had ripped off my blindfold. I got to my feet and ran.

Dodging between boulders and scrub, I gained yardage on burning lungs. Lettau had the altitude advantage: his steps pounded hard behind me. Then came his hand on my shoulder. I tucked and somersaulted. The man flew over me, then lay face down against a boulder he'd met with a crack.

Sucking air and staring at the unconscious man, my options narrowed to one: cut and run, but I needed to get his cuff keys out of his pockets. Backing up to Lettau, I sat, twisted, and stretched until I located a lump in his right front pocket, a lighter, as it turned out. His other pockets were beneath him. I stood, puffing like an old man, and rolled the deputy over with my foot.

Lettau moaned and moved a leg. He groaned, grabbed his head, and curled into a fetal position. He coughed, then directed one eye to me. "You son of a—" He pulled himself up and lunged. I dodged, countered with a kick to his knee. The joint buckled. He screamed and grabbed at it. I finished with a low roundhouse kick to the chest that laid him out. The impact stole his air and he gasped like a dying fish. A kick to the head ended the fight.

I sat again and fished around his left front pants pocket and found the rough edges of keys and slid them out with numb fingers. A ring held a fob and numerous keys, but none for handcuffs. Deflated, I grabbed Lettau's pistol, shoved it under my belt, the steel frigid on the crack of my ass.

I started for his cruiser, the very model I had recently lobbied my pueblo's governor and council to buy. I rifled through the vehicle as best I could with hands cuffed behind but found nothing. The cruiser's radio, its signal masked by the San Juan peaks, crackled with static.

No keys for cuffs. My sigh sparked a last-chance idea. I trotted back to Lettau and fingered behind his badge. Sure enough, a small key was attached to the back; the New York Tuning Fork.

As I removed it from the back of the badge, Lettau made a grab for my neck. He squeezed, I twisted, got on top,

162

but cuffed as I was, I could not break the hold. His fingers crushed away my air until I jammed a knee into his nuts. He released my neck and I head butted him back to neverland.

Fat-fingered, I managed to unlock the cuffs. Lettau had not moved since I had knocked him out, but I checked his pulse. It beat strongly. I cuffed his right hand and left ankle together. Awkward, yes, but it would make it that much harder to get around once he revived. I didn't want the man to get too far.

My FBI rescue hadn't arrived, so I drove the cruiser to the highway, parked it with the light bar on, and called Durango dispatch. Without identifying myself through the static, I gave the cruiser's location, reported the driver lost nearby, and hoped Reel's people were listening.

This model of Interceptor can run with the keys pulled. I pulled them from the ignition and stuffed them in my pocket.

Grabbing blankets from the trunk, I covered Lettau with one after dragging him closer to the road, then I headed up the nearest hill to hide and wait for my FBI tail to show. Reel had promised she had me covered. I found a small area behind rocks and stunted pine. From here, I could view the road in both directions, the place where I had left Lettau, as well as the cruiser on the road below. If anyone used the highway, I would see them first.

I waited. Far off, great horned owls hooted and answered. The night carried the whines of a bull elk bugling deep and resonant, then pitching to a high squeal, and ending in a sequence of grunts. The animal seemed as distant as the white peaks of the San Juans and as detached from me as the black sky punctured by countless stars.

I waited as stars crept across the sky. To my disappointment, no headlights lit the road. So far, no feds to the rescue.

Alone and hopeless, I started to feel sorry for myself. My headbutt to Lettau had caused an acorn-sized lump, so I rubbed my forehead to sooth it.

Down on the road, the cruiser sputtered and stopped. Out of gas. I took it as proof Lettau had taken me far from civilization to kill me. Soon the cruiser's lights would drain the battery and leave me to the high-country night and my sole distraction, a moon so brilliant its reflection off the snowy peaks made me blink.

I wrapped myself in the blanket. The Milky Way, Earth Mother's answer to the Las Vegas strip, reminded me again how cold alpine nights could be at ten thousand feet. A breeze strong enough to throw grit dropped the temperature and smelled of snow. Any plan to walk out died right there. Denver papers are full of people who died making that mistake.

In my hillside hiding place, I shook from the cold and busied my throbbing head with details of Reel's mission. She wanted to prevent violence at the hospital groundbreaking and I had identified a few of the players on both sides. Grizz ripped up both groups before I could ID the leaders. Not only had I failed at my task, somebody had wounded Walker, Grizz had mauled No Name, and set his sights on me. In the recesses of my mind, my old drill instructor bellowed, "You got a high casualty rate and shit to show for it." My face, neck, and ears heated with embarrassment. If there was a way to duck out of this scene, I would have.

Chapter 28

Snow, moon-lit diamond dust, fell and muffled night sounds. A typical Colorado mountain summer night.

"Time has come."

I jumped, swiveled, pulled the pistol from my belt. Only stars and shadowed pine met my eyes. I must be hearing things now.

"You're not hearing things." The voice came from the nearby trees, but I saw nothing.

"Come out or I'm coming after you," I said, without the faintest idea of who I was dealing with.

"Yawn. I'd dance circles around you."

"Nice talk. Tryin' to scare me?" I asked.

"I don't need to try." The voice came from the opposite direction. Close.

I spun. Deer stood inches from my face. Antlers stretched beyond my field of vision on both sides. His large ears swiveled, listening everywhere, then faced me. The dark V on his forehead separated huge brown eyes. His nose twitched as he sniffed me.

"Jesus, man," I said, heart beating like a quarter horse at the finish line.

Deer turned and bounded off, looked back, then disappeared in the tree line.

"Hey, goddammit!"

Deer returned in a heartbeat, said, "No need to get pissy."

"What do you want from me?" I asked. I held out my palms, pulled them back not sure Deer would understand the gesture.

"Oso," he said.

"Oso Walker? No way. Reel wants him."

Deer shook his head, his antlers amplifying the movement into wide sweeps. "You owe him to me."

"Why?" Annoyance painted his eyes, so I said, "I damn near get killed by sheriff's assassins, then by a car wreck. I get attacked by wolves—"

Deer said, "Some things must be done."

165

"What?"

"The wolves were required to get you near Oso," Deer said, big-eyed.

"I couldn't just walk up to Oso, shake his hand, and say hello?"

Deer recoiled, ready to sprint. "No one walks up to a skinwalker and shakes his hand."

"Those wolves bit the crap out of me." My stitches tingled.

Deer said, "Your need for medical care disguised the reason I wanted you there. He puffed up, as if enjoying it. "Right outside his place, too. I found it quite creative."

"You sent wolves after me? Jesus, how could you—"

Deer pulled back. "Me? You killed two of them."

"Why am I even explaining this to you?"

Deer said. "You're boring me." Snow layered on Deer's back, giving him a ghostly appearance.

"You want me to give up the only hard suspect I got?"

Deer exhaled. "This isn't about you."

This guy burned my ass. "Who the fuck're you comin' out of nowhere demanding' my perp?"

Deer raised up on his hind legs. His antlers atomized, then drifted away like pollen in the night. Ears, brown and long, shriveled to round, flat, and hairless. His black nose vanished, the white snouted face morphed to rounded and bronzed human features, front legs reshaped into arms, hind limbs straightened, hooves turned to hands and feet.

Deer, no, not a deer. A man. The man stood before me dressed in finely-beaded leather with epaulets and a vest sporting red stars on a blue field. Crow wings adorned his dark hair. His furrowed, copper face attested to a life in the sun. Around his neck he wore a bird-bone choker accented with turquoise. A pendant with red feathers and white beads hung from his neck. A fox tail draped over one shoulder. In his left hand, he carried a carved horsehead staff, his right gripped what looked like tiny clusters of galaxies, constellations and stars. A small celestial body circled his hand.

I gawked at the vision, speechless. Snowflakes drifted into my open mouth.

"I've been following you since you found that dead horse," he said.

This man, at least one who looked like him, had stood in front of my house holding an AK-47. A few days later, I visited his office in Ignacio, looking for information on the horse killers. Clement Ouray Pokoh.

"Ain't you dead?" I asked.

"Not in the way you're thinking."

"Who are you?"

"Call me Pokoh."

Pokoh, a spirit the Utes say created the world and formed every tribe out of the soil where they lived. The legend of Pokoh was not in my pueblo's tradition, but that made him no less powerful. A man carrying stars in his hand commanded respect.

"What do you want from me?" I asked.

"I told you. Oso. Grizz. *Ursus arctos horribilis.*"

"The man or animal?" I asked.

Pokoh said, "Both the same. Oso is the skinwalker."

"Reel gets him, first."

"You owe him to me." Pokoh eye-balled me while juggling his miniature constellations, waiting for me to absorb what he'd just said. The stars he held, billions of miles reduced to inches, twirled and flashed like a prize from the county fair.

"See these?" he asked.

"Hard to miss." If juggling parts of the universe was meant to impress me, it did. I hoped Pokoh didn't notice my knees shaking, hoped he didn't hear my fat tongue.

"Do you understand their origin?" He pointed upward.

I shook my head. "Those real?" I asked, pointing at his shimmering hand.

Pokoh lifted his eyes to the sky, looked self-satisfied doing it. "I placed them there, long ago. Hard work. Asteroids proved touchy, though." He pointed to the glowing object circling his hand. "Asteroids are hard to control. Now I learned to direct them at will. Anywhere. Anytime. The right time."

167

I was in the presence of a powerful god who was working an agenda in the background. It was he, the man-deer-spirit, who'd connected me to Southern Colorado, the Utes, the Chivingtons, and Oso Walker. I didn't even try to understand what he was planning.

"So, it's agreed?" he said, taking my expression as approval.

I wanted to scream, No, I didn't agree, but my lips wouldn't move. Pokoh had not only read my mind, he'd entered it.

"Follow," he said. "You need to see this."

I did without knowing why. Together we travelled, in a way I cannot describe. We flew through a place without reference, so I couldn't judge direction, speed, or surroundings.

"Where are we going?"

"Not far."

We came to a lake. The water was dark, impenetrable. Around it, pine grew tall in places, stunted in most.

"Where are we?"

"The Doorway of the Rainbow, *Shipap*."

My people originally came up from the ground through a large hole. But the hole in front of me was a lake edged by a steep rock outcrop on the far side. *Shipap* was located in a place now called Southern Colorado, the ancients say. I said to Pokoh, "*Shipap* is not Ute, not your world. Why are we here in mine?

Pokoh laid out his palms, "I'm not the one in doubt."

We walked around the lake through fallen and shattered scree, then came to a huge boulder that Pokoh pushed aside with ease. The rock had covered a tunnel.

"Follow me," said Pokoh, the man-deer-spirit.

We walked. I don't know how far because darkness hid the length. We came to a bright place that looked like my pueblo, the old one I have seen only in history books: the paths, the buildings—some two and three stories—rocks, hills. Sun. No cars, no telephone poles.

The dead. They were here. People I hadn't seen in years. The Herreras, the Suinas, old man Trujillo. I'd been to their funerals. Even Ramon Chalan, a childhood buddy who'd

168

died of polio. As kids, Chalan and I always managed to get into trouble.

Over there, Ha'ro Velasquez, a paratrooper killed in 'Nam, talked and laughed with a man who died in the Korean War. Some ancient ones who'd lived long before my time chatted near the kiva. Everyone went about their business. People talked. Kids ran and laughed. Everyone seemed content.

I didn't recognize some people. "Who?" I asked, pointing at young, fresh faces.

"Those waiting to be born," he said.

"Here, now? Why?"

"Time is an illusion. Everything that has ever been and ever will be is happening here. Now."

"When Grandfather told me these things, I didn't understand. Still don't," I said.

"No past. No future. Only now," Pokoh said, looking around. "See for yourself."

I smiled at Rosendo Montoya, but he looked through me as if I were mist. Another man I'd known since I was a boy, Clofe Arquero, walked through me. I stood dumbfounded until Pokoh grabbed my arm and led me to Juan Pecos and his son, Jason, the men murdered at my pueblo. Their lifeless eyes looked directly at me.

I greeted them. They remained wordless, motionless.

"What's wrong with them?" I asked.

"They want to come here, but can't," Pokoh said.

"Why not?"

"They seek justice. They cannot reside here until they find it." He stuck his chin up and out, folded his arms, said, "Until you find it."

So, there it was. Justice. At first, I had assumed this visit to *Shipap* was some sort of payback for the teen-aged tweeker I'd killed years ago back home, or that woman—a walking IED—back in Iraq. But now I understood it was more immediate than that. This wasn't payment for what I'd done long ago. This was a chance to redeem the sins of my immediate past by excepting the responsibility for the deaths of people I was sworn to protect and serve.

"I'll find the killers of Juan and Jason Pecos. And "I'll find Oso, too." I said nothing about handing Oso over to him, then banished the thought hoping Pokoh could not read my face or mind.

Pokoh smiled when he said, "But, be careful. Looking for a skinwalker carrying a grudge for over a hundred years can be risky. Bad blood between the Utes and Navajos goes way back. It came to a head when Utes helped Kit Carson end the Navajo's way of life in their last stronghold, Canyon de Chelly. From there, they were marched to the swampy Basque Redondo on a brutal journey called the Long Walk. Hundreds died of starvation and exposure. The old and the sick. Children. Navajos are still furious. Can you blame them?"

His eyes darted about when he said, "Shooting is inevitable at the hospital groundbreaking ceremony. When the first shovel digs into the ground, the trouble starts. Utes, and bystanders die. Chivingtons, too. Then the finger pointing starts and everybody blames everybody else until the Navajos end up holding the bag.

The Navajo and Ute reservations shared a border, but I thought Pokoh might be exaggerating the threat. I sensed his desperation, though.

"Why now?" I asked.

Pokoh sighed, said, "The past always finds a way to haunt the present. People like the Chivingtons are still around looking for a chance to hate Indians and the groundbreaking is a good opportunity to take care of two tribes with one blow."

I'd experienced this kind of hate in the past, but I had hardened my heart against it. Combat duty in the Marine Corps put stiff armor around my emotions. War was business in the Marines, and I had earned my body armor. But, an attack on my people by outsiders who sought to use a 150-year-old massacre as an excuse to reward their hate was personal.

I owed every one of my people who suffered and died from these cowardly acts, past, present, and future. I owed my people—all Indians—justice.

I asked, "Okay, you brought me here to *Shipap*. Why? You're a Ute. So is Oso. Why do you care so much about the Navajos?"

"What harms one, harms all. It is time to end the feud."

I locked on Pokoh's eyes as it struck me that my connection to the potential deaths was also a link to my heritage. We were all connected. I knew that. I just didn't realize how much.

Then, he disappeared. A blue light lingered, then faded away, leaving me alone to think.

Everything went black.

Chapter 29

I awoke back on the mountainside. The high moon edged the pines with silver-blue, a color like the lake above *Shipap*. The snowy peaks fluoresced a brilliant white.

The moon's blue cast invoked memories of Grandfather. He knew the old ways and told me the color blue was a call to power. My mind ran with vague recollections of past supernatural events that had appeared then vanished like last night's nightmare. Like my blue skin. I looked at the back of my hand and rolled up a sleeve to double check. No blue. My skin was colored normal except for the stitched bites from Wolf.

Pacing helped me think. Pokoh had slipped something into the conversation, almost as an aside. The spirit made it a point to tell me he could control asteroids. Putting stars in the heavens was a monumental feat, and I could understand his pride. But he took the time to tell me about his power over those smaller celestial fragments hurtling through space to who-knows-where. Was he merely proud, or was his attention to the asteroids circling his wrist a threat?

I shivered, but not from the cold. I was now in the middle of the Ute-Navajo feud.

Pokoh, in the form of Deer, reappeared in a blue flash.

"Jesus, man," I jumped a foot. "Hey, you an' me gotta talk."

His gleeful eyes, the first hint of humor I'd seen from him, focused behind me. "Have you found Grizz, yet?" asked the man-deer-spirit, chin-pointing to something behind me. "No need." He bounded off.

I whirled. Grizz stood not twenty yards away drooling, crouching cat-like, closing-in on snow-muffled paws.

I broke downhill for Lettau's Ford Interceptor. Grizz snapped at my heels, snagged my pants leg with a claw and jerked me off balance. Airborne, I expected life's end to come fast. The bottom of the hill arrived faster with a lung-busting

172

thud on the road. Grizz, hot on my heels, crashed on the pavement next to me so hard the impact made me shudder.

Jumping up, I fished through my jeans and found the Ford's key fob and thanked the gods as the doors unlocked. I jumped into the police car and used the fob to lock all the doors. Sucking air, I checked the rearview. Outside, Grizz sat up, stared off at the snowy peaks, dazed from the fall.

The starter responded with a click when I twisted the key. There had been enough juice to operate the locks, but not enough battery to start the engine. I had become a victim of my own plan to run the gas and batteries down. Fortunately, the cruiser faced downhill, so gravity was on my side, at least. With a shift into neutral, the Ford rolled.

Not too soon, either. Grizz eyeballed me, shook his body like a wet dog, then ambled my way. Making five miles an hour, I muscled the cruiser around a curve just as Grizz broke into a trot. His front leg hinted at a limp, but Grizz could outrun a horse, limp or no limp.

By the time the road straightened out, Grizz had worked into a lope, trailing me by twenty yards. He seemed stronger, all claws, jaws, and fangs, while my prospects for survival had turned weaker.

Another turn in the road and Grizz was ten yards closer, bigger, crazier. His rapid breathing beat inside the cruiser. My foot instinctively pumped the gas, but stomping the accelerator returned nothing from the dead engine. Grizz gained distance, claws clicking on the blacktop, pads thumping like a boxer's heavy bag. The bear swiped at the rear bumper, missed, then stumbled and fell on his face. Curves sharpened into hairpins. With one eye on the two-lane, another on the rearview, road and abyss blurred as the paw footfalls grew louder.

Scraping the length of a side rail robbed the SUV of speed. Grizz closed again, swatted at the vehicle's rear, the shock so forceful, I had to oversteer to keep on the road. Part of the bumper dragged along behind me. In the mirror, bumper parts littered the highway.

The SUV rolled down the mountain at twenty, but now Grizz cantered alongside, tongue slapping his jaw, eyes wide and red. He wheezed but seemed strong .

With no power-steering, I hugged the two-lane's high side with all my strength. Steering into the next hairpin, a VW-sized boulder sat in the right lane, the product of a landslide. I swerved, scraping metal on the stone bank to my left. I avoided most of the smaller rocks, crashed over others with the skid plate.

Grizz slammed into the Ford like a locomotive, pushing it sideways, stopping it in its tracks, up against the roadside cut. A huge paw smashed the rear passenger window. The beast rammed again, clawed at the rear door until it opened, then tore it off with a swipe, sending a wrenching jolt through the SUV.

Scrambling and grabbing for purchase, Grizz squeezed into the cruiser's prisoner compartment. I wanted to bail out, but my door, jammed flat against the side of the mountain, opened less than a few inches.

Rivets popped when Grizz shouldered against the prisoner barrier and crushed me against the steering wheel. I couldn't breathe. I drew my pistol out of my belt but couldn't angle an arm to aim at him.

Grizz dragged two-inch canines across the plating that separated us, his hot breath reeking of putrid meat. I dropped the pistol while fighting for air. Grizz's ear-splitting roar destroyed my hearing and expelled every rational thought in my head.

Grizz snorted, head-butted the passenger rear door. The blow caused the vehicle to bounce away from the rock. He rammed again and the cruiser bounced free of the rockface and started to roll down the steep road.

Another roar deafened me. Stuck half-in half-out of the prisoner cage, Grizz fought to keep pace with the accelerating vehicle with rear legs like pistons. He bit at the mesh screen between us, fangs scraping like fingernails on a chalkboard. I oversteered the SUV left and right as the trapped animal's violent thrashing pin-balled the Ford against the road cuts and safety rails.

Grizz inched backward as he struggled to free himself. I jerked the wheel hard right and aimed the cruiser off the road toward a drop-off. I yanked the door handle. No luck. Another tug. And again. Roadside gravel crunched under the tires as we

174

rolled toward the cliff, Grizz yowling in my ear. I pulled the door lock toggle, then handle.

The door opened and I rolled out. Impact with the road took all of my air. Pain shot through my left arm. I missed the rear wheel by an inch and slid to a stop. I lay there and watched the car disappear over the edge of the precipice.

The sound of sheared metal and shattered glass exploded from the canyon. I sat on the cold ground soaked in sweat, too exhausted to celebrate with more than a weak smile at each echoing return. I listened for screams of an injured animal but there were none, just the final tinkling of glass falling against rock.

The bushes rustled against the silence.

"Hm." said Deer.

Too drained to muster surprise at his sudden reappearance, I stared at the ground.

He shook his head, said, "It's too early to count your victories."

My patience had been sucked away with my energy, but Deer vanished before I could say a word.

175

Chapter 30

I patted my legs and arms to take inventory. All parts hurt but were present. I grimaced at the thought I'd just taken this same inventory a few days before. Numerous scrapes and abrasions stung, but I wasn't bleeding anywhere important. The cold had penetrated my wet clothing and I shivered. I was dressed for summer, not a three-inches-of-snow mountain summer.

I tried to touch my right shoulder with my left hand but could not. My left shoulder had dislocated from the fall and racking pain shot to my spine when I moved it. I tried shallow breathing, but the technique at this altitude made me dizzy.

The level of pain was so high, I knew that I only had one option. I'd seen a few dislocations treated, so with an amateur's idea of how, I sat.

I placed my left elbow between my thighs. I relaxed as best I could, then squeezed hard with my legs. I leaned back and pushed against my knee with my good arm. The joint popped back in. I stifled a cry, but tears clouded my vision. I swung my arm in a circular motion. It hurt like hell, but at least I had regained movement.

It took all my strength to stand. I held my left arm close and started uphill. Every breath of frigid high-mountain air scratched at my throat and left my lungs begging, but now was not the time to stop. I had to get to Reel and report my conversation with Pokoh and his accusations that Grizz planned to create fatalities at the hospital groundbreaking.

First, I had to check on Deputy Sheriff Lettau. He'd tried to kill me more than once, and I wouldn't give a shit if he froze to death, but I had to keep alive my insurance policy for the Deputy Jones killing.

I'd run into people like Lettau before as an MP. Lettau was up to his ears in the Jones shooting, but he was in fact a coward—shooting a sleeping man in his bed is low-life and spinelessness. A man hiding behind a badge is a weakling, not a Boy Scout.

Lettau would turn against his mates to save his own skin, and testimony will be crucial to my defense. Of course,

176

Lettau could lie on the stand, but assholes like him inevitably
sell out fast to save their own miserable asses.

The two-mile uphill hike turned out to be three. Snow
trickled off the road in rivulets. My cowboy boots, a gift from
my wife—ex-wife—provided little traction on the slush. I
would've given my good arm for a pair of hiking boots.
At the road where Lettau had driven me, I turned left.
New snow hid the tire tracks, but I spotted the blanket I'd
abandoned while escaping Grizz. I didn't see Lettau. In this
black and white place, every rock and bush appeared as a
featureless mound. I searched farther but the snow hid the
man's tracks. Backtracking showed only my prints and no
others. Cuffed hand-to-foot, Lettau could not have escaped. I
had the only key to his cuffs.
Lettau had sustained a serious head injury when I had
thrown him. He could've staggered off half-dazed. All I knew
was he had not made it to his cruiser.
A groan, then another, floated over the snow from a
quivering snow-covered mound. Underneath the snow, Lettau
lay curled up. When I pulled him to a sitting position, he
mumbled gibberish, half-frozen.
His carotid pulsed weakly against my fingers.
I admit I slapped him harder than I needed to, "Hey.
You in there?"
"Wha…?" he asked. "Where?"
I slapped him again. Hypothermia would kill him if I
didn't get his body heat up. Pissing him off might help.
Lettau's face seemed cold to the touch and his waxy pallor
showed the beginnings of frostbite. His eyes darted until they
focused on me in a mix of gratitude and hatred. I retrieved my
blanket and wrapped it around Lettau's shoulders. He clutched
one end with a palsied hand. I rubbed his cheeks roughly to
draw blood to the skin.
Then he vomited. The man needed medical attention.
"Can't walk," he said.
He shivered uncontrollably, his breathing rapid,
shallow, and choppy. Vapor clouds drifted away with each
breath. I fished around in the snow for his lighter, found it next

177

to his leg where I'd dropped it before, then set about gathering dry wood to build a fire. I began shaking, too, but I got the fire going.

As Lettau thawed and I watched the fire grow, I began to question the nature of Pokoh's comment on asteroids. At first, it sounded like a boast borne from his arrogance. Now it seemed more like a threat. My exhausted mind played a scene featuring a space object looming above Southern Colorado, teasing the earth with a near miss only to return. A miss then a return. Then, again.

Rather than accept Pokoh's word that he controlled celestial bodies, I wanted to talk to my favorite Aunt, Priscilla Romero, PhD, who could tell me if there were any asteroids headed our way. If not, I could forget about Pokoh. If true…well, we had a whole bigger problem.

Lettau stared at me for a good ten minutes. The fire flickered in his eyes as he said, "You think this's gettin' you off the hook, Injun?" His teeth chattered as he spoke, but his pupils seemed normal in the flickering campfire.

"You got an explanation why you dragged me up here?"

Cuffed hand to foot, he managed to pull the blankets tighter around his shoulders. He focused on the fire, said nothing.

"Thought so." I held out my hands to gather heat, relished the warmth on my palms, pressed them to my face.

"They're coming."

"That a fact?" I asked.

"You didn't have to come back."

"Ain't no love fest, man. You gotta sing at my trial."

Lettau stared off, said, "Fuck you. What happened to my cruiser?" he asked.

"Long story."

We sat in silence until the fire glowed and my supply of wood disappeared. Lettau had recovered enough to walk and I wanted to get him to FBI custody where Reel could keep him under wraps.

"We're gonna walk out of here," I said.

"They're coming."

"You got a credibility problem, Lettau. Get up," I said.

Lettau made a face, but he stood on shaking legs, then fell over. I moved behind him when he tried again, steadying him when he needed it, ready for whatever mischief he'd planned. Still weak from the cold, he could do little hunched over with one ankle handcuffed to the opposite wrist.

I almost laughed at his semi-crouched discomfort. "Gotta fix that," I said. Grabbing a piece of firewood, I jammed it into his kidneys. He dropped, wheezing for air. He groaned as I put a knee on his backbone and switched one of the cuffs from his leg to the un-cuffed wrist, my own arm jolting every time I applied pressure.

"What the fuck, Romero?" he said, gasping.

"Needed to occupy your thoughts while I switched the cuff. Let's go. You first."

Lettau coughed as he struggled to get up. I grabbed his arm.

"Asshole," he said, jerking away.

"You're welcome."

We started down the highway, hoping that a random vehicle would drive by and call for help, or that the failed FBI tail would finally show up. The deputy shuffled like an old man. I let him keep both blankets though I still shivered.

"Romero, you have no idea who you're dealing with." He stink-eyed me, then the road.

"Makes two of us."

The moon had set, so we walked under starlight offering meager help on a road lined with drop-offs. Fortunately, the snow contrasted with the roadway and kept us from walking into thin air.

"So, your pals are comin' for me? A little clean up, huh?"

Lettau said nothing.

"Taking care of me is only half your problem." I said. "You're the other half."

He stopped in his tracks. I'd hit a nerve. Lettau knew if it were convenient for his cohorts to kill him, they'd do it. He just stared.

179

"Keep moving." I pushed him.

We passed the spot where I'd jumped into the cruiser to avoid Grizz. A mile later we stepped around the bumper parts Grizz had removed from the Ford with a swipe. We turned sharply with the road, then came to where the rockslide had nearly stopped me. Lettau turned to look at me, said, "What happened to my cruiser?"

"Gets worse," I said.

I checked for approaching lights, but the twisting road and big hills limited my view in both directions.

At the roadside cut where the beast had jammed the vehicle up against the rocks, chrome trim and glass granules were sprinkled everywhere. The detached door lay on the blacktop, a monument to Grizz's brute strength.

Lettau chuckled, said, "Don't worry about wrecking my ride, Romero. Your ass is dead, anyway."

"You're lookin' at a needle." I said.

Lettau stopped, turned, lowered his eyebrows. "What the fuck are you talking about?"

"You were involved in the capital murder of Deputy Jones and the attempted murder of me. Move it." I looked both ways. No lights.

Lettau laughed until we passed the place where I drove the SUV and Grizz off of the cliff. In the light of ten thousand stars, tracks led off to a black canyon. He said, "If you're looking for a character witness, better kill me now, asshole."

We turned a sharp hairpin and continued down the road. Blinding lights appeared. A light bar flashed.

"May not have to bother," I said, expecting my long-lost FBI tail.

A siren whooped. Deputies, Lettau's thugs, stepped out of a La Plata County cruiser.

Chapter 31

I sprinted off the road, crashed through scrub, took my chances with the night and weather. I slipped, then grabbed at branches, but my left arm sent stabs up my shoulder and weakened my grip. Lightning flashed through my head as my banged-up bones protested. I tripped and fell. Voices from the road fueled my crawl as I scrambled like a three-legged dog through a thicket growing on the edge of a precipice.

The sound of pounding footsteps grew closer. Someone yelled. I looked over the edge into the void.

Deep in the gorge, Lettau's wrecked cruiser reflected the moonlight in gold letters from a white door panel. Wheels revolved pathetically in the dark.

I searched for the best route to climb down, but a dark, featureless slab extending to the bottom offered no purchase. I would have to solo slippery rock without the slightest knowledge of its fissures, cracks, or ledges, with every bone twinging, one good arm, a bad ankle, and not an ounce of common sense. If this was my night to die, I had plenty of opportunity.

"Not gonna happen, Romero," a voice pulled me away from the face of the cliff. Before I could yell, my captor threw me over his shoulder and started trotting. The shoulder on which I rode was huge. Oso.

Oso crashed through thick brush downhill. The big man navigated the stiff ground scrub in silence. In the starlight, Oso never lost direction nor footing as we descended into the canyon down a path of broken shale.

"Easy, man," I rode his shoulder like a one-strap backpack. My bruised bones protested every step.

We made it to the bottom of the canyon, a trough with dark rock stretching upward. Voices followed, Lettau cursing at his men to find me.

"Put me down, Oso." I had trouble drawing air while carried like a duffle bag.

Oso dropped me into a shallow cave and blocked the door with his bulk, a man-mountain. Grizz in human form. I imagined teeth and claws, the eyes of a predator. He must've sensed I assumed he was going to kill me. He said, "You don't get it, do you?"

"What are you talking about?" I asked, hiding fear with volume.

"Pokoh. That star-juggler is a liar."

"Liar?" Oso Walker's claim was as surprising as it was bizarre.

"Gettin' even for the past is what he's doing."

Ute-Navajo conflicts were constant and deadly long before European arrival in the Southwest. Spanish and Mexican governments promoted that enmity as part of a brutal divide-and-conquer strategy to acquire more land. Later, American policy promoted an Indian Armageddon and theft of Native resources. Tribal conflicts continued today heated by a history of abuse and hate.

"What are you saying?" I asked.

"He's blaming all the trouble around here on a skinwalker. That's complete crap."

"Oso, Grizz has killed at least a dozen so far and who knows how many will be hurt during the hospital groundbreaking. You don't call that trouble?"

He smiled. "I call it payback, but you still not getting it."

"Get what?"

Oso moved in close, breath like spoiled milk. "There's no goddamn Navajo skinwalker. There's no Navajos involved, period. Pokoh's the one doing the killing. Pokoh is Grizz. Plain as day. He tried to kill you, close up. Killed those Chivingtons and us Utes. Blamed it on the Navajo skinwalker hoping to start a shoot-up. That didn't work so he's gonna kill a bunch of Utes and rednecks at the hospital groundbreaking then blame it on the Navajos. Again. Both Chivingtons and Utes are armed to the teeth. Gonna be real retribution, this time."

If I wasn't sitting, I would have fallen over. I clutched my chest, a sharp pang shot through my injured arm. Pokoh was planning to kill his own people, sacrifice them to an age-old beef with the Navajo.

"What? I just kick you in the balls?" Oso asked.

182

Hurt like it. I said, "Bullshit. I saw you with Grizz from behind your house and up the hill. You danced with Grizz then took him inside."

"Jesus, man. That's old Sash. Raised her from a cub. You think Sash's been killing these people? She has no teeth. Eats nothing but milk, porridge, and raw eggs. Sound like a killer to you?"

"A pet? A grizzly? You're shittin' me, Oso."

"Found her near Mexican Hat, skinny as hell, mostly ribs. She'd lost her fur, skin was blue and purple. Her teeth were black, man. Poor cub was way the hell out of her territory with mama gone or dead. When she saw me, she ran up and rubbed against my leg like a cat. I bent over to pet her, she licked my face. What would you do?"

"A pet bear? C'mon," I said.

"Got fifteen grand in vet bills over the years. Don't regret a penny."

Turning my world around like that made me dizzy and the only thing I believed was he was lying. "How in hell does a career Navy man have time to raise a grizzly?"

"You still buying the shit Pokoh's sellin'? My last tour was at the Albuquerque recruiting station. Gave me plenty of time to look after Sash."

"And when you went to sea?"

"Had four tours with the Marines, mostly at the Camp Pendleton hospital, so I didn't deploy much. Gave me plenty of time to care for her. I kept her at home 'til she got huge. Otherwise, she hung around my place on the rez. Still does. When I couldn't take care of her, my cousin did."

Oso's cabin had broken chairs, I remembered, so it made sense a big bear might've busted them up. "You said she had no teeth."

"She's twenty-three which is like seventy bear years. She's got no teeth. I bottle feed her, no shit."

I still wasn't convinced, but he blocked the only way out of this cave. I hugged my bad arm close and kept my mouth shut.

"See anything?" a voice asked from outside the cave. I could not see the speakers, but they were just below our cave.

183

Oval light beams raked the cliff from near the SUV, not seventy-five feet from our cave. Oso moved away from the mouth of the opening. He put a finger to his lips.

"Nothin'," said another voice.

"Look at my cruiser. Fuckin' Romero ran it off the cliff," said Lettau. "Anything in it?"

"Nothing I can see," someone said.

The deputies' voices faded as they walked away.

Oso poked his head out of the cave, looked left and right, then back at me. He said, "Pokoh's got plans for you and me. He's gonna end it all. All of it."

"What are you saying? How?"

"The constellations. You see him with stars in his hand?"

"Yeah. He told me he put 'em in the sky."

Oso crossed his arms over his chest. "The man's a god and he's gonna put a stop to the Ute-Navajo feud. He's got stars in his hand, constellations, asteroids, for chrissakes. You know what asteroids can do to the Earth?"

"Killed the dinosaurs. Pokoh have something to do with that?"

Oso said, "Can happen again, right?"

"Maybe," I said, stone-faced.

"Pokoh says he built the whole sky and everything in it." Oso held out his arms, then leaned in like I was hard-of-hearing. "He's got one heading this way now."

"He's got a small one coming in from the sun. Small enough so no one can see it. Gonna fuck up the hospital ground-breaking, for sure. Kill everybody there." Oso waved a hand in my direction. "You'll have plenty of time to think about it while walking. It's fifteen miles to the trailer. Stay in the canyon. You'll avoid being spotted."

Oso stepped out of the cave.

"How do I know you ain't bullshitting me, Oso. Navy says you're dead." I got no response, so I limped after him. He was gone.

Chapter 32

Sand and gravel made the bottom of the canyon easy travel despite the darkness and an occasional slap in the face from a low branch. Distracted, I tripped on a small log landing on my knees. I stood, brushed myself off and trudged on.

I tripped again and fell on my shoulder, swore, spat sand, and moved on. It seemed every case I have ever investigated injured me.

The morning sun warmed the nape of my neck, a welcomed relief from the night's cold. The walls of the canyon seemed more distant and I began to breathe easier. Deep shadows and cold remained where the canyon switched course. My calves cramped as I put one stone-dead foot in front of the other.

Farms and fields replaced the cliffs, arroyos, and boulders as my descent exposed a broad valley.

My chapped, cracked lips tingled. Grit clogged my throat. The long night, the altitude, and the exhausting walk had dried me out. Mind games red-zoned my brain, weakened my legs. My feet had numbed to a constant pricking of needles. When I flashed hot and cold, I knew I'd approached meltdown. I wouldn't make it to Reel's command post. Out of beliefs, ideas, and steam, I sat on a rock.

I covered my face with my hands. A blue light filtered through my fingers. Blue? I looked at my hands. My blue hands. Blue like the high-altitude sky, blue like a far mountain range, blue as the alpine dawn. Blue as my cold, dark mood. Was I hallucinating or dying?

Rivulets cut the snow and formed a small stream that trickled away. I sucked handfuls of snow and waited for my energy to return. I examined my hands. My blue hands. The color led up my arms. I pulled up a leg of my jeans past my boot tops. My shin showed blue. My face tingled like being washed by a warm, tropical rain. This wasn't frost-bite.

"Get off your ass, private," a voice said. My DI, resplendent in Smokey Bear hat, ribbons, and creases. When my DI said jump, I jumped, but my rubber legs failed me when I tried to stand.

Hands on hips, my old drill instructor, said, "Winning is a mindset. It's not about talent. It's about effort. It's not about sitting on your ass on a rock, Romero."

"Sir, no sir," I said, one of two responses ever allowed. My quads kinked up like cables. I pounded them with my fists looking for life.

"Winning is for champions. You throw a champion to the wolves, he returns leading the pack!" he said, voice grinding like gravel rolling in a drum. "You a champion, Romero?"

I still had stitches where the wolves had bitten me. I stood. It hurt, but I did it. "Sir, yes sir." The second allowable response.

"Winning is what happens when champions tire of losing. You tired of losing, Romero?"

I was tired. "Sir, yes sir."

In my face, breath like old coffee, he said, "Make sure your opponent knows you're ready for war. Look him in the eye and make sure he knows you won't stop. Look him in the eyes until you see his fear. And win. You want to win, Romero?"

"Sir, yes, sir!"

"I can't hear you."

I bellowed, "Sir, yes, sir!"

"Then move. Time is going to run over you like a tank. When the situation is impossible, charge, Romero, charge!" he said, then he was gone.

Fifteen miles. Blood rushed through my wrecked heap of a body and charged me. Even in my sad state, my former drill instructor had inspired power and wisdom. I put one foot in front of the other.

I raised my arms high. "Bring it." The canyon walls echoed my voice. I inhaled the day, the scent of pine, clean sand, and melting snow.

And wet fur.

At the shuffling of gravel upstream, my heart jumped. Grizz bawled, a frightened and wounded animal. I quickened my step.

I made time as the trickling water developed into a stream cutting through flat, open land. Fields of grazing cattle spread out before me. Farmhouses and barns dotted the plains. In places, silos penetrated the high-country horizon.

Wailing from the injured animal animated my pace. I stayed concealed in the high-banked streambed to avoid being sighted by Lettau's deputies, but I now trotted at a painful half-run. No matter how fast I moved, the howls got closer.

The stream bed, deep and narrow, hid all but my head. Twists and turns provided even more safety from detection. It also hid the location of the beast howling behind me and closing. I hurried as fast as I could.

The sun rose as the sides of the creek bed flattened. The flat, ranch country revealed a wooded area in the distance where Reel had hidden her command post. I still had a lot of walking to do across a wide bowl surrounded by mountains and exhaustion was setting in. Random thoughts of self-pity subjected my mind to images of driving my Jeep—my stolen Jeep—across the plain in front of me. The sound of the big engine's glass packs rumbled in my ears until reality intervened.

Fifty yards to the front, a highway crossed a bridge spanning my stream's course. Next to it, parked a La Plata County black and gold with three deputies on guard. Two leaned against the cruiser and Lettau sat behind the wheel. I stayed out of view. Grizz's yowling grew louder, but the deputies seemed not to notice as they smoked and talked.

As I observed the men, I calculated my chances of making it alive across ground void of cover except clumps of grass, yucca, and cactus. Chances: zero.

To my front, the river bottom passed beneath the highway through a culvert too small to walk through upright. Passing through the corrugated pipe was too risky. I pictured Lettau's posse blasting away at me from both ends of the culvert and leaving my hidden body to rot beneath the road. Probability of survival: less than zero.

187

The river bottom stayed shallow on the other side of the road. On the off-chance I made it to the other side, I would be spotted easily. Odds of escaping detection: zip.

The likelihood of surviving Grizz's four-inch claws offered the best way out. I back-tracked toward the bawling sound. The twists and turns of the dry riverbed blocked my view, so I peered around the corners of each, until I found him. Grizz was sitting, panting heavily. When he spotted me, his eyes slitted and burned red. A low growl issued from his chest, then he roared. I grabbed at my ears. Birds exploded from the trees. When the grumble stopped echoing through the valley, I walked towards him. He stood on all fours.

I did what any Marine would do, what my DI said I had to do. I charged. At fifty yards, Grizz growled his menace, again. The animal favored his rear paws, holding each off the ground alternately. At thirty yards, I pulled up my sleeves and waved my arms to show my blue skin.

Grizz cocked his head, first left, then right, as if puzzled. He chomped his teeth, then charged.

Blue skin or not, I turned and ran, trusting I could outrun the injured animal.

The animal's hot breath warmed the back of my neck about the time I made it into the view of Lettau and his guns. I ran straight at them.

The deputies startled, unholstered and fired. Bullets flew everywhere. Some whistled past my head, missing by fractions, others thudded against Grizz who lumbered inches from my heels. I flew between the deputies, Grizz swiping at my feet.

One deputy got off a round at close range that diverted Grizz's wrath to them. Behind me, the crescendo of pistol fire faded and turned to screaming.

I crossed the road, running with all I had. Shrieks and growls faded behind me.

I ran until my legs failed. I dropped to my knees, then crawled until my arms gave out. I lay gasping on the sand until my heart and lungs settled down. Only then did I look back. The La Plata County Sheriff's SUV was gone.

Too exhausted to rise, I watched the area for twenty minutes, but neither activity nor sound interrupted the soft hiss of the wind and the twitter of birds.

Hot pokers burned my ankle when I tried to stand, so I crawled to the scene. Two deputies lay mauled, deep gashes had opened their chests. One of them had been decapitated. Grizz had dropped off to one side with his legs spread out like a bear rug. Blood stained the fur on his face, front legs, and torso.

I hesitated to approach the animal and waited on hands and knees at a safe distance. Grizz was a great warrior and worthy opponent. This beast had tried to kill me several times over the past week but had never given up. Grizz, in life, was a magnificent creature worthy of respect and I mourned the passing of his soul. I created a chant in his honor.

But this bear was the last earthly embodiment of the skinwalker, Pokoh. I had also seen Pokoh the man, Pokoh as Deer and as Pokoh the spirit in all his constellation-juggling glory.

For years, Costancia's mother told me stories about skinwalkers. I listened wide-eyed but Costancia couldn't stand it. She said calling out the name of the creature for all to hear would dispel all the psychic energies of the creature who would then reveal his human form.

I was certain Grizz was the earthly embodiment of Pokoh but seeing is believing. I wanted proof and it couldn't hurt to try.

"Pokoh," I hollered. "You, Grizz, are the Ute, Pokoh." I said it again, louder. No reaction came from the dead beast. I said it several times in English, then Keres. I chanted over and over a mantra containing all the spiritual power I could muster from a position on my knees.

"Your pathetic ditty didn't work, Romero," Pokoh said, from behind me, "and it isn't over."

I whirled, faced a scowl from a mouth twisted downward in an anger so strong, I could smell it. Despite his denial, his appearance confirmed the mantra had worked.

Pokoh, Ute god of the heavens, stared down at me, a man-vision dressed in beaded leathers and crow-wing

189

headdress. The deity—from my hands-and-knees viewpoint seemed ten feet tall—juggled constellations and stars in his right hand. His left curled into a fist, close enough to hit me.

Pokoh studied his handheld stars, then me, with mouth pinched flat. His narrowed eyes revealed contempt, disgust and hate. "They are beautiful, aren't they? Just lonelier than before." He snapped the words, bit off the ends. The small asteroid previously circling his hand was absent from his cluster of glowing stars and constellations.

"Where is it, Pokoh?"

"Waiting."

Before I could ask any more questions, he vanished.

Chapter 33

Pokoh's asteroid. My mantra designed to destroy the skinwalker had not only failed, it might've escalated his power. Boxcars of questions piled up, one against the other in endless collisions of improbable events, irrational conclusions, and impossible consequences.

I stood as best I could. If I put little weight on my foot, the pain was bearable. I studied the two dead men and tried to separate the real from the unreal.

The men's mutilated bodies were real. One deputy's head lay next to the skid marks of the sheriff's cruiser. Lettau had deserted his own men quickly, the SUV nowhere in sight. Real enough, for sure. Grizz lay where he'd died. Real?

I needed Reel. The Cherokee in her would listen, understand what I could not. She had a way of making sense out of nonsense. If she rejected everything I had to say out of hand, I still wanted to be near her.

I had ten miles to go but I didn't think I could make it. I would have to wait for a ride, but this road was a secondary highway and lightly travelled.

The smell of death wafted past my nose and coated my throat. I considered staying with the dead men, but anyone coming here would end up pointing fingers at me, the cop killer. Despite claw-marked bodies, severed head, and a dead bear, I was the only one left standing, thus Suspect Number One.

Rattles and squeaks preceded a vehicle coming from the west. Out of caution, I headed for the drainage pipe crossing under the road, the only hiding place around here. As it neared, I recognized the vehicle, a Bondo and bailing-twine junker that must've caused celebration every time it started.

It was driven by the Peruvian who'd given me directions to Rafi Maestrejuan's *campito*.

I waited by the side of the road and waved. The Peruvian slowed, studied the dead deputies, recognized me, then smiled. He stopped, stepped out, held out a hand. "Looks like you've been busy." he said in Spanish.

"No, not me." I said, pointing to Grizz.

He winked, asked if I needed a ride. I answered yes but his glee over the dead deputies and dead grizzly made me uneasy. "Anywhere you want," he said, with a grin.

At our last meeting outside the bar, the Peruvian had made his distrust of white cops clear. Ordinarily I steered clear of cop haters, but I was in no position to refuse a lift.

The truck's threadbare seat was the most comfortable thing I'd ever collapsed on. The water he gave me was the sweetest I'd ever swallowed.

We talked in Spanish about mundane things, but I eased the discussion toward things celestial. I asked if he knew about any Incan asteroid-throwing deity.

"Ombligo de la tierra, Señor," he said.

Navel of the Earth. The term applied to the ancient Peruvian capital, Cuzco. In *Nahua, Cuzco* means "center of the world" in the same way the navel is the center of the body. All roads led to Cuzco's gold-lined, emerald-studded structures until the Spanish pillaged the place, but his answer did not satisfy my question.

When I asked again, his eyebrows dropped, and his smile disappeared. Many Indians did not like to talk about their religion because of fear. Fear they would be ridiculed, fear they would be evangelized, or, worse, fear their religious beliefs would be stolen.

Inca religion was closely tied to astronomy. So, I said, "Tell me more. Start at the beginning. Tell me how Cuzco was founded," I asked. I looked at him seriously and he seemed to understand I was. The Peruvian was not an educated man, but I did not want learned knowledge, I wanted myth. Myth is where Pokoh came from, and somewhere in the depths of timeless lore, I might find clues to Pokoh's true capabilities.

The Peruvian launched into a legend about the city's founding prior to the Inca. "Five thousand years ago, the Inca were born from the sun god, *Inti,* at the ancient city of *Tiwanaku* in Bolivia. They migrated to the Cuzco valley to fulfill an earlier prophecy claiming they would settle where a golden staff could be easily driven into the ground. With the

192

help of stone giants, they defeated the local tribes and the great Inca capital was built."

I listened as he told the story, using his hands lavishly to tell it, while driving on meandering roads. "...So, you see, Cuzco was placed by the children of the sun," he said.

Children of the sun? Every tribe says that. No help.

Then he said, "Our great empire fell to the Spanish as foretold by a great asteroid sent by the gods." With suppressed excitement, I asked, "By the gods?"

"Sí, Señor. Los dioses." By the gods.

Both Utes and Incas believed in legends of destruction from space. My cheeks burned. I wanted confirmation. I needed to talk to my Aunt Pris. She could confirm if the earth faced imminent danger. "I need a phone. Fast."

The Peruvian found a Circle K in Durango and waited while I called. I went for the phone feeling like every eye in town was on me. I walked as fast as I could to an outdoor booth, probably the last one in New Mexico, and faced away from the street. I called collect to Aunt Pris' home phone hoping she was not at work. The university would not accept a collect call.

She picked up on the fourth ring.

"I need your help," I said.

"It's the only time you call. And collect?" She exhaled. "What do you want, Peter?" she said, voice like icicles on my handset.

"I really need help. I need to know if there's an object in space that could present a danger to Southern Colorado, Durango area."

"You have a lot of nerve calling me after leaving Costancia like that. Shame on you, Peter."

"She left me, Aunt Pris."

"And you, Peter Romero, had nothing to do with that?"

I loved my aunt. She adored me but loved Costancia more. Everyone did. "She hated my job."

Silence loitered like a bum on a busy street corner.

"Aunt Pris? Please?" I told her what I needed.

"Of all the requests over all these years, this is the most bizarre. Space objects? Really, Peter?"

"Really."

"You know this is out of my discipline?"

Doctor Priscilla Romero, PhD anthropologist, was my go-to on all things ancient. "Yes, but you know people who know these things."

"I really don't have time for this," she said.

Pris seldom denied my queries and never asked why I needed information. It was our understanding. This time it seemed important to fill her in best I could. I told her of Pokoh's threat.

"I respect spiritual power as much as you do Peter, but this is nonsense," she said.

I told her what the Peruvian told me.

"Oh?" She asked. The line went silent.

"Aunt Pris?"

Another sigh of exasperation. "I'm off today, but I'll see what I can do."

"Aunt Pris, I need it now."

"The nerve," she said, as she hung up. Aunt Pris would find the information. She was part bulldog, part locomotive, if something got in her way.

The Peruvian dropped me off at the mouth of a small canyon near Reel's mobile command post, but not too close. Her operation would remain secret as long as I could help it. I thanked my friend and set out through a narrow canyon as fast as I could limp.

The Pierce RV was well hidden, but the grumbling generator made finding the mobile command center easy. The cool air refreshed me when I stepped in.

Reel's command post hummed with voices and ringing phones. Keyboards clicked out a rhythm as I hurried toward the conference room where Real worked. Thousands of people's lives, maybe more, were at stake and we had less than twenty-four hours to protect them. I had to convince her she needed to cancel the ceremony and keep people away from the area.

Reels' assistant Dean blocked the conference room door, looked me up and down, then said, "She's busy and doesn't want to be disturbed."

"Get out of my way," I said, pushing past him.

He grabbed me by the arm. "You hard of hearing? I said, she doesn't want to be disturbed."

The sloppy research by Reel's assistant was responsible for one of this investigation's bizarre turn of events. "She's gonna be disturbed when I put my boot up your ass. Get your hands off of me."

The conference room door opened, and Reel stuck her head out from behind it. "What's going on here?"

Dean said, "I told him he can't—"

She gave me a look like one would give to a dying animal. "What hap—? Never mind, get in here."

Chapter 34

Reel sat with a pile of paperwork in the conference room.

Reel looked at me when I sat, sniffed, made a face. "You look a mess, Peter."

"Would've been here sooner, but your tail never showed."

"I'm sorry that happened. Lettau shook them early on."

"Armatures?" I asked.

She flushed. "I recommended them for a tour in Minot."

FBI's version of hell minus the heat.

My mud and blood-stained shirt, and my shredded pants gave the appearance of a street dweller, but not as clean. When I closed the conference room door, a look of dread crossed her face. I pulled up a chair a short distance from where she sat, embarrassed at the way I must have smelled.

"You don't look surprised to see me."

She pointed around the perimeter, "Cameras. Peter, you're hurt."

"That's the easy part," I said. I pondered how to explain Pokoh to her. I had to appeal to her Cherokee spirit while skirting her FBI practicalities.

I detailed my kidnapping by Lettau, the confrontation with Grizz, then Oso, then the constellation-juggling Pokoh and his threat that an asteroid was coming to destroy everyone at the groundbreaking. I felt relieved when I unloaded it all.

"An asteroid? Really?"

Her eyes said I was crazy, and I couldn't disagree, but I had seen what I'd seen.

"Jean, if I had a story, why would I come up with this one? Deer morphed into Pokoh. He held parts of the universe in his hand. Weirdest thing. He's a man when I first met him, then an animal guide, then a spirit."

"Three-in-one? Seriously?" Her eyes widened, then narrowed.

196

Her comments were either sarcastic or dismissive, at least, that's the way I took them. I said, "Deer, uh, Pokoh, told me not to trust Oso. Pokoh said Oso was Grizz. A skinwalker."

"A bear? A skinwalker?" she said. She lifted an eyebrow. "My problem with this story is Oso is dead according to the Navy."

"Hard to get around that. But there's something weird about the Oso we're dealing with. He showed up in the San Juan Range in the middle of the night after I ran Grizz off a cliff. Oso saved my ass from Lettau and his deputies. It gets weirder because Oso told me Pokoh was Grizz."

Reel wore a frosty expression, asked, "You're saying Grizz is dead?"

So much for skirting her practicalities. I wanted her Indian, but all I got was her FBI. "Looked that way."

Reel said, "Then it stands to reason Oso, whoever he is, is dead. Then, Pokoh, either man or deer or both, is dead."

I said, "Not sure reason plays any part in this."

She ran her fingers through her hair, then pressed a hand to her forehead, looked at the floor. "Find Oso Walker."

"What is your fascination with Oso? Why don't you believe me about the asteroid?"

"Peter, you tell me Oso Walker, a man we thought we knew but don't, is Grizz. Oso says no, Pokoh is the grizzly. Then you tell me Pokoh denies it. Then you tell me Grizz is dead. A dead spirit? Really? Then you tell me Pokoh, a man-deer-bear-spirit has asteroids on call. Pardon me if I have my doubts, Peter. The only thing I can take away from this story is that my investigation has been compromised. I want to know how Oso penetrated my organization. If he's alive, find him. If he's dead well, I'll think about your Grizz story."

"This is not about your investigation and it's not about who's who. This is about Pokoh's asteroid blowing the shit out of the ceremonial groundbreaking and half of Durango, too," I said. If she heard the anxiety in my voice, her eyes conveyed her last answer was the only one I would get.

"Jean, right now, I need your Indian more than I need your FBI."

She raised an eyebrow, nodded. "Okay. Call your Aunt Pris right now and verify if this whole asteroid thing is true."

I wanted to pause, let the relief sink in, but there was no time for that. I fat-fingered numbers on Reel's table phone.

Aunt Pris picked up on the first ring. "I've been waiting for your call. Peter, your question about dangerous space objects was, let's say, unusual, but I found an answer."

"I have you on speaker phone. Jean Reel is here, too."

"Oh, Jean, how are you, dear?" Effusive to a fault, Aunt Pris became even more animated when she talked to Jean. She loved Jean. Loved everybody, come to think of it. Well, maybe not me so much, right now.

"No one here at the university can answer my questions, don't worry, I was very discreet when I called NASA and talked to an old flame, head of NASA's Planetary Defense Coordination Office who oversees Spaceguard efforts. Brought back memories. He was quite hot back in the day."

"Aunt Pris," I said. If not checked, my aunt would replay stories of her love life, which by all accounts was rich and full. As she'd grown older, she showed a willingness to reveal more than I cared to hear.

"Spaceguard?" Jean asked.

Pris inhaled, ready to launch into endless technical detail suitable for technocrats and scholars, but not for people like me who wanted to know if we were going to die soon.

"Well," Aunt Pris, said, "The term refers to a number of worldwide efforts to discover and study near-Earth objects; asteroids and comets big enough to reach the Earth's surface and do substantial dam—."

I said, "I hope you're going to tell me there are no such objects."

"Not quite, Peter. There are fourteen hundred."

My jaw must've dropped because Jean's did. "What"?

"The good news is none of these objects pose a threat to Earth within the next hundred years, and there are no known objects capable of catastrophic destruction likely to hit us."

"How about the possibility of unknown objects?" Jean asked, looking at me.

198

Aunt Pris explained the risk of undetected bodies was real. She gave two examples: the 1908 Tunguska airburst that levelled seven-hundred square miles of Siberian forest, and the 2013 airburst over Chelyabinsk Russia that damaged thousands of buildings and injured sixteen-hundred people.

"Any more surprises out there?" I asked.

The line was quiet for a moment, then Pris, said, "I don't think that risk will ever go away. The problem is space objects can strike at a low angle from the direction of the sun, which makes them difficult to detect."

Oso had said the same thing. "Don't these things radiate? Can't they be picked up by frequency detectors or radar?"

"Even if they discharged like a TV tower, the sun's own emissions would mask the signal. We just cannot discover them in time to react."

"What if we did see one coming?" I asked.

"In theory, if we had enough time, there could be an interception, but NASA needs a warning first," she said.

"How much of a warning?"

"A few years would be ideal."

We had a one-day warning. Tomorrow. Saturday. My chest constricted like someone was standing on it.

While Reel chatted with Aunt Pris, I rose to satisfy an urge to step outside and look into the sun for foreign objects. I needed air. Reel gestured, demanded I sit. I sat.

Once off the phone, Reel dismissed her Cherokee side by saying, "Well, that settles that."

"Settles what?" I knew the answer.

"Trust me, I want to believe you, but you heard Pris as well as I did. There are no objects coming this way."

"And you heard her say objects blocked by the sun give no warning. That gives Pokoh plenty of room to slip a space object past detection."

Reel's face reddened as she said, "You also heard her say we had no ready defense against them. Detected or not, we can do nothing about it."

"You could call the Durango mayor and ask to postpone the ceremony."

Reel looked at the ceiling, said, "And the reason I'll give is?" Her eyes were determined but her forehead wrinkled.

This was my final chance. "Pokoh's threat is a call for action from the ancestors. *Your* Great Spirit is calling. Won't you listen? Tell the mayor there's a threat to the security of the ceremony. Tell him the Chivingtons are bringing automatic weapons. Tell him the Utes are bringing hand grenades. Shit, tell him anything."

Her eyes bored through me as she said, "I talk to the mayor regularly. He knows what the threat for violence is and we are prepared. In the past, I have asked for a postponement to protect my case and he has refused. No, he will not delay.

"And, based on what Pris had to say, I think Pokoh is blowing smoke." Reel crossed her arms, body armor that welcomed no argument.

She was through listening and I had lost. "We can't take the chance, *dammit*," I said.

She held up a palm. "Officer Romero, you listen to me. I have a very sensitive operation going on here. I cannot give out information, some of which is classified, to just anyone. Not law enforcement. Not the mayor. As it is, I'm pushing the envelope by talking to you.

"The ceremony is tomorrow at noon, Officer Romero, and we have done all we can do. No one will believe a Ute god is going to disrupt the hospital groundbreaking with an asteroid, especially when NASA says there is no threat. The only thing I can take from this whole story is the question that the Oso Walker we think we know is an imposter. Find him and get him in here. Now."

"There will be hundreds of people at the ceremony. How many are going to die because of this, Jean?"

"Find Oso," Reel said, gathering her stack of papers before storming out of the conference room. Agents tending their monitors glanced up as she passed. I ignored their gaze as I followed her down the hall, my mind fixed on tomorrow's disaster.

200

Outside, I hopped into an FBI sedan, "bucar" in FBI-speak, black and non-descript, and drove toward Oso's cabin. I had no idea where Oso was, but his home was a place to start.

Oso was the man-of-the-hour by Jean's reckoning and I was to bring him in for questioning. Whoever this man was, this bogus Oso, was destined for jail if he could not justify his role as an imposter and for his infiltration into a classified FBI operation.

I wanted him too, but for what Oso knew about Pokoh's power to direct a destructive space object to earth. I suspected he knew much more about Pokoh than he let on.

My deadline crept closer like Cougar. In complete silence. Looming unseen, undetectable, and inevitable. If Oso was still alive, this would be my last chance to find out what he knew.

Chapter 35

With an eye on the side and rearview mirrors, I punched the sedan all the way to Oso's place. I drove like a drunk, swerving in-lane, careless on the curves, distracted, and unable to wrap my mind around what had happened. I kept an eye out constantly for approaching sheriff deputies on the prowl even though they had no jurisdiction here. A sense of unease spidered up my spine.

The flash of a light bar jacked my discomfort to alarm. The black Ford interceptor riding my bumper must have been hiding in the bushes along the road. I slowed and pulled off. He passed without looking over at me and cruised out of sight. Good thing, the cruiser's gold markings identified him as a La Plata County deputy, but I didn't recognize him as one of Lettau's goons. If he'd intended to pull me over for a traffic violation, the federal plates on my bucar must have persuaded him the required paperwork would not be worth the effort. I allowed myself to breathe, pulled out, and continued.

Things had gone terribly wrong, and I fumed over Reel's orders as I drove. Hunting down Oso was a distraction from the real threat, Pokoh's asteroid. Now, I alone carried the awful certainty of pending disaster and I had less than twenty-four hours to prevent it.

When I neared Oso's cabin I stopped just out of view and took time to watch and listen. The area seemed clear, so I parked in Oso's driveway hoping the man's pet bear, Sash, was not inside the cabin. My knock on the front door was met with a low growl from behind. I whirled. The beast stood between me and my car. I cursed myself for letting my guard down.

Old Sash had no teeth, according to Oso, but she did have claws. Four-inch claws. Pet or not, the massive brown grizzly could crush me to death by just sitting on me.

Sash sniffed the air, then walked toward me. The roof had no visible access, so a hard shoulder to the front door knocked it open. I lunged through and slammed it behind me. The bear did not follow. Instead, she scratched herself against the front bumper of my sedan. The car bounced on its shocks. As I studied her through the window, she stared at the cabin for a moment, too bored to follow it seemed, then shambled off, looking more exhausted than enthralled.

Oso's place was small enough to see at a glance no one was home, but I took a quick look through drawers in the kitchen and rummaged through the only closet.

In a bedroom dresser with missing handles, I found some well-thumbed books: *Maya Cosmos: Three Thousand Years on the Shaman's Path* and *The Shaman's Coat: A Native History of Siberia.* Oso's interest in shamanism only added urgency to my search. If he was not Grizz, as he claimed, why the interest in shamanism?

Quickly, I examined the backyard from a rear window, then stepped outside after listening for Sash. I found her around a corner of the building in a heap, snoring. After checking the other side of the house, I trotted to the car.

My next destinated was the clinic where I first met Oso. As I grabbed the door handle, the sound of many metallic slides chambering bullets sounded like the hiss of so many snakes.

"On the ground, Romero. On the fucking ground. Now!"

I did exactly as told. I hit the deck with arms splayed. I didn't dare move. Move a hair's breadth and he would pull the trigger.

Boots and camouflage-clad legs rushed in. I counted sixteen legs. From the ground, everyone appeared ten feet tall and smelled of gun oil and testosterone. They cuffed me, jerked me up by the arms, nearly pulling them from their sockets.

"Jesus. Easy, man," I said.

My escort fast-walked me to a La Plata County Sheriff SUV. So much for jurisdiction. While one deputy pushed me into the prisoner's cage and fastened the seat belt, another in the front passenger seat told me I was under arrest for the murder of Deputy Frank Jones and recited my rights. He asked if I understood. I remained silent.

On the way to the jail, Lettau sat in the front passenger's seat. No one spoke. I'd figured Lettau, the man I'd kept alive last night, would not risk turning me in, given the fact he'd kidnapped and tried to murder me. Keeping him alive was a bad move. Lettau, grinning at me from his seat, had ratted me out.

In Durango, we came upon the slab-sided one-story jail as inviting as road tar. We passed a white street sign announcing the place with a blue arrow and the word Jail. The lowering sun jacked my nerves. The faster the night came so did the morning, and disaster.

After in-processing and a cursory medical exam by a male nurse who took photos, but clearly didn't give a shit about my torn stitches and bruises, I was escorted to my cell: gray-green door, two wall-mounted bunks, a stainless-steel toilet and sink.

A huge man lay motionless, facing the wall on the top bunk.

The jailer uncuffed me. As the door slammed shut, I sat on the lower bunk. Stuck in this cell, frustration pushed my heartbeat into my temples.

"Watcha in fer?" said my roommate, his voice unusually high for a man his size.

I told the truth, hoping to shut him up. "Killing a cop."

"You da man," he said. This time the voice sounded familiar. I jumped up and looked at him.

"How'd you get in here?" I pointed, worked to get words out.

Oso sat up. "Ya' know, they really don't make these bunks for people my size," he said. Looking at me, he said, "Not nice to point, Romero."

"Answer my question." I dropped my arm.

Oso said, "Not much to it. Walked through the wall."

"What are you doing in here, Oso?"

"Wasn't you lookin' for me? Got to correct some misinformation and protect your lame ass, too."

"Start correcting," I said.

"First of all, I am not, was not, Grizz."

"Navy says you're dead, Oso."

"So?" Oso hunched his shoulders.

I stared at him.

The cell door opened, and a deputy appeared. "Keep it down in here!" He looked around the cell, didn't acknowledge anyone but me, and slammed the door.

"You're invisible, too?" I asked.

"No."

"That guy…" I said, pointing to the door.

"He doesn't believe."

"*I* believe you're not Oso."

"Trust me and you might learn something."

"All I'm learning is you won't answer my questions. And trust you? No." I held my head in my hands. "Here's my problem with you. You say Pokoh is Grizz. It was Pokoh that led me to safety after I rolled my truck near the *campito*. He warned me Grizz was about to attack last night in the mountains. Been tailin' me since I arrived in Colorado. Protecting me."

Oso snorted. "That what you call protection? He's stalking you. He knows you got the power. You're the only one who can stop the asteroid."

"How the hell am I supposed to believe you?"

Ropes appeared in Oso's jaws and neck. "I just walked through the wall and you ask a question like that?"

"Yeah, so did a two hundred pound deer last night." I sat on the bunk; my brain had given up trying to figure out what was going on. "Shit, I don't know."

"Come with me. I got somebody you need to talk to," he said.

"Who?" I asked as he disappeared through the wall. "Hey, wait! Who do you want me to talk to, Oso?"

His head poked out from the wall. "You coming? Haven't got all day."

"Through a block wall?"

Oso held out his palms. He said, "For a guy in a hurry, you got a lot of questions."

"You —" I almost said no one could walk through walls, but there he was, partly-in, partly-out of a thick partition with only his head and two hands jutting from it. "I can't just…it's physics!"

Oso stepped into the cell. "To hell with physics. Look at your skin," he said, rolling his eyes like I was some dumb kid.

My hands and arms were blue.

"Well?" Oso asked. "You can't recognize a sign?"

Until this moment, my occasional change of skin color had not registered a purpose except to scare Grizz. Now, it was a gift from the ancient ones, a spiritual directive, a call-to-action. Still, I could not get past the physics problem.

I stared at Oso not knowing what to say. At this point, I didn't understand a thing.

Oso stared at me. "You want out of here?"

"Bet your ass."

Oso said, "Leave all you know behind. Say goodbye and let your guard down. Let it go. All of it." Oso had a leather bag hanging from his shoulder and he pulled a small bottle from it. "Here, take this. It'll help."

"What is it?"

"Peyote. The hell you think it is?"

I can take or leave peyote. Some truly believe one can't commune with the ancients without it. That was not my problem. My immediate goal was to get out of this cell and Oso, or whoever he was, clearly knew how. I nodded.

Oso smiled, led me in a ritual to honor the six sacred directions, North, South, East, West, Earth, and Sky, an exercise in imagination because all four walls, the floor, and ceiling of my cell were identical in nearly all respects. Only the toilet, bunks and sink broke the sameness.

"We have no drums, but you get the idea," Oso said.

We finished the ceremony, but I experienced no effects of the peyote. "I saw Oso looking at me. "What? Nothing's happening."

Oso started to chant. My body warmed and my knees weakened as Oso's songs traveled straight to my soul. The walls began to warp, pulsing as if they were breathing in time with his songs. The walls curled and pulsed more as Oso's chanting got faster. His voice blended with unseen others. The singing got louder until it enveloped me, the walls pulled away.

206

Oso's face contorted, elongated. His arms elongated until they touched the ground. I laughed, his smile reached his ears, I grabbed my sides.

Oso said, "I see you're ready." He disappeared into the cement blocks.

I walked toward the wall in a haze not caring I was about to receive a busted nose.

Chapter 36

We didn't run, walk, or ride, and moved in no particular direction past sparse vegetation, mountain lions, eagles, and mountains, all in luminous, vivid colors. We stopped in front of a cave. Inside, a cathedral of stalagmites contained scattered fragments of pottery. Next to them lay a small skeleton belonging to a child. The tiny bones had calcified to shimmering crystal. Nearby, a body of sparkling water glowed. Walking on, we passed more human remains, adorned with meticulous care, they looked like sacrifices to various gods and spirits.

My thoughts summoned up *Xibalba,* the Place of Fear, ruled over by Mayan death gods and inhabited by vampire bats. Places like this contained rivers of blood and scorpions ruled by demonic gods. "Is this *Xibalba?*"

"No," Oso said.

The high-ceiling cave exited onto an endless plain, an undulating sea of grass rimmed by a white-capped range gleaming like silver. We followed a brush-lined river, I drank water pure and sweet. Buffalo by the thousands grazed, ran, and rolled in wallows. Birds swirled in vast clouds that cast shadows on the green earth.

Everything I touched was real; brush, the ground, the grass. We came to a hill with dramatic views of towering, three-hundred-foot rock slabs of pink sandstone against a backdrop of snow-capped peaks and brilliant blue skies. The wind whispered voices I didn't understand while I admired stone spires and humpbacked formations lined up like migrating dinosaurs.

Oso said, "My Ute ancestors lived here. Rivals laid down their weapons and gathered here in peace. This is sacred ground. Our spiritual way of life started here." He spread his arms wide.

"Our elders grew up here and the bones of our forebears are part of this earth. An elder, a blind man, brought me here for the first time when I was a child. He led me to spots where the tribe once held religious ceremonies. Whites call it, Garden of the Gods, now."

"Why are we here?" I asked.

"You'll find your answers here. Go." Oso leaned against a tree, panting, but there was a glow around him. From the beginning, Oso had been my guide and I'd misjudged him.

I walked on. My answers were here. Somewhere, they were here.

A path, overgrown with thistle, meandered through sheets of upended stone. Bones, big enough to belong to dinosaurs, stuck out of the rock. Rib cages big enough to walk through curled overhead.

I looked back. Oso was gone and I wondered if I might ever see him again.

A plateau overlooking the rock formations produced a better view. The sun stood straight up and baked my head. I'd worked up a sweat from the climb, so I unbuttoned my sleeves and rolled them up past my elbows. The injuries from Wolf's attack glowed an angry red laced by black stitches over my blue skin.

Under a rock formation resembling kissing camels, a ribbon of smoke drifted upward. I hiked downhill to a small bonfire where an old man sat cross-legged inside a circle of stone. He chanted and tossed bone fragments on the ground, studied them, scooped them up and threw again. The man wore a full eagle headdress and a loose smock of tan leather without decoration. His nut-brown skin contrasted with white braids that hung low and brushed the ground. The old one took no notice of me until I neared his stone circle.

"Stop," he said.

I did, then asked his name. He looked at me as if I should have known. His black eyes seemed heavy, half asleep, his thoughts in another place, perhaps. "You have travelled far to talk to me, yet do not know who I am. Why?"

"I seek answers."

"And you, in your arrogance, expect that I, Senawahv, have the answers and will provide them?"

I stepped back. I was in the presence of the creator, Senawahv himself, who had created the mountains, rivers, rain, snow, wind and wildlife for the Utes. He created the Utes themselves from loose logs falling from his knapsack. He normally lived in the sky, but now he sat before his earthly campfire eyeing me with an intense, unswerving stare.

"Pokoh said he put the stars in the sky."

"Pokoh is my creation. A spirit, yes, but only one of many. I've made spirits who heal the sick, another for thunder and lightning, a spirit of war and one of peace. Pokoh is a self-indulgent fool, a legend in his own mind. Yes, Pokoh put the stars in the sky, but only as I commanded. Clearly, he's bored. Fear him."

"He intends to send an asteroid to earth," I said.

Senawahv's chest expanded and his face reddened. "Justify your sacrilege or I will kill you where you stand." Senawahv's voice shook the earth. Stones rattled off the rock slabs. Sand trickled down like hissing snakes.

I could barely control my shaky voice when I said, "Pokoh intends to reignite Navajo and Ute hostilities. People will die at a ceremony, then more will die from the revenge war." My voice caught.

Senawahv's glower suggested I lacked worthiness to speak.

"What is it you want from me?" he asked.

"How do I stop Pokoh's asteroid?"

His grimace burned my skin. "Get out," he said.

"What? Why?"

"Power is obtained from knowledge received through one's own dreams or visions. I can give you none."

I stared, hiding my rush of anger and disappointment. Senawahv looked down, threw the bones and scooped them up. He threw the bones again, scooped them up with no attempt to study their meaning. I dared not move.

He gazed at me with red eyes. Bushy white eyebrows shadowed his pupils. "I see you were sent here by your spirits. I recognize the blue of your skin, but I have no aid for you. Be gone." he said, through tight lips.

I stood fast, rooted like the rocks surrounding us.

Senawahv rose, his human form stood eight feet tall, his menacing gaze that of Cougar. His face colored as he judged me, "It is time for you to go."

210

My pounding heart said run. My knees weakened as
nerves twitched in my legs, but I would die rooted here if I had
to. I wanted answers. I puffed up my chest fearing Senawahv
could hear my amped heartbeat ricochet off the towering pink
slabs. If this was the end, then it would be the end.

Senawahv balled his fist, then threw a lightning bolt
that exploded at my feet. The blast knocked the wind out of me
and peppered my legs with gravel. I gasped when he threw
another bolt that passed between my thighs and heated my
groin. Rock shards from the impact behind me stung my ass,
but I dared not flinch. Senawahv had the power to incinerate
me.

Senawahv said, "The next one is the last. I will not
tolerate your impudence."

I steadied myself for the end and would have sung my
death song had I possessed one. Senawahv stopped, then turned
his attention to the bite marks on my arms. "How did you
receive those wounds?"

"Wolf. Pokoh sent a pack of six. They attacked me. I
killed two."

"*Shinab* are sacred here," he said, slit-eyed. "You killed
two?"

"They were trying to kill me." I stretched out my arms,
offered the sutures as evidence.

Senawahv growled, "How did they die?"

"Bravely. In combat by my hand. One with a kick. The
other by a broken neck."

"Those were my children." Senawahv looked at the fire,
paused, mouthed a prayer ending with the kissing of his
tobacco pouch. He looked towards me, then smiled. "I knew
they had died in battle, but I needed to hear how," he said.

"I am sorry for your loss." I braced for a lightning bolt
straight to my gut.

Senawahv looked at me with kinder eyes. "My children
fought and lost but did not shame their kind. A warrior's
destiny is unalterable and death in battle is the only reward.
But, as their father, I demand justice. I command that you face
Pokoh."

"How do I face a mighty Ute spirit?"

Senawahv shook his head. "Do you fear death? If you want to live, breathe, and evolve, you must conquer that fear. You must figure out how. I have spoken, now go."

Before I had a chance to speak, another form materialized out of nowhere. Pokoh stood in front of Senawahv wrapped in smoke and quaking like the yellow aspen that flecked the far hills.

Gone was the straight posture and spread-legged stance of the powerful. His once beautiful clothing hung in tatters. Pokoh hunched over Senawahv's fire as if collapsing into his rib cage. He clutched his constellations to his chest as if protecting them. Tangled black hair over his face failed to hide wet tracks on his cheeks.

Senawahv, towering above Pokoh, pointed and said, "You may no longer smoke the pipe at my council fire."

Pokoh howled and begged. Pointing to me, he said, "This miserable wretch blocked my path to justice for our people!"

Senawahv chastised him, "You sent my children to their deaths! Your only salvation is they died bravely at the hands of a worthy warrior. I withdraw your invitation to my fire."

The conversation continued in Ute and ended in a loud scolding that caused Pokoh to cringe at each stressed word. Senawahv pointed a lightning bolt at Pokoh. Instinctively, I put my arm up to cover my face.

I had become a forgotten bystander. I felt reluctant pity for Pokoh, but nothing I could do now would alter his destiny.

Pokoh vaporized to a mist.

The sun pierced my eyelids.

Chapter 37

A generator exhaust pipe pumped poison over my face. I coughed and rolled away. I sneezed until the exhaust smell faded from my nose. My head throbbed as I stood on rubber legs and dusted off my jeans. Somehow, I'd ended up behind Reel's mobile command post.

I rubbed the lump on the back of my head, no doubt a result of a farewell gesture from Senawahv. Time slowed as my heartbeat sped up.

A path led to the front door of the command center. I trotted as fast as I could on shaky legs. Reel needed to know what I had learned. The steps up and into the command post seemed higher and the short hallway to the conference room rocked and rolled with every step.

Reel blanched when she saw me. "Peter? I can't believe —"

"I don't believe it either," I said. My experience with Senawahv had both exhilarated and exhausted me.

"Where have you been?" she asked. Her feminine side showed in her eyes.

Talking through my pounding headache, I told her what I had learned during my peyote trip. "Pokoh said the asteroid would strike at high noon. Less than four hours."

She asked, "Okay, so where is Oso?"

"I left him at the sacred garden." Her question irritated me. "Did you just miss the point of my story? There's no time to worry about Oso. Everything happens at twelve."

She raised a palm, said, "I sent you to find Oso's imposter. You were to bring him in for questioning. I need to know who we've been dealing with."

"I don't understand you. I just told you of a potential catastrophe and you're worried about your investigation? The ceremony is on Indian land. Evacuate everyone from the ceremony site before it's too late. Use your damn authority."

"We keep having the same discussion on this distraction. And, I don't like your attitude, Officer Romero."

I said, "Distraction? Are you serious? Since when are mass casualties a distraction? What do I need to tell you?

213

Danger is not coming from a perceived security threat to your investigation, it's coming from the sky. Today, Jean. Today in less than four hours. It's a real fuckin' disaster."

The wall clock showed eight-fifteen and my breath shortened with every twitch of the second hand.

"I'll determine what's important in my investigation. And I'll say it again. I am not cancelling the groundbreaking ceremony based on the threats of a spirit who claims he can control a space object, an object which you know damn well cannot be verified by anyone at NASA, or your own aunt."

"I can't shake the feeling you're sleep-walking through this entire Pokoh threat. Because no one can see the object, doesn't mean it isn't hidden by the sun, damnit. I'm also beginning to wonder what you think is more important: your job or your Indian. You're losing your instincts, Jean."

If I could have caught those words in mid-air, I would have. Her face darkened, and I saw more than fire in her eyes. Fear, pain. I suspected she was up against it, dealing with things I knew nothing about and afraid she'd lose her job.

She stood, pointed to the door. "Get out. I've had it with your antics."

Alarm stuck in my throat. I had wounded her. My jaw clamped shut.

I rose from my chair, headed for the door, then turned. "That's not what I meant." I held out my hands. Paused. "This day is not going to end well if that ceremony proceeds."

"Get out, or I'll have you arrested." She pointed to the door, her outstretched arm a lance straight me through.

"This will be on you, Jean." I stepped outside the conference room. She wouldn't have me arrested because she was the one who hijacked me and dragged me into her investigation. I wasn't supposed to be here in the first place without a security clearance. I turned to face her. "Jean, I—"

"You're taking advantage of our relationship." She slammed the conference room door, said, "Don't come back."

She had cut me off at the knees.

Every pair of eyes in the command center avoided mine as I hurried outside. The last thing I saw when I stepped from

214

the command center was the digital wall clock showing eight-twenty.

I opened doors of the few vehicles parked in front of the command center hoping an ignition would hold keys.

"Maybe you better quit feeling sorry for yourself, first," Leslie No Name Ponsford said.

I was so blinded by self-pity; I'd almost run into the man sitting in his sedan. "How'd you kno—." Apparently, my private thoughts were written on my face. "I thought you was dead."

"Me too," No Name said.

"I need your car," I said.

"Your ass," he said.

"I gotta get to the groundbreaking. Gonna be a shootout for sure between the Chivington rednecks and the Utes. Lot worse, too." I didn't want to turn him off with my asteroid theory.

No Name smiled as he stared through the windshield. "Shooting? Get in."

I hurried around the car, climbed into the passenger's seat. No Name stomped the pedal before I could close the door.

From the passenger seat, No Name looked like a mummy. Bandages circled his skull to hold in his brains, for all I could see. Bandages covered wounds on his face. Discolored skin peeked out from under the gauze. He wore an arm sling and a neck brace. The shaking Grizz had given him must've bruised every vertebrae and cartilage from head to tail bone. "You doin' okay?" I asked.

He kept his eye on the road. He hit seventy on the dirt road. He said, "What kind of dumbass question is that, Romero?"

"Right." I took comfort in his testiness. The Lakota would recover from Grizz's attack.

"You?"

"Lost my job," I said.

"No surprise." He kept the sedan at a smooth eighty-five once we hit the hard surface road.

"Listen," I said. No Name lifted an eye when I described my peyote trip to Senawahv's sacred place. I figured

215

his survival from the jaws and claws of an eight-hundred-pound grizzly might have increased his sensitivity to the works of the spirits.

"So, what happened to Pokoh?" No Name asked. "That son-of-a-bitch Grizz tried to kill me."

"Been fired."

"Bullshit. A spirit? Fired?"

I said, "Canned, busted, disenfranchised, stripped of rank. You know, defrocked."

"Well, it's an interesting story you got there," No Name said.

I leaned over for a better view of the speedometer. Ninety. "Faster, dammit."

No Name chuffed, then punched it and we flew low until traffic near the ceremony slowed us. "What time?" I asked.

"Quarter to nine."

"Shit." I got the words out as my heart crawled up my throat. "Push it."

The big Lakota put his red flasher on the dashboard, and we made time cruising the left lane. If No Name ever worried about his future, it wasn't while driving. Visions of a fireball heading toward the center of the ceremony burned in my brain.

At the ceremony site, we passed two groups of men gathering at opposite ends of the parking area. No Name parked in a roped-off lot reserved for VIPs and slid the keys under the seat while eyeing me.

"What?" I asked.

"Them," he said, facing the two groups. I recognized them: Chivingtons and Utes. Indian-haters and hating Indians. Some Chivingtons wore cavalry shirts, the old dark blue kind, some of the Utes wore war paint on their faces. Wannabes, every one of them: pseudo warriors wearing blue jeans and cowboy boots and fake soldiers—recruiting rejects too drunk, stoned, or wacked out to make it in the military. Everyone packed heat.

"What time is it?" I asked.

216

"Ten to nine. Calm down, man."

I nodded to shut him up. My only concern was to get everyone out of here.

Traffic was building on the road and more people congregated near the area roped off for the golden shovel ceremony. I scanned the sky looking for evidence of Pokoh's asteroid but only managed to white-out my vision.

I said, "Let's check out the area, see how hard it is to get everyone out of here without creating a panic."

No Name shook his head.

The Utes and Chivington gathering in the parking area complicated matters. Both groups, intent on creating trouble, could jam up traffic easily.

Elsewhere, people were working hard. A sound truck parked near a cleared patch of scrub while a technician placed microphones on the podium erected on a square of red carpet. Workers prepared displays, tables, and tents. Others hung banners on poles.

Red Pine hardware displayed Southern Ute tribal wealth: mobile drilling rigs, flatbeds with huge gas valves strapped on, and mobile field lighting lined up like big-eyed robots.

A half-dozen natural gas tanker trucks ringed the ceremony grounds. All Red Pine equipment sported the corporation's circular, two-feather logo. Each sage green truck was personalized with Ute spirit names, an homage to the tribe's traditions; *Queogand* for Bear, *Teahshooggoosh* - Deer, Coyote - *Yeodze*, Wolf - *Shinab,* and *Pari* for Elk. One truck's name, the closest to me, was hidden by a pile of brush. I wondered if those trucks were empty or full of natural gas. They made me nervous.

Food trucks set up shop. The smell of red chilé beef enchiladas, fresh corn tortillas, and the crackling hiss of onions frying in iron pans reminded me I had not eaten since yesterday.

A county fair atmosphere evolved as a mariachi group offloaded their instruments from a panel truck. The local post of the Veterans of Foreign Wars rumbled in with a World War

II, M-3 Halftrack. Sales booths took shape for Colorado Ski
Country USA, the Telluride Ski Resort, and Telluride's historic
Hotel Columbia. The La Plata County Sheriff's Mounted Patrol
pulled in towing horse trailers. Members of the mounted group
were volunteers, and to my relief, Lettau's thugs were not
among them.

The image re-formed in my head: a sun-hot asteroid
closing in on men, women, children. A hot flash followed by a
skull-crushing explosion. A pile of ashes, everyone here,
smoldering in the cratered earth.

I shook the image away and turned my attention to the
Southern Ute Police Department officers directing traffic on
the highway and at the entrance to the site. As Utes, they were
my best bet to reverse the traffic flow and I rushed toward them
devising a believable plea about evacuating the area. I came up
with zip—Pokoh, Ute spirit, asteroid. Nothing. *Nada*. No one,
not Reel, not No Name, took my story seriously. I couldn't
expect strangers to even listen. I abandoned the idea and trotted
back to No Name, blood pounding in my brain.

As I passed the armed Utes and blue coats, I took a
quick weapons count. Open carry is legal in Colorado, and I
counted three dozen pistols and a dozen rifles between the two
groups. Know the enemy, my DI used to say.

To No Name, I said, "I'm gonna use that sound truck
over there and close the ceremony." I set out for the truck, "I'll
tell' 'em the whole thing's been cancelled. Won't say why, I'll
just say go home."

"Won't work."

I stopped, turned. "Why?"

"After they stop laughing, they'll stone the shit out of
you for ruining their weekend entertainment. Some of them are
half in the bag already."

Loud yells came from the direction of the Utes and
Chivingtons. Hostility had deepened with a flock of middle
fingers and raised fists.

"We've got to get everybody out of here." I pushed my
face upward into No Name's mug, my anxiety secreting from
my skin like sweat. "I'm gonna talk to the Utes. They'll listen
to me," I said pointing in their direction.

No Name glared down at me. "Who's gonna believe your shit? Look at those assholes eye-locking each other like a bunch a coked-up wolverines. They're haters, both sides are waiting for an excuse to shoot," he said. "Your crazy-ass story will just get 'em riled up. One shot and a full-blown firefight breaks out. Innocent people will get hurt." He pointed to the road. "Look at the traffic," he said. "No one's going anywhere."

Traffic had jammed up and stopped dead as the Ute and Chivington hate bubbled like a steam cooker. Like my head. When the shooting started, everyone would be dead and done. Exactly what Pokoh had hoped for. And an even better reason to shut this down.

No Name studied me for a minute, then said, "Reel's got SWAT teams hiding out. Just in case."

"She never told me that."

No Name shook his head. "Need to know don't include you."

"What time is it?"

"Jesus, Romero, its ten-goddamn-thirty."

"I gotta call Aunt Pris to hear what's new, but I got no phone."

"I'll call Reel, maybe she knows." The big Lakota got her on the phone and said he'd heard stories about an asteroid and wanted a warm and fuzzy that they weren't true. He listened without expression, then punched off.

"She said a telescope in Hawaii discovered an unusual object. *Oumuamua* they call it. Means messenger who reaches out from the distant past. Came from another solar system and travelled here at super speed."

"Could you get to the point?" I kept my eyes on the testosterone baking at the edge of the site in the high-country sun.

No Name said, "*Oumuamua* broke up last night. Hawaii tracked the debris until solar flares obscured the picture. Couldn't relocate it due to a software failure. Anyway, they expect some big chunks headed for the Southwestern U.S. Can't tell exactly when, where, or if, they will hit."

A messenger who reaches out from the distant past. I
recalled the Peruvian, my bar stool informant, saying an
asteroid had been sent by their gods to warn the Incas of their
cataclysmic demise by the Spanish. My gut twisted into a knot.
Oumuamua linked the distant past and present with a warning
of catastrophe.

More armed men arrived. All armed. I paced back and
forth, to dampen my blood pressure.

"You got a firearm I can borrow? I'm feeling a little
naked, here," I said.

No Name shook his head. "Isn't La Plata Sheriff's
Office looking for you?"

"For sure." I said.

No Name crossed his big arms over his chest. "So you
want me, an FBI agent, to give you my weapon? You? A
fugitive? A cop killer, no less. Ha! Forget it." No Name walked
away chuckling. I watched him tour the area, check out the
Utes as they glowered at the Chivingtons who returned the
expression in a macho stare down. He walked to his sedan,
opened the rear door, closed it and returned.

"I'll be damned if I can't find my personal Glock.
Must've fallen out of my belt when I was driving," he said,
walking away. "Damn!"

No Name wasn't the best actor I've ever seen, but he
kept his back to me as I walked over to the sedan and groped
under the driver's seat. I found a Glock 26 and slipped it under
my belt at the small of my back and covered it with my shirt
tail.

I walked over to where he stood. "What time is it?"

No Name checked his phone, said, "Eleven. Give it a
rest, Romero."

I seethed in frustration. A door in my aching head
opened and my Marine drill instructor walked in; dressed in
Smokey Bear hat, knife-edge creases, and mirrored boots. He
glared at me like I was the lowest life form to ever pollute this
miserable earth.

"Obstacles got you defeated, Romero?" he asked.

"Sir, no, sir." I lied.

220

"When trouble comes, they send for the hunters, not the hunted. They send in the sons-of-bitches. You a hunting' son-of-a-bitch, Romero?"

"Sir, yes, sir."

"You do not fight because you hate those in front of you. You fight because you love those behind you."

"Sir, yes, sir!" My voice grew stronger.

"What do Marines do in the face of obstacles?"

"Charge, sir!" I yelled.

My DI nodded at the hostile groups behind me. "What do Marines do when outnumbered?"

At the top of my lungs, I said, "Marines don't count that way, sir!" He smiled, then faded to a green haze and drifted away.

To my left, people milled about the displays talking, eating, and buying souvenirs, oblivious to the loathing between the Utes and Chivingtons not thirty yards away. Shouting and racial epithets erupted along with a flock of bird-fingers shot towards the sky.

The rivals inched closer to each other, chests inflating the closer they came. A few more feet and there would be fists, chaos, and shooting.

My smoldering frustration turned to rage. I said. "Let's get those lovebirds out of here and herd them down the dirt road over here. I pointed to the road that lead to a farmhouse and away from the highway. That'll make room to get the others out."

"What lame-ass scheme you got now?" No Name asked.

"Walk in like we own it." I could taste my anger. "Go violent. Go crazy." I headed for the belligerents.

"What the fuck, Romero." No Name said, to my back. "You're gonna get your ass killed."

I'd had it with the doubters and the haters. "I'm done with talk."

"Get your ass back here and help me," he said, pointing to his neck brace and arm splint. I helped him remove the bandages and brace.

221

I walked over to the group. My arms pulsed with blood, ready for anything, but my mind was as clear as a mountain lake. Most of the belligerents paid no attention to me as I elbowed my way through, their eyes glued on each other.

I announced my presence with my best son-of-a-bitch, a sidekick to the leg of the nearest Ute. The victim buckled. No Name put down a Chivington with a punch to the throat. He collapsed like a wet sandbag.

"Enough! Nobody wants trouble here! Pack it up and leave the area!" I said, holding my badge in the air. "Now!"

No one moved.

The Chivington lay gagging on the ground until his fellow rednecks recovered enough to pull him aside. The Utes made no move to help their comrade while eyeballing me, stunned, it seemed, by two fools inserting themselves between sixty armed belligerents.

"You heard me," I said. "Get the fuck out of here. Take that road." I said, pushing the Ute nearest me toward the dirt road. I stood ready to throw feet and fists. A few Utes turned to go, then stopped when the Southern Ute Police, who had been watching from the highway, trotted our way.

The tribal police's arrival provoked the Chivingtons into a thunder of profanities. The Utes reciprocated. Some shook their fists. Others glared, then palmed their pistols.

No one gave ground. My evacuation plan had started and stalled in less than a minute.

Chapter 38

The warble sirens grew louder as La Plata County Sheriff's vehicles approached. My cue to exit.

I abandoned No Name and the Ute police, while the La Plata deputies trotted toward us. I scanned for a hiding place. I spotted a Red Pine truck fifty yards away and sprinted toward it.

The sirens had generated new booing and yelling from the two hostile groups. I couldn't make out what they were saying but I didn't need to. The trading of offensive labels had raised the belligerents' temperatures to boiling.

I scrambled behind a Red Pine tanker truck. Crouching near the front fender to see if I'd been spotted by the deputies, I glanced up at the vehicle's door. In the middle of the two-feathers logo, the word Pokoh had been painted. How strange that name would end up on the very truck I had picked. I crawled underneath.

Brush piled up under the truck's frame hid me, offering some safety until I focused on an object directly above my head. Taped between the 3500-gallon LPG container and the truck's fuel tank was a bundle of explosives—six bundled sticks of GEL-X Extra—wired to a cellphone. I'd seen this sort of improvised device in Iraq.

Then it became clear. An explosive devise rigged under a truck named Pokoh had to be the defrocked spirit's Plan B to create bloodshed and ignite an Indian race war. The bomb under this truck was payback for my testimony before Senawahv. Pokoh's grand fuck you.

Pokoh had threatened a space object for mass destruction, but it was a hollow threat because he'd lost his power. And I'd fallen for it.

I'd had no explosives training in the Marine Corps, but I had explosive ordnance demolitions buddies who, when drunk enough, shared their favorite tips. I flexed my fingers to remove the stiffness and breathed in deep to clear my head.

I craned my neck to find any hidden cables from the yellow bundle, then rubbed lightly over and around the explosives with my fingers and found none. When my hand passed close to the phone, it lit up. My heart stopped. The screen read eleven-forty-five then went black.

Fifteen minutes.

The techs at the podium began sound checks. Pokoh had said he planned for high noon. With everyone gathered at the podium, mid-day would allow him to achieve maximum effect.

It was now or never. Fuck the possibility of arrest and chances of getting shot, I would grab the mike on the podium and tell everyone to run. I would scream "bomb" until they did.

As I pulled myself toward the rear of the truck, No Name's alligator boots passed by my hiding spot along with the black trousers of three others. Sheriff's deputies. Lettau talked among them.

A plan suddenly flashed. I could drive the truck down the dirt road where the GEL-X would blow far away from everyone. I'd been down that road before: it led west to the old farmhouse where Grizz had mauled No Name.

If I could drive through the middle of the crowd and get some distance down that road, the separation would save lives when the truck exploded. If I could get behind the wheel without being stopped. If the keys were in it. If I could get it out of here without getting shot. I hate ifs.

Fifteen yards away, No Name talked loudly to guarantee the attention of the La Plata County deputies. No Name pointed in every direction but mine yet stole glances in my direction. As the deputies looked away, I pointed to the undercarriage and signed *bomb* then gestured with hands at two and ten, *drive truck.* His eyes grew wide. He nodded, turned his attention back to Lettau.

Crawling from beneath the truck, I kept the vehicle between me and the deputies. I jumped into the cab and lay on the seat praying to my ancestors the driver had neglected to remove the keys.

No fucking keys. No tools to hotwire the truck. No driver. No time.

"I'll tell you one more time, Deputy Lettau, Romero is in federal custody at a place I will not disclose," said No Name.

His voice came from just outside the truck. I lay on my stomach, trying to melt into the seat.

"We have a warrant for Romero," said Lettau. "For murder of a law enforcement officer." He had raised his voice, playing the bully against No Name. This was getting interesting.

"This is reservation land. Federal jurisdiction is not—get that paper out of my face—your responsibility. Clean the shit out of your ears, Lettau." I expected the next sound to be the crack of No Name's fist against Lettau's jaw.

"No need to get personal." Lettau said.

"Get your hand off your weapon, deputy. Things gonna get a lot more personal if you don't back off. Now get the fuck off the reservation before I take all three of you into custody." No Name said.

I couldn't help smiling and wished I could take a peek.

"Ladies and gentlemen," the loudspeakers blasted. "Please make your way towards the podium where representatives from the Centennial State, La Plata County, the City of Durango, and our hosts, the Southern Ute Tribe, will conduct the ceremony. The festivities will start in ten minutes."

Ten minutes.

"You haven't heard the end of this, Ponsford. I'm taking this to the DA," Lettau said, voice fading away.

No Name laughed.

He opened the passenger door. "You still here?"

"No keys," I said.

"Hotwire?"

"Maybe."

No Name angled his head to one side. "Here," he said, handing me his pocketknife, an all-in-one like mine still sitting in property-hold at the La Plata County jail.

Pulling my upper body under the steering column, I removed the cover on the steering column. I was not familiar with this truck, but I identified the battery, ignition, and starter wires among the bundles by color. I snipped, then separated them, fumbling with sweating fingers.

I stripped insulation from the end of the battery wires and twisted them together with the ignition wire. I poked my head up and could see that the dash lights had come alive. So far so good.

The starter wire was a charged wire. I held it tight, but it quivered in my hands. A spark in the wrong place could short the fuses and I would have a dead truck, a bomb-laden dead truck.

I touched it to the battery wires and used an elbow to depress the accelerator. The truck started with a cough and a rumble, then stopped. *Fuck.* I touched wires again and the truck restarted and rumbled rhythmically.

Squirming out from under the steering column, I slid on to the seat behind the wheel.

No Name hopped in. "Get this truck out of here."

With slight pressure on the accelerator, I eased forward, honked the horn, to get people out of the way. Some just stared at me until No Name yelled at them. Some flipped the bird, strolled reluctantly out of the way. I had about one hundred yards to get to the road and clear the crowded ceremony grounds.

Honking and yelling, I eased through the crowd, turned left, then accelerated down the road. The route seemed clear all the way to the abandoned farmhouse at the end. The surface was recently graveled, but I kept the speed down. Riding on six sticks of explosives with 3500 gallons of liquid fuel behind me made me cautious. I concentrated on avoiding every rut and pothole.

"What the fuck?" No Name asked, voice pitched up.

"What?" I nearly jumped out of my seat.

"Look." No Name said, pointing to the horizon. The sun was straight up, but the skyline showed a bright spot growing as it rose.

I could only stutter, "N-no."

The ball glowed brighter than the sun. I looked away. "You think—"

"No shit."

Pokoh's asteroid. Fragments of *Oumuamua* at minutes to noon. "The son-of-a-bitch wasn't lying after all."

I hit a pothole. The entire truck shook.

"Hey!" No Name yelled. "You're gonna kill us before the asteroid does!"

I corrected, paid attention to the road.

The fireball streaked overhead, and with it, intense volcanic heat. Contrails streamed behind the asteroid like those of a dozen jets.

A projectile's buzz hurt my eardrums. I knew that sound too well. Shots fired.

"What the fu—?" I yelled.

"There!" No Name pointed to a man in the middle of the road. He held an automatic weapon, aimed straight at us and the truck-bomb.

Out-of-range at first, we closed in fast when I stomped the pedal. Bullets pinged off the bumper, grill, and radiator. Steam geysered from the front of the truck. The engine began to miss and sputter. The shooter snapped in a new drum of ammo. Rounds shattered the windshield but missed both of us.

Bullets ricocheted off the LPG tank behind me. Some rounds penetrated the tank with a loud crack. I had visions of fire and a terminal explosion as cold jets of propane hissed like snakes through the bullet holes.

Clement Ouray Pokoh stood directly in our path, aimed in, pulled the trigger. The muzzle flashed full-automatic. Pokoh emptied the AK's drum. The big tank rang like a mission bell as rounds glanced off the steel. My heart skipped at every peal, but I held the wheel straight at him. If Pokoh was human, he was going to die. Now.

No Name grunted. Blood blossomed above his collar bone. "Run that prick down," he said, jamming a handkerchief against his wound.

Pokoh disappeared under the truck with a sickening thud of steel against flesh and bone. The truck's rear wheels bounced with a sickening thud. Pokoh reappeared in the rearview, crumpled on the road. I jammed on the brakes. We skidded to a stop.

"One minute 'til noon," No Name said, his face white, pain written in a grimace.

I jumped out of the tanker, bolted to the passenger side, opened the door, pulled hard on No Name's arm. He fell out, but I got my arms under his. Still, his lower half hit the ground hard. No Name's big frame was limp. I dragged him across the dirt road toward a drainage ditch and threw myself over him and waited for an explosion to kill us all.

No Name choked words, "Cell phone."

I glanced in Pokoh's direction. The man, torn and broken, struggled, reached out toward a cell phone lying on the road with a palsied hand, red with blood. His pained determination emphasized the spirit's evil.

I left No Name and ran thirty feet to the phone, kicked it away, and hit the deck. Time was up.

Pokoh lay on the road staring up at me with one eye, the man's body a mishmash of broken flesh, blood and imbedded gravel. A leg and arm were bent at odd angles.

"You are a great disappointment, Romero," he said.

"What?"

"This was our chance," he said, coughing.

I walked over to the man. "*Our* chance?"

"To return to the old ways, you fool. Once the Utes were a great power, rulers of plains and mountains, mother of the Shoshone and Comanche. Now, our traditions are forgotten. Our ancestors have forsaken us. How long until we are all gone?"

I had no words. I glanced over to No Name. He had not moved and I feared the worst. A form emerged above No Name's body, shapeless and ghost-like, and I knew. A hole ripped open deep in my chest. There was nothing I could do now except grieve, and that would have to wait. I returned my attention to Pokoh.

Pokoh looked up with lidded eyes, "You must never forget, old gods never die. They sleep in the deepest recesses of our minds. We need them. They give meaning to our souls. Where is your soul? Why do you think I picked you?"

"What are you talking about?" This man stood in front of my house a week ago with an AK-47 and an attitude.

"Your power. You can talk with the spirits, make things happen." His voice sounded far away.

"I tested you with *shinab*, a challenge you met well." Pokoh coughed again. A pink spray misted, red drifted across his face. Blood ringed his lips and stained his teeth. The test, sending a pack of Senawahv's children against me, proved to be Pokoh's undoing as a spirit.

"I took you to your sacred place, where all of your people are born, die, and are reborn. I thought that would remind you of your heritage, but no. We could've done great things, you and I. We could have rid our earth of the invaders. I tried to tell you, Romero. Now it's gone, everything is gone." He tried a sweeping gesture with his arms, but the broken limb flailed pathetically. The evil this shattered man planned overwhelmed my empathy for him.

"You and Grizz?" I asked.

Pokoh grinned with red teeth. "Aggression of the predator is useful when fighting spiritual battles. It was given to me to drive away the degradation and pollution of the new, and to frighten cultural sickness away. As Grizz, I had great spiritual power and physical strength, enough to stop our spiritual rot. I could've saved us, Romero!" He retched blood. "Saved us, were it not for you and that fool Senawahv—" He spit. "There's no future for us, now."

When Senawahv had expelled the star-juggler from his council fires, Pokoh lost his spiritual status. As a mortal, he'd substituted the truck bomb for the asteroid.

"Save us through the killing of innocents?"

"It is the old way, the best way. You—"

I glanced up at the truck when it coughed and sputtered, then died. The hissing of the propane continued. I looked back down at Pokoh. His eyes had glassed over. I watched him breathe his last. Again.

Just before he died, Pokoh had said I had something special going with the spirits. I could talk to them, he'd said. We could have done some great things together. I tried to tell you, he had said. I never had the chance to ask what he meant. Perhaps he wanted my help to join him as he worked to reignite the Ute-Navajo war. Thank the gods, I never had the opportunity to refuse.

Chapter 39

Voices from a loudspeaker at the ceremony grounds
drifted my way as I rushed over to No Name.

Special Agent Leslie Ponsford lay crumpled on the
road, eyes open, face paled in death. Blood stained the gravel
under his neck. I chanted a death song in Keresan. No verse
had come to me when I faced my own death, but over my
fallen friend, it bloomed from my heart.

Singing No Name's eulogy did not relieve me of my
guilt. Had I not talked with Pokoh after kicking the phone
away, I might have saved him. I pressed my hands into my
face, a gesture that allowed me the temporary self-deception of
denial.

Selfishly, I hadn't recognized what a friend he was.
He'd taken a mauling—walked right into Grizz's jaws—and
saved me. His warning about the cell phone saved me again by
disabling the truck-bomb detonator. His laconic advice, wise in
its way, always set me straight. Now he's gone. How sharp was
the razor-thin line between life and death?

Marines do not leave our dead on the field. No Name
was at least twice my size, but I would drag this man back to
the ceremony site if it killed me. The propane in the tanker
truck might, if I didn't get out of here.

The big tank warned with a loud, propane hiss. The
smell told me a volatile mixture was forming. Electrical wires
crackled in the truck's engine compartment. There was nothing
more to do here but die.

I would never get my arms around No Name's chest
and lifting his limp bulk was beyond my strength. I slipped off
my belt, then removed his. Buckled together, the two belts
barely made it around his rib cage, but it gave me something to
hold on to.

I pulled backwards with both hands gripping the belt to
gain motion. One step at a time. Pull, rest. Pull, rest. I set a
rhythm, progressed foot by foot. Pull, rest.

The air smelled of gunpowder and burning sulfur from
the asteroid, but I'd heard no explosion. The ceremony
continued on; life as usual. If *Oumuamua-The Messenger Who*

Reaches Out From the Distant Past, had exploded, it was too far to hear. Proof enough Pokoh was not in control.

Pull. Catch air. Resting periods grew longer, my energy drained away like a desert creek. Pull. Not enough air at this altitude. I didn't stop. My hands stung, my arms and legs burned, but never would I stop. By the time I dragged No Name to the edge of the site, the ceremony had concluded and much of the crowd had dispersed.

The FBI SWAT team had things under control. Camouflaged men surrounded the Chivingtons and Utes, automatic weapons at the ready. Some agents carried stubby M4 Commando rifles. Agents, not otherwise armed, packed .45 Colt pistols. Supervisors barked commands to everyone, detainees and arresting officers alike. A few moved from kneeled hostile to hostile, disarming and plasti-cuffing them while another aimed a shotgun at their head to encourage cooperation. A pile of confiscated weapons grew in the rear of a pickup.

With Pokoh dead, the principal players in custody, and the bomb-rigged truck immobilized, the Ute-Navajo feud could not reignite. I mourned the loss of No Name and would not forget him, but the fact that the ceremony had ended without greater loss of life brought me relief as well as overwhelming fatigue.

I sat, unable to speak or raise my arms to signal for help. Someone in the SWAT noticed me with No Name's body and came running with a medic in tow. They asked me questions, but I gave them the minimum necessary. Anything I had to say would be to Jean Reel.

I wanted to go home. I would return Tommy Palafox's retainer, rescue my Jeep from Wookie Gutierrez if I had to beat it out of him.

I'd had it.

I found No Name's sedan, fished the keys out from where he'd placed them under the seat, and headed off for Oso's cabin.

The only thing I needed in this world right now was sleep.

Chapter 40

I woke with Jean Reel stroking my hair with her long fingers. I held her hand against my face and inhaled. Her soft skin reminded of fresh rain. Her scent enslaved me. Maybe I was dead in my final resting place, *Shipap*.

"You had me worried," she said, "running off like that."

"You fired me." I rubbed my eyes.

"Ponsford didn't make it," she said, her voice trailing off. She looked into my eyes searching for pain to share.

"I know." It was too painful to live my hurt. Too soon. Much too soon.

She said, "We're holding the Utes and the Chivingtons on charges of conspiracy and inciting a riot. We've had wiretaps and informants for the last six months. Our evidence, bullet-proof."

"What about Lettau and his hoods?"

"In custody. With your testimony, all three are good for felony murder, because it happened during their attempt to kill you," she said. "They're facing life-without-parole."

"Lettau's gonna say I shot Jones resisting arrest."

"The last thing you have to worry about is Lettau's veracity on the stand," she said. "The case is solid. Had to pull teeth, but I gathered Alcohol, Tobacco, Firearms and Explosives, and Drug Enforcement Administration cases, as well. Got them all wrapped up in a nice package for the prosecution."

"Have any luck finding Pokoh's corpse?" I asked.

Jean started stroking my hair, again. Embarrassment heated my neck. I hadn't bathed in a week. "My search party says no," she said.

That answer kicked me out of my sluggishness. "Really? I ran over the son-of-a-bitch. Broke most of his bones, far as I could tell. No blood, scuffmarks, impressions in the dirt?

"Loads of physical evidence, but no corpse, Peter."

So much for Pokoh being human.

"No AK?" I asked. I lifted my head off the pillow. She pushed me down, her palm cool on my forehead.

"We found the Kalashnikov and expended shells at the roadside once the LPG tank quit expelling gas. It took the fire department all afternoon before we could get near it. Fortunately, it didn't explode.

"You know, I have to test you for gunshot residue, Peter."

"I never fired a weapon."

"Procedure is procedure," she said with affection in her voice. I saw it in her eyes, too.

"The asteroid?" I asked.

"Pris said fragments of *Oumuamua* passed high over Colorado and burned up in midair. No reported injuries."

"You think Pokoh had something to do with the asteroid?" I asked.

"Peter…" she said in a tone of disbelief.

I didn't have the energy to convince her.

Jean continued to stroke my hair and said, "You are the most dedicated man I know." She smiled. "As long as I've known you, you've been willing to place yourself in danger to help others."

My feelings were the same toward her. "I've always admired your strength. There's nothing you can't do," I told her.

She smiled, kissed my forehead. "Flattery will get you everywhere with me."

My lids weighed heavy and I had a hard time staying awake until I remembered how she'd kicked me out of her command center. The very thought alarmed me to the point I almost didn't ask, "You 'n' me. Is it over?"

Jean smiled, said, "You tell me." She leaned forward and caressed my neck with a cool hand. When she kissed my cheek, shivers ran down my spine. She unbuttoned her blouse slowly. Too slowly.

We lay on Oso's bed, lit by a window casting leaf shadows on the wall and floor. For the night, the cabin became our sanctuary from the rest of the world.

I slept until I heard Jean rummaging around in the kitchen. At the table, she placed a plate of breakfast burritos

234

plump with eggs, meat, potatoes, and intense red chilé, followed by a mug of hot coffee. I inhaled the first serving and she made more.

"Where did you get this wonderful food?" I asked.

"I called the command center and they did some shopping for me last night."

"I didn't hear you call."

"You were dead to the world," she said.

We ate in silence as the sun rose behind the hills and painted the cabin in tones of red that changed to orange and gold. The soft, diffused color made the dilapidated cabin pleasant, even welcoming.

After the light show I asked, "You make Wookie for the killing of the Pecos men at my pueblo?" My question was not random, Wookie Gutierrez remained unfinished business.

"Yes, I think Wookie killed Jason and his father, but I don't have the evidence I need. Fortunately, I can hold him for dealing firearms and drugs to the Chivingtons. That will give me some time." She busied herself at the sink. I took comfort in the morning sounds: running water, the clatter of dishes. "I have to find him, first."

I asked, "Want to hear my theory of how this whole thing went down? How Pokoh set it up." I said.

She turned off the water. "Okay, but I've already developed my theory of the—"

"Hear me out. It was Pokoh, Pokoh the man, who goaded the Chivingtons into killin' the horses. You know, a weird but offensive hate crime against the horses' owner, a Saudi. Pokoh wasn't sure I would investigate, so he convinced Wookie that Jason Pecos was about to rat him out. Poor Juan was just in the wrong place at the wrong time.

"When I went to Colorado to investigate, he got the Chivingtons to kill the sheepherder who may have known too much. Poor hikers were in the wrong place, too. Pokoh had the Chivs by the balls by then and extorted them to participate in his plan to start a race war."

"Okay, who shot Pokoh, the man, and why? You know, the truck and the sniper?"

"Well, Pokoh put the stars in the sky, why couldn't he put a bullet in his own head?"

She cocked her head. "That doesn't sound right, Peter."

"Anyone find evidence of a sniper? Shells, footprints, tire tracks? Anybody hear anything?"

"Well. no."

"Okay, then it sounds right to me. Then Pokoh, the spirit, played on my beliefs in an attempt to make me his ally. I fell for it 'til Oso set me straight. Then, when Pokoh, the spirit, figured things weren't going his way he became the skinwalker, Grizz, and came after me."

"Where is Oso, now, Peter?"

Her change of focus told me she was not buying in. "Colorado. Last I saw him was at Garden of the Gods. I think he's gone forever."

She cocked her head. "Okay, the crooked cops. Lettau and his cronies? Where do they fit in your theory?"

"Not related to Pokoh's plans. Lettau was affiliated with the cartels through the snowboarders and he believed my investigation would uncover his activities. Truth is, I figured him as a run-of-the-mill redneck until he tried to kill me."

"That's my belief on Lettau's involvement, too." She went back to washing the dishes. "Part of me believes you, but I can't take any theory involving Pokoh to a federal prosecutor," she said.

I said, "Any prosecutor would jump on Wookie with both feet."

She looked up. "I know what you're thinking. Stay out of it, Peter, Wookie's a dangerous man."

As exhausted as I was from the events of the past week, I had no intention of staying out of it. The fucker had my ride.

After breakfast, I gave the leftovers to Oso's pet bear, Sash, and I became her newest best friend. I twirled my arms above my head the way I'd seen Oso do it and she whirled about. Then she gave me my first real bear hug and lumbered off. It tugged at my heart to see her go. Later, I gave Oso's cousin a call and he agreed to see after the old bear.

Jean and I went our separate ways after a long, tempting hug. "I appreciate you listening and your support of my beliefs," I said.

She smiled, said, "I believe in you, Peter."

Jean loaned the bucar sedan to me and said she would pick it up in New Mexico.

As I drove home, I suddenly felt giddy. Just thinking of Jean gave me a reaction I hadn't had since I met Costancia thirty years ago, and that feeling wouldn't let go.

At home in New Mexico, I sorted through my emails, many of them from women with Russian names wanting to meet me.

In the mailbox, I found a one-week load of catalogs and brochures, maybe a pound's worth, and a short stack of letters. Two of the envelopes were from BandelierQuickLoan marked, "Urgent". That sort of bad news would have to wait.

I called Tommy Palafox.

"The FBI is locked on the Chivingtons for the horse killings. They got DNA evidence from one of their trucks," I said.

"Reel told me the same thing. She also said she was finished in Southern Colorado and returning to Albuquerque," Palafox said. "Know what she was working on up there?" he asked.

My heart jumped at the idea of Jean returning. I said. "Classified is all she told me."

"Typical," he said.

"One more thing." I asked, "Any idea where Wookie Gutierrez is hanging out?"

"Española last I heard. He's on my radar for a backdoor heist at a Walmart. Insurance case. Wookie bribed forklift drivers to load his truck."

I had planned another day of rest, but this information energized me. I retrieved my .45 semi-automatic, a necessity when dealing with Wookie and placed it in the sedan's glove compartment. At noon, I hopped in the bucar, pushed the pedal to the floor and kept it there. This sedan was a hog and if I have ever needed the big engine in my Jeep, it was now.

Dealing with a life-long criminal like Wookie could be dangerous, and I would have to catch him off guard. He'd asked me to find his toddler when we met at the lowrider show. Of course he left out the part where he may have murdered his wife, but I sensed emotion in the man when he talked about his daughter. I would tell him I had found her. Playing on his emotions didn't bother me. Wookie was a killer and as street-smart as anyone I ever met, but my scam just might work.

In Española three of my usual informants clammed up or played stupid. In the evening, I found JJ Chavez, a homeless man I've known for years. JJ was an ex-paratrooper who'd experienced a failed chute and never got over it. He lived behind Lowe's, outside the gardener's tools, pottery, and fertilizer section.

"JJ, I'm lookin' for Wookie." I didn't get too close to the man. JJ seemed too comfortable with his unwashed aroma, a mix of body odor and dirty feet. Downwind, he secreted a hint of shit, too. "Keeps the riff-raff away," he once told me.

"Ain't seen him," said JJ.

"Forty bucks if you tell me where he's at," I said.

JJ looked to the right, left, shot a glance behind him. "Rumors goin' around gonna be a heist over to the Big Five tonight. Ain't sayin' its true. Ain't sayin' it's Wookie, neither. Just what I heard." I shoved forty bucks in his filthy hand and fast-walked back to the sedan.

Wookie would not show until later, so I ate then drove to the store on Riverside Drive, arriving at ten-thirty. I circled the building. In the back, loading docks were serviced by three tall cargo doors. Everything seemed locked up and quiet, but the standing lights were off. I found that more than strange.

A dimly lit rear entrance at a nearby clothing store had a good view of the loading dock. On this moonless night, my black Ford blended in perfectly. Any observer would conclude it belonged to a store owner working late.

Eleven o'clock came and went. Stakeouts were the most boring activity a cop could perform. By eleven-thirty, I was sleepy and hungry. I rubbed my eyes and fought to keep them open. I was dead on my feet and feared driving the twenty miles home would not end well. I reached for the ignition just as a light duty box truck pulled up slowly to the loading dock. I slouched down in my seat as the truck backed into the Big Five dock and braked, motor running.

Wookie stepped down from behind the wheel. Up went a loading door and someone drove a forklift with a stack of pallets into the truck. Another stack followed, then another. Wookie handed over a paper bag, then pulled himself up to the wheel after slamming the truck's rear door. The Big 5 employee disappeared into the building with his forklift and rolled down the cargo door with a crash. I could have nailed him then, but I had no idea if his hoods were waiting nearby.

Wookie drove out of the dock going east. I stomped it on a side street and beat him to the intersection. A tree concealed me as I hid behind it. I stepped out when he stopped at a sign. I stood on the passenger step, my pistol aimed at his head. He held up his hands.

"Get out of the truck, Wookie."

Wookie raised his head, then chinned in my direction. *"Chíngate, cabrón."*

"How 'bout I put a bullet in the engine block? Then what will you do with three pallets of jocks and tennis balls?"

"Hey, this is a fuckin' rental, I got a damage deposit. I'm goin' straight, man."

Wookie had an interesting definition of going straight driving a truck full of stolen goods.

"That's a fine way to speak to the man whose found your little Ximena, your *preciosa.*" I lied. Wookie's daughter had been fostered out; a fact wisely kept from him.

Wookie stepped out of the truck, but left the engine running. He walked around the front of the truck toward me but kept his hands raised chest high. "Where is she?" he asked.

Wookie had gone from aggressive banger 'tude to a father with open hands and heart. So far, my diversion had worked. I didn't have his daughter, but the possibility of seeing her again caught him off guard.

"We'll meet tomorrow. I'll have Ximena, you have my Jeep," I said.

Wookie glared, asked, "How do I know you ain't ly—"
His jaw dropped. *"Estúpido.* I don't have no fuckin' Jeep." He
dropped his arms. *"Estas loco en la cabeza,"* he said, pointing
to my head. He started to laugh. "Repo man got it, *tonto.*
Flatbed took your Jeep. Funniest shit I seen in a long time."

I flashed to the two letters sitting on my desk, both from
BandelierQuickLoan. *Fuck.* I was so intent on getting my Jeep
back from Wookie that I lost focus on everything else.

"If you're lyin' to me, Wookie—"

Wookie sank to his knees in hysterics, then fell to the
ground clutching his chest fighting for breath between spasms
of laughter. He could've been lying, except he wasn't.

I took advantage of his temporary helplessness and
cuffed him.

"Hey, what the fuck, *cabrón?*"

I half-carried, half-dragged him to my sedan and stuffed
him into the back seat. I hopped behind the wheel and took off.
I called the Rio Arriba Sheriff's Office and told them I'd found
Wookie and informed them he had pending federal murder
charges. I also told them where to pick up the rental full of
stolen goods.

The next morning, a knock at the door woke me. My
first notion was Wookie's thugs had come for reprisal. When I
peered through the peephole, I held my .45 at my hip.

Jean winked and placed her finger over the peephole
when she spotted my eye behind it. When I let her in, she gave
me a long kiss.

I'd made breakfast, if you want to call toast and coffee
breakfast. "I found Wookie late last night." I looked for an
expression of approval, but she gave none.

I asked, "Sheriff say he spilled anything in
interrogation?"

"He lawyered up," she said.

I showed her the letter from BandelierQuickLoan and
asked her for a ride. I was too embarrassed to tell her it had
been impounded and Wookie had not taken it.

She said she'd drive me to the impound lot. "Later," she
said, grabbing my hand and pulling me toward the bedroom.

Much later, she drove me to the impound lot to retrieve my Jeep. While driving we talked.

"I think I'm going to miss No Name, as you call him, for a long time," she said.

"He was a good man. I'll miss Juan Pecos, too. We grew up together. Like so many parents, he had the misfortune of having a son who got into drugs." Suddenly, I missed my own son and felt relief that he'd grown up without getting into serious trouble.

I said, "It's disappointing you got nothing from Wookie."

"He had a driver when he committed the murders. Told us all we need. The DA's pushing for life-without-parole."

I was torn on Wookie. Yes, he was a killer and I'd put most of his male family members in jail at one time or another and that's where he belonged for the rest of his life. But I saw something human in him when I'd lied and told him I'd found his daughter. Wookie had lived a bad life and would be sentenced to prison for life. A life squandered is a sad thing to witness.

"And Lettau?"

"Gave it all up: gun runners, bad cops, Sinaloa operatives. Nine in custody at last count. Couldn't shut him up. He'll probably do five, maybe less, then witness protection after that."

"Jesus. Not bad for two murder attempts on me."

"Greater good, Peter. For the greater good." She sighed.

"Ute Traditionals?"

Reel said, "Looks like they'll do nine months then probation."

"Chivingtons?"

"The horse killings belong to New Mexico and Colorado law enforcement. I gave them all I have."

She pointed, turned into the driveway. "Here we are."

"And Pokoh?" I asked.

"What about him?" she asked.

"He's still out there. I know it. I was responsible for Pokoh's defrocking by Senawahv and I broke his body when I ran over him. No human could have walked away in his

241

condition. Pokoh kept a grudge alive for over a century. Will I be waiting for his payback for the rest of my life?"

She gave me a look of doubt. "Looking back is not a good way to live. It's better to believe there will be happiness forever." Her face lit up. "Oh, by the way, Palafox says the ranch owner has an impressive token of appreciation for you."

"I couldn't accept—"

"Hush, I already bought a new bikini, a very small one," she said with a wink.

"You can model it this evening." My turn to wink. "What do you think of Cabo?"

She didn't wait for my answer, said, "I love you, but I'm late for work." She drove off.

THE END

Acknowledgements

I would like to thank all who supported me in the writing of this novel. Thanks goes out to my long-time writing compatriots Ken Kuhlken and Maynard Kartvedt. My beta readers not only get thanks, but a big hug: Craig Blakey, Judy Hamilton, Gene Riehl, and Ken. My Thursday writing group led by Rich Farrell gets a hearty thank you as well for helping me add magic to each scene. A super hug and kiss to my editor, Molly Knop, for her in-depth editing and innovative cover design.

The Author

David E. Knop is a retired Marine officer with twenty years of service. He served two tours in Vietnam as an artillery forward observer and naval gunfire support officer. As a staff officer, he authored numerous military operations plans. Dave also wrote feature articles for the *Field Artillery Journal* and *Marine Corps Gazette.*

In civilian life, Dave became a technical writer and produced many electronic and automotive manuals for industry leaders such as SAIC and Computer Sciences Corporation. Dave's work for the Eighth Air Force received an award of excellence in a Northern California Society of Technical Communications competition.

Dave's first novel, *The Smoked Mirror,* a supernatural thriller featuring former Marine, Cochiti Pueblo police officer Peter Romero, placed honorable mention in both the Maryland Writers' Association and Reading Writers contests. Dave's second mystery, *Mining Sacred Ground,* brings the role of spirit warrior to the subgenre of Native American detectives. This novel was a semi-finalist in a recent Amazon.com Breakthrough Novel Contest and placed top ten in the Killer Nashville competition. Dave's third novel, *Poisoned by God's Flesh* was awarded a bronze medal by the Military Writers Society of America.

David E. Knop   Dead Horses

Animal Parts, a Peter Romero mystery, received honorable mention in the 2016 Public Safety Writers Association writing competition and achieved finalist in the 2017 New Mexico-Arizona Book Awards.

An alumnus of Book Passage Mystery Writer's workshops, Taos Institute of the Arts, and Maui Writer's Retreats, Rose Tyson Seminar in Forensic Sciences, and Crime Scene Investigations, UC Riverside, Dave is a lifelong student of Native American mythology.

Also by David E. Knop

Mining Sacred Ground
Poisoned by God's Flesh
Animal Parts

Please visit me at https://davideknopbooks.com/

Please post a review at:
https://www.facebook.com/DavidEKnopBooks